SALEM'S SON

By M. Chandler

DEDICATION

For Our Forgotten Soldiers
Our Anonymous Suicides
And My Youngest.

CONTENTS

ACKNOWLEDGMENTS

Special thanks are in order for Brittney and Sarah, real women who shared their light to breathe life and beauty into these pages. I also wish to thank Aaron and Bob who inspired characters and encouraged me to keep going despite my own misgivings.

I take angry shots at government in this, even singling out one officer for personal scorn. I met this fellow and my dislike of him is deeper than institutional. I don't apologize for this, with one exception.

The much maligned Department of Veterans Affairs has saved my life, particularly the Puget Sound Area doctors and the PTSD clinic at American Lake. I might not be here without their tireless dedication and professionalism.

I would separate the VA from the rest of government I criticize relentlessly, for a special thank you. From the bottom of my heart, thank you to the VA staff and volunteers.

CHAPTER 1

ERIC

"Why are we so careful with the dead?" I wondered as they unloaded Eric from the cargo deck of the tiny jet we recently shared. I took in a deep breath, happy to be out of the coach cabin hell of recycled, toilet-scented air. I tried not to breathe more than I had to on the plane. Each breath was an unwanted kiss from a dozen filthy hobos, coughing and clandestinely picking their noses all around me. They seemed to be hovering, closing in—waiting to breathe into me their hatred of what I had done.

I know they could see my guilt, all my faults. I know that they hate me for killing him. They all blame me even as he sat silent, burning in the corner trying to kill us all. I fought the urge to scream, stand and strangle any nearby asshole. The urge screamed that it was okay—that all would be right if only there were one less hobo breathing hot shame into me. I had won against that urge, and would reward myself with a drink or three as soon as I could find a bar.

Eric had sat there at the emergency exit in the corner of my eye for the entire flight. He was slouching, looking crestfallen but ablaze with a vengeful rage. Thick oily rivulets, black and orange tentacles flowed from him, seeking me, seeking revenge. I thought it odd that he was silent during the flight. From Germany to Dover to Harrisburg, he made no sound but the hissing of burning blood and the popping cracks of bones bursting from the heat that killed him. Flying with a dead man bent on murdering everyone aboard was a new brand of hell I could not endure again. The worst of the trip was over now and I would never set foot in an aircraft again if I could help it.

But off the plane in the fresh open air I was happy, until a slovenly beer-gut in a reflective vest shouted over the whine of jet engines that they had lost my luggage. I shrugged, and shouted back to the poor fellow, no doubt a victim of the same lousy guidance counseling as I, that it was alright, "As long as they didn't lose the fucking casket." He shook his head and cupped his hand to his ear. I shook my head and walked away.

1

I still smelled the coach cabin air. It seemed to be stuck in my uniform. With my luggage lost, I was resigned to the possibility of remaining in my hideous dress uniform forever. It was made of green polyester, never fit right and was festooned with too many gold buttons. My shoes were shined like mirrors, which seemed wrong somehow, like something a pervert would wear.

"Whatever, fuck it," I thought as I trudged to the waiting hearse. Inside it smelled pleasantly of lavender and stale cigar smoke. I liked the sounds the overstuffed leather seats made. The driver, an appropriately grim fellow, made no attempt at small talk or even a smile. I was glad for it. If another civilian thanked me for my service and told me about the time they almost joined the army back in 1969 or the first Gulf War, I was going to punch someone the fuck out. There I caught a glimpse of Eric as he finally appeared again. I hoped he would stay on the plane. Now he was beneath the plane's wing staring at me via the hearse's side mirror, fresh accusations and hatred burning in his eyes.

I ignored Eric, I was learning to since that's what the docs advised me to do. I was satisfied that he was a figment of my imagination after he failed to cause the plane to explode in midair. I inventoried my carry-on bag. "Fuck." Not even a toothbrush. Just some pills the army gave me and half a packet of airline almonds. "Why did I even bring this fucking bag?" There were some official papers in it, mashed and crumpled beyond the point of being worth the trouble to try and read anymore. Those would be thrown out as soon as I got to a trash can, and looks like my stupid wool beret made the trip successfully as well. That damn thing, what a disaster that was.

In 2001, the good idea faerie dressed as General Shinseki decided to switch all our hats out. Perfectly good, functional, easy to pack and transport hats, were replaced army-wide with wool berets. These served no purpose, looked stupid and pissed off all the special ops guys who wore berets since forever. Then there was the logistics debacle.

The law says our uniforms have to be made in America. Well the army in all its wisdom bought something like two million from China. Even though the money was already in the hands of the Chinese, on the principles of the matter, they shipped those hats, something like half of all the hats the army bought for this purpose, to Canada to be destroyed. Even now, in 2004 I don't think everyone in the army got one. I hated it and thought to throw it away but kept it in case I ran into some ornery colonel who would hassle me if he saw me in uniform without it.

Eric appeared again in the back of the hearse, scrunched up beside his body. The black car carried us three souls, one separate from its body, south towards McKnightstown. Though I had been there many times before on visits with Eric, and thought I had been looking forward to being there again, I was beginning to dread it.

It was a small town without a lot to offer. There were bars everywhere, a college and community college but little else. It had a minor role in the Civil War that it hyped for profit. It was close enough to Gettysburg though that no one gave a shit about McKnightstown. The college was at one time an all-girls school, though it was coed now. There was a girl there that I now allowed my thoughts to rest on.

I thought of Emily and how I would explain what had happened over there to her brother. I worried that she would blame me, too, and I'd never see her again after the funeral. Thinking of Emily, I dozed off. I dreamed of her and it was horrible. Like so many of my dreams of late, this one was full of death.

I killed her in the dream and she would appear again and I'd have to kill her. I wished to wake but the hellish visions kept coming. I killed her with my hands, strangling her and drowning her in a tub. I snapped her neck or watched her burn tied to a stake. I watched her being sacrificed ritually to some dark god—a machine of war three stories tall. I tried to stop it but failed every time. Mercifully something jarred me awake, finally.

The hearse scraped the steep driveway as it turned into the funeral home parking lot. The sound and bumping jarred me back to consciousness. The building sat at the far north end of town. Beyond it was only orchards, a gas station and a highway interchange for highway 15. I got out of the car and observed the black clad experts load Eric into the back of the funeral home, taking pains to ensure the flag draping his coffin remained perfectly in place the whole time. There wasn't anyone to impress with this display of precision, I wondered who it was for. I didn't care and I'm pretty sure Eric couldn't give a fuck either. I looked for him again, nothing.

I walked to the roadside and lit a camel. I saw a blue and gold historical plaque in front of the property and craned my neck to read it. The sign was far too high to read comfortably from the ground, "Historic McKnightstown" it declared. I was sure I was the only person who bothered to stop and read it. I wondered who the hell it was for. It was very wordy, explaining the original establishment of the town as New Salem, settled by a McKnight family from the Massachusetts Territory, that's as far as I got before I stopped giving a fuck.

I was more exhausted than ever now, sleep refusing to let go of me. But I was happy to be able to stand and smoke. It had been misting rain since we landed and I had my fill of the damp for today so I went to stand beside the hall under an overhang. One of the undertakers was having a cigarette there and I inquired with him about my accommodations. He said there was a cot for me. He asked if I planned to stand vigil over the "fallen" and I nodded squinting through my own smoke as the misting rain became a squall, bringing a cool misery to an already ugly sunset and a welcome end to another useless day.

When I sought shelter inside, I wished I hadn't. I was met by another of the undertakers and he wanted to make a show of shaking my hand and thanking me. I attempted a smile and nodded.

"Thank you for your service," the mortician said. I thought about a response, I'd heard it so many times before yet, I still hadn't figured out what to say to that. "You're welcome," perhaps, like I had poured him some coffee. Maybe if I was quicker on my feet I'd tell him not to thank me but to enlist and take my spot, I was not going back. So I just nodded and decided to be grateful. I was too fatigued to throat punch him. He showed me to the cot next to the flag-draped casket and offered me coffee or tea. He denied having anything stronger so I took him up on the tea.

I sat on the cot and shed my wet uniform coat, laying it out at one end so it would still look marginally presentable tomorrow. The mortician brought me my tea and I thanked him. I pulled some pills out of my bag and after the tea had cooled I washed a handful down with it and laid down for a little shut eye.

CHAPTER 2

EMILY

I awoke to someone prodding me with a delicate finger. I complained, "For fuck's sake." I had forgotten where I was and blearily sat up trying to get my bearings. The room was dark. There was a casket beside me and Eric was here now, too, near the door on the opposite end of the hall. Burning low and crackling, he cast little light making his appearance haunting, ominous. The finger-jabbing culprit ended up behind me as I sat up. It was Emily, Eric's beautiful younger sister.

She was talking but I couldn't hear her over the ringing in my own ears and the pounding headache I had. I raised a hand and nodded muttering something that stopped her jabbering. She pressed a bottle of water into my hand and I took a sip. Now I was aware of an intense bladder pressure and I eased my way up out of the cot. I looked around, asking her if she knew where the facilities were. Then I remembered.

Last year when I was here for her father's funeral, I had been here. It's the same place. I hate this place. I made my way to the restroom and did the best I could to clean up, brushing my teeth with a crumpled up paper towel, thrilled they didn't have one of those blow dryers bolted to the wall. Eric followed me there.

"Leave her alone."

It sounded like a warning. "You told me to look out for her if you didn't make it back, remember?"

"You know what I mean."

That was definitely a warning, there was the old rage I remember from the hospital where I first saw him. Eric had screamed at me and tried to strangle me, beat me and kill me in the hospital in Germany where we were evacuated to from Baquaba after the crash. When he wasn't yelling at me or trying to kill me, he was telling everyone that I had killed him or begging someone to kill me for him. I was getting used to that loud ghost. The peaceful respite he afforded me on the flight left me unprepared to once again confront his wrathful tirades.

5

"Fuck off, Boss." The mirror cracked in response. I fell backwards and crawfished across the floor ending up with my shoulder jammed under a urinal, and my heart beating out of my chest. Eric was gone but had somehow found the power to affect the living world. Or did I break the mirror? I found the courage to return to the sink and washed the fresh sweat and stale airplane stink from my body. I leaned my head against the broken mirror and cried. I don't know why. I was shaking and realizing I was hungry. A check of my watch, it was just a little after nine pm. A last look in the cracked mirror–I looked like hell. I found another pill in a pocket and washed that down and decided to face Emily.

Back in the parlor Eric was not waiting for me. I checked every corner and saw no sign of him. She was standing beside the casket with her hand resting atop it. I apologized for my condition and she shook her head.

"It's okay I should have let you rest after such a long flight."

"Dover to Harrisburg isn't very long." I looked at her and wanted to reach out and touch her, to comfort her, to be comforted. She had obviously been crying. Even so, she was a wonder to behold and her gentleness threatened to crack me.

She turned towards me. "Did you get a chance to eat anything yet?"

"No, I was just thinking about getting something." So I followed her to her car and we went out into the night.

We wound up at "Kildare's," an Irish pub on the town square. The menu said it was named for some obscure Civil War army soldier, Captain Kildare, who died ignominiously during a battle here no one remembered. That's how we remember the dead men who serve. An obscure footnote on a menu, a name on a highway overpass if you're really important like Major Dick Winters. I was happy not to have died ignominiously in some unimportant battle that had no meaning but washed away the happiness with a few pints.

Emily was talkative. She peppered me with questions about nothing. The flight, what happened to my luggage, did I have a place to stay or a car. Was I going back? But she asked me nothing about her brother. Finally I had to ask her what she knew about what happened, how it happened. Her demeanor changed in a blink.

"No," she shook her head, "the army didn't say. Just that he died in a combat operation."

That was a lie. It may have made it sound worthwhile but it wasn't quite true. It wasn't our combat operation. It was the enemies, but not ours. Why the lie? To make it seem less senseless than it was? I wondered if I should dare disabuse her of this illusion. Lies are nice places to hide.

I think she could hear me thinking about this and before I could decide what to do, she asked if it was true. I decided his death was no less senseless if the truth were known. Even if we had won some major battle for the cost of his life, in the end he was still dead. Her world was shattered and winning in Iraq wouldn't fix that for her.

"No, I can tell you what happened if you think–I don't really want to but, if you think it would help. I haven't shared it with anyone who mattered. Just the doctors and the intelligence guys who needed to know what happened so they could lie to the public about it properly."

She begged me. Taking one of my hands from the table into her warm, trembling grip, she pleaded and I surrendered. Then, he came through the door.

"Just tell her you killed me you dumb bastard. She deserves to know."

I looked at him in disgust for a moment, Emily noticed me looking away and searched for what I was seeing but I looked back to her, and with a squeeze of my hands brought her eyes back to mine. She released my hand and I sat back, wiped my brow, smiled, cleared my throat and started the story. I failed to ignore Eric as he slumped across the room making a mess of the place, leaving a trail of burning waste behind him. He was going out of his way to be a nuisance–tipping over glasses and lighting a woman's hair on fire. She didn't seem to notice so I looked away again just as his eye burst and its jelly oozed down his face, fresh steam rising from the withering socket.

"Ironically we were heading out of our fob for a much-deserved break. Your brother had orders to attend a supervisor course since before the invasion. So the army, not ready to admit we were in for a long fight yet, was sending him back to the world, temporarily, to attend the course. He was furious. But he had some leave to burn so he was gonna stop home to surprise you. I was in the chopper with him as a porter. I was just carrying his bags and had a shopping list for the company commander. I was going to fill the boss's order at the foreign exchange where you could get good booze cheap. Our army didn't allow us to have the stuff but our foreign partners have no such rules. The idea of fighting sober was wholly alien to them." I finished my pint and ordered another.

Emily pondered what to make of my story and muttered, "Makes sense," then drained her glass.

"I was going to be returning to the base for a promotion ceremony, take over a squad of my own. I would be replacing still another dead fellow. Well, we didn't get very far before we saw some sporadic fire, typical and nothing to worry about usually, but then we started catching rounds–big ones and in a few blurred moments there was a fire. Then a big jolt, alarms and screaming."

She saw me beginning to change, saw me hesitate. I felt myself changing. My body tightened and joints cracked from the strain of muscles in full panic. She was hanging on every word and her eyes were watering. "Please go on."

"Next thing I knew we were on the ground. I was choking on dust and smoke. My helmet was gone. I had lost a boot from the impact. My clothes were on fire. There were pieces of the crew sprayed across a field of twisted metal debris." I had to stop, I was trembling and she was in tears. She apologized to me. I wondered why. Then I felt eyes upon me. It felt like the whole bar was staring at me. I noticed I was crying again, tears warming my cheeks. The waitress came to ask if I was okay. I nodded but hid my face behind a napkin wiping the tears away.

Emily asked for the check, the waitress turned to look at the bartender who shook his head. "It's on the house, son."

Emily slapped a few bills down for a tip and we left holding each other, resting our heads against each other, out again into the night. Neither of us was in any shape to drive. Though not quite drunk, we were shaken by emotions. We sat in the car talking again about nothing, both of us stammering through apologies for upsetting the other. Finally she worked up the courage to brave a trip home.

"I can't take you back to the funeral home. You need a shower and a clean bed. I will get you back to the funeral parlor in plenty of time tomorrow." I nodded thinking she meant I should get a hotel. There was one near where we were parked. "I'm staying in my mom's guest house right now and there are three rooms there, you're welcome to have one for as long as you need." I didn't even feign a polite protest and jumped at a chance to be near her a little longer. I took ease and comfort next to her, immersing myself in her scent. She held my hand while driving with her other hand, scarcely letting go of me for more than a second during the trip to her home.

Her family estate was a ridiculous sprawling affair. Three main buildings in the Tudor style, in the middle of a few hundred unkempt acres fifteen minutes out of town and a hundred years ago. We entered the guest house through the kitchen door, inside there was no light. Emily explained, "I've been using candles and hurricane lamps since the guest house hadn't had electricity for years. The water works, so a hot shower will be no problem. That was run on a propane furnace at the main house sent over here somehow. It would just take a few minutes for the water to get here from there." No sign of Eric so I was able to breathe a little easier.

"The guest house kitchen was the kitchen for the main house, once upon a time. Servants would prepare everything here and schlep it over to the main house or the garden for meal service." I marveled at the kitchen that was big enough to play hockey in and I thought I might get lost in it. Eric wasn't there, though I couldn't be completely sure—there were lots of places to hide. She brought me a towel and lit several candles, plopped down a pair of whisky glasses and a bottle of scotch. I asked about the label and Emily described it as being from her late father's collection. It had been in the house since the Vietnam War and it sounded like it was easily worth a month's pay, maybe three.

I resisted her offer. "It's kinda late." I wanted the drink but needed sleep.

"No, just have one with me." She pretended to pout, I detected some cheer restored to her, I could not refuse now. I nodded and she poured. One turned into three as we talked.

"Thank you, I can't drink alone. I mean, to be honest, I have been of late. But I don't normally."

"No judgments from me. I've been trying to drink alone but people keep coming up to me to talk. Every airport stop, I have to get some civilian clothes."

"Did you say the air force lost your luggage?"

"They might have yes but, the airport in Harrisburg was the first to tell me about it."

"What's in the bag you got there then?"

"Just some bullshit." I took the papers out, the pills and the almonds that had spilled dust and skins all over the inside of the bag. I tossed the whole bag in a nearby trash bin. I started to smooth the papers out and she looked at them curiously.

"You want me to iron them? I think if we steam 'em in the microwave they go flat again, like a donut tastes fresh after a few seconds."

"You can nuke a donut?"

She nodded and poured another round. We threw that back by candle light and she poured more. "Makes it brand new, I swear, a few seconds and it's better than new!"

"Did we eat?"

"I don't remember!" She giggled and I joined her.

"I know we had menus at one point." She looked around her stool for them. I looked for them too. Then she rocked off her seat and made her way to the pantry. She found some Pringles and explained how they can't call them chips, then made duck lips with two of them, laughed them into crumbs on the floor and tried to get two more out to eat. "You got some fine learnin' in college."

"I also learned how to make a bong out of stuff. That was like day one."

One of the papers I had been flattening said I had an entitlement to the GI Bill and had instructions on it saying to give these papers to my institution's financial aid people. "You should totally do it, school's awesome." We had finished near half the bottle now between the two of us.

"I dunno what I'm going to do."

"Well you're not going back to the army, right?"

"Never, no fucking way. That place is beyond stupid. It's like a new kind of dumb. Like if dumb were a critter, like my dumb is a dog, the army is Godzilla." How did I tell her I only wanted to be near her and would do anything to make that happen?

She giggled and pretended to smash Tokyo with her hands, breaking up a small pile of Pringles she had liberated from the tube.

"I was hoping to eat some of those." I feigned protest and joined her in laughter.

"What are those other things there?" She pointed at my pills.

"Most of those are for erectile dysfunction." She just stared blankly at me a second and I thought I had gone too far. Then she laughed, catching a spray of Pringle crumbs in her hand and we laughed ourselves off our barstools.

I tried to excuse myself to get to the shower but she made me take another shot with her, which I did, after securing a promise from her to show me to the shower. In a few moments she graciously, but clumsily, guided me to the bathroom lit by candles in brass wall sconces. The water was hot. She asked my shirt size, I handed her my shirt. She looked for her glasses, sitting on top her head and read the label saying, "Right!" then went out of the room.

I wouldn't fit Eric's clothes but she shouted from down the hall, "I still have Dad's clothes in boxes, he's more your size." She rooted around in another room and returned with a collection of soaps and a set of pajamas. "It's warm in here now, do you mind if I stay with you, just to talk?"

"Sure." I couldn't refuse. Then Eric appeared scowling at me an inch from my face I fell backwards and clutched at the curtain, bringing it down with me. Darkness took me.

Emily was wrapping a towel around my shoulders when I could see again. I was shaking. "Are you cold?" she asked through the now deafening, ever present ringing, in my ears.

"Yes," I lied. I wasn't sure where Eric had come from, I had checked every corner. Where were my pills? I think I shouted the question in a stammering staccato. She brought me water and the wrong bottle from the kitchen table where I had left them. I asked for the bag, I think, or complained and she went back downstairs to search for the correct pill bottle. She delivered them all.

"Sorry, those two rolled under the kitchen island and I didn't see them the first time."

I found the pills I needed and choked down two and let her wrap me up in a comforting embrace. When I stopped shaking she helped me up. I think my leg fell asleep so I was gimpy as she guided me to a bed. I can't remember hearing anything, just a painful buzzing. But I know she was talking to me. I tried to read her lips but I couldn't make out what she was saying. I could only make out something about a "fish burger" and a "big-foot meatloaf." It made no sense.

Eric stood there accusing me with a pointed finger from the bathroom doorway. "I didn't kill anybody Eric!" I yelled. Emily recoiled in fright. I apologized a dozen times as I tried to calm down. I could hear again, the buzzing was almost gone. I was crying.

"What are you talking about? Who are you talking to?" I was staring past her, through her, when I shouted at Eric who vanished now, the pills worked fast. "You said 'Eric,' is he…is he here? Eric?" She looked around for him but he wasn't there.

"He's not here right now."

"Right now? Was he here?" A flash flood of fresh tears poured down her cheeks. She became sallow and broken somehow. Now she knows I'm crazy. She thinks I'm a fucking nut case, nothing left to lose, maybe she would understand.

"I imagine I see him sometimes. The docs say it's normal after what happened." I didn't sound convincing, of course I didn't know if I believed the damn docs.

"Does he talk to you?" Now she had grabbed me and looked directly at me. Do I lie?

"Yes. Not always, just sometimes."

"What does he say?"

I wondered how that would matter but I didn't want to tell her. I shook my head. "Crazy shit, he's angry and does things. Mostly he just stands there in a corner someplace looking mad."

She embraced me, sobbing. "Is he suffering?"

I shook my head and wept. I couldn't drag her into my madness. I couldn't bear to have her wondering if what I saw was real. I couldn't have her join me in this insanity. So I lied. "He's a figment of my imagination…I just imagine him, Eric is…" is what? I wondered. Was he fine, in a better place? What the fuck do I say now? I apologized again. We just stared into each other through tearful veils and fell together into bed and drifted to sleep.

I wish I could have held her all night. Instead, I arose after a while, fresh nightmares full of murder and fire jolting me awake. I was careful not to disturb her as I rose from the bed then sat in a nearby chair watching over her until the morning.

As the sun came up I noticed the three panel painting above the bed, prints of one of Monet's Water Lilies from a discount store. Light entering a wall of windows revealed there were doilies on the nightstands and pastels and plaid everywhere. It was a bizarre accidental gramma-married-a-lumberjack motif. I worried I would have a seizure and wondered if that wasn't why they didn't have electricity in the guest house. She roused from her slumber soon after the sun was up and studied me pitifully. "You slept in the chair?"

"I did. It's a comfortable chair." I couldn't stop lying to her though I loved her.

She showered and dressed quickly. I made my way to the kitchen and looked for food. Emily found me there. "You look lost, just take a seat. I know how to work the stove." She lit the stove with a match and excused herself, heading to the main house where I guess the refrigerator works.

I watched a limo arrive at the main house through a leaded glass window that distorted the images of the disembarking passengers comically. I watched a spider in a corner of the window for a minute then squashed it with a cigarette after taking my last puff. Death comes for us all and without warning. I felt worse about the spider than for any of the men I had killed in the war. What was wrong with me? Were puppies next?

Emily spoke little as she prepared breakfast, I should have offered to help but I was miles away then I asked if we would be late when I noticed the crooked limo pulling away.

"No, Mom is going to a service with her book club before the funeral. We have time…" her voice trailed off and she smiled brightly at me. With care she placed a perfectly round fried egg in front of me on a bagel. She had cut up a grapefruit, garnished it with vanilla cake icing or yogurt, beside it she had placed some fried spam.

I made a joke. "Are you in school for nursing or chef-ing?" She smiled and poured some scotch into a pair of mugs and asked if I wanted some coffee with it. I didn't see any coffee around and so shook my head. She was drinking her scotch straight too.

"Mom hasn't cooked since Dad died. I got a crash course of sorts, Eric was the chef. He taught me. Even when he was away with you and we talked on the phone, it was usually mostly about recipes and food." We finished the scotch and soon we were feeling giggly again. After breakfast I remembered I needed a toothbrush and she took me to a pantry stocked for Armageddon and excused herself. I found my way to the bathroom and got myself together. I took a handful of pills and decided I didn't need a shave and so wouldn't bother her for a razor. I felt like I still needed a shower so I stripped out of the pajamas and got in there. Eric didn't bother me.

After I got out of the shower, I brushed my teeth and stood staring into the sink hoping to make the ringing in my ears go away. I felt something warm and soft pressing against my back. I felt her arms wrap around me as she pressed more of her skin against mine, laying her head between my shoulders. My heart raced and sang. She tugged at my towel and I let it fall away. We were both unencumbered by modesty. She gently turned me to face her. Her eyes met mine for a moment. Then she kissed me. I didn't want to go the funeral anyway.

CHAPTER 3

MARA

We arrived late, shared an umbrella across the parking lot and Emily held us close against a stiff unseasonably chill breeze. We shared half a cigarette before going in and we embraced again before entering through the side entrance I had used last night. I found my coat, pressed and on a wire hanger waiting for me in the antechamber. One of the staff pressed my hat into my hand and led me to a seat in the main room. I lost Emily. As soon as we entered the main hall of the funeral home, she had been absorbed by a sea of black-clad women, relatives and friends and now I was alone again.

I searched for Eric and found him standing beside his casket, his flames were gone, his flesh just smoldering embers now. He was sad it seemed, examining his casket. They would not be opening it for what remained of him was never going to be put back into a form suitable for public viewing. There was a large oil painting of his last official army photograph. He was smiling, he was always smiling. Nothing got him down. He died, I told myself, because it was a tragedy.

It seemed God liked tragedy. You always see people talking on the news about the guy who died unexpectedly: "He was the greatest" or "everyone loved him" and "he had a good heart, would do anything for you, give you the shirt off his back." No one ever tells the news that they were glad that bastard was dead. It's never "I fucking hated that cunt! Thank God he's dead, now I don't have to do time for killing his ass." I avoided being that guy. I was an asshole. I didn't try to impress anyone. I never gave a shit about anybody. Fuck people. If I died people on the news would say "who?" God wouldn't get any punchlines from my death, so I survive. Fuck God.

While I sat, a group of men, uncles and neighbors, teachers, Eric's doctor, his mailman, everyone that knew him even slightly came by to shake my hand and I was asked to say a few words. I looked to Eric and he ignored me, he walked out of the hall and I think I heard him weeping. I tried to refuse but gave up and finally agreed to speak, just to shut the old men up.

I could have been kinder. They were just a well-meaning contingent of the local Veterans of Foreign Wars post. They had irritated me, though, and I was searching for a way out. I knew where all the exits were but that wasn't enough. I wanted out of this whole situation, only the chance to be near Emily kept me here.

During the service, led by a priest, I was introduced and led to the podium reluctantly. My eyes darted about the room a moment. I thought to bolt through the door but my eyes caught Emily, seated beside her mother, Mara, watching me with a plaintive look seeking something healing. I silently prayed, not knowing to whom, asking that I not embarrass myself. Then I found the courage to speak.

"Eric, Sergeant First Class Eric G. Salem, was the man I wished to be. I loved him as a son loves his father. He was at once my boss, my friend and a brother. His loss will be felt by so many..." I began to cry. "I'm sorry. I was with him when he died. I don't know what I can say to help you people take comfort. I miss him so much." I wept openly now and didn't care. "He died a hero." I was choking back tears and struggling to go on, "Not a TV hero, or a comic book hero or generic hero in the way every veteran is called that once a year on veterans day to help sell mattresses." I was angry and looked to Emily, "Eric gave his last breath to save me. I was trapped in a burning wreck. He tried to pull me free but could not, so he climbed into the fire and lifted me clear. I was the only one to survive that day...that's the man who God took from us, who we lost. He was what was best in men and still the one I want to be." By that I meant I wished I had died that day.

Mara Salem stood and fixed me with a murderous gaze. She seethed then let out an inhuman howl that shook every soul in the hall. A fresh sweat covered me as she stalked toward me, screaming that I had killed her son, that it was my fault. "Murderer, murderer!"

I tried to flee but she grabbed me before she was restrained. She swiped at me and pulled my hat from my hand as I made for the door. I ran from her, all the way to town where I found a dive bar next to a laundromat and climbed inside a bottle looking for oblivion.

Emily found me there some time later. I was drinking for free as there was fresh news of another horrible "setback" in Iraq on the TV. Twenty dead in an ambush, a suicide bomber killed a score of my brothers, people who would be missed unlike me. Emily sat beside me and ordered a drink. She apologized for her mother and for her relatives putting me in that awkward situation. I feigned indifference with a gesture but couldn't find words. She inched closer and wrapped an arm around me and leaned her head on me. I breathed her in. I apologized to her for being a mess and for upsetting her family.

Emily explained, "It doesn't matter, everyone understood. After her mother died, Mara was never the same. She withered overnight. Eric took a leave of absence to care for her. Dad was busy with work, his mistress and died a short time later. This loss hit her so hard—I do hope you'll forgive her." Emily had another drink and fought back tears. I looked at her. She had weathered so much tragedy in so little time. I had no one to lose. Before the war, before Eric, I had lost no one. Before Emily, I didn't worry about losing anyone.

"Of course I forgive her." I lied, if I could kill her and get away with it I might. I was angry right now and capable of carrying terrible grudges.

"That's when you met Mom for the first time. At Dad's wake, remember?" I would never forget our first meeting.

Eric was thinking about leaving the military to go back to college and be near his family home to help care for his mother. He was going to have a life. It was just after 9/11 and knowing our unit would be called up I had been trying to convince him to re-enlist. Only because I would be lonely without my best friend and the replacement supervisor would have been a dick. It was as much my fault as Charlie Daniels and the rest of redneck America and its relentless pantomime of support. Somehow despite all of that, our unit still shipped out under-manned. But Eric was there and I was there, glad to be with him.

Eric had explained to me one day in Iraq that his mom had made me a symbol of his decision to stay in the army, she told him in a letter to "be shut of me" as quickly as possible fearing something bad would happen to "the fool." I had never heard the phrase "be shut of" someone and had to look it up on the internet. It was at a dinner in the days following the funeral for his father that Eric announced he would be re-enlisting and expected to be sent to fight in the months ahead. Mara had made a dramatic exit after chastising Eric for the decision and informing me I was no longer welcome in her home. I never thought of either incident again until now.

Emily and I finished another round of drinks and she phoned a friend to pick us up and take us home. I reminded Emily what Mara had said a year ago and suggested I should get a hotel but Emily laughed that off, "I'm not hooking up in some no-tell motel." She stayed with me that night but I felt that she perhaps had begun to regret it, that there was something in her kiss that said this would be the last time. I didn't sleep but held her tight, staying awake and aware hoping to remember every breath and heartbeat together in the night.

Eric appeared just before the dawn and asked me, "Why? What had I done wrong? Why were there no angels? No Heaven? No peace."

I embraced my own madness and asked my hallucination, "What did you expect?"

"That if nothing else, the pain would stop!" He raged, "I feel myself dying! I burn! And I'm not alone here, there are so many dead and with you there is another—can't you see the 'Other?'"

CHAPTER 4

RACHAEL

I had almost forgotten about Eric. I had been wrapped in Emily. Now I found myself trying to calm him and make sense of his new explosion of emotion. I forgot what he said of another, one ghost was enough to drive me mad. I could not bear to be haunted by another. Soon, I noticed Emily cringing behind her blanket and wearing still more tears–I don't know how much of my half of the conversation she had witnessed but the strain on her was breaking my heart. I had to stop.

I fled to the bathroom and found more pills. I shook there, waiting for Eric to disappear. Eventually he did. The pills killed him, sometimes they did that. When I emerged from hiding, she was gone. I dressed and half-heartedly searched the cottage knowing I'd never find her. I didn't.

That night I found a dream apartment, a room for rent above a bar I stumbled into around dinner time. I found a friend too. A petite blonde student named Rachael who I'm pretty sure was underage, but had a convincing fake ID. I let her share some cigs and fries with me while I forgot about Eric standing by the pool table setting the balls on fire to amuse himself.

Rachael had a car and offered to take me shopping before the stores closed, after I shared the story about my luggage being lost. I choked down some pills in the bathroom before going with her and grabbed two quick shots at the bar while waiting for her to return from the washroom.

Rachael was exciting, and excited. Her eyeliner was too thick but I liked the contrast with her porcelain skin. She wanted to know everything. "Did you kill anyone?"

I lied, "No." I joked, "No one you'd have heard of anyway."

"What's it like over there?"

"Hot, bullets and bugs, it stinks. Everything is covered in dust that is mostly atomized shit it turns out."

"Gross!" She lit a camel, kissing it with her lipstick and passing it to me before lighting another for herself. "Are there women there?"

I thought of Jessica Lynch. The hoax the army had used to make her a hero, the lie to cover up the hell she had been through and what was done to her. The friends involved in her recovery and the heroes that died who wouldn't have a book and a movie for them. Hollywood was making movies about wars against aliens and bullshit right now and completely avoiding the real wars. The army was doing enough make believe I guess.

"Yes. There are women there. A lot of the locals are just tents with eyes. Though not all the Iraqi women live like that."

"Did you have a girlfriend?"

"No. I tried. I really did. It was stupid. Eric told me not to date at work. He always said you shouldn't shit where you eat."

She looked at me askance, "Most people meet their spouses at work, that's kinda how it works."

"That would explain all the single army guys then." We laughed.

"Who's Eric?"

"Oh, he's the fellow whose funeral I was at yesterday. I escorted him here, we were friends."

"Ooh, I'm sorry." She put her hand on my thigh. "I heard about that at school, that was a big deal, he's the first soldier from our town killed in a war since the last world war. My professor offered a free pass to skip and go to the funeral."

"There were a lot of people there. He was a great guy. Everyone loved him."

"Wait—I know his sister, you know, her name is Eugene or something!"

"Emily, yeah."

She remembered something she didn't like about Emily. "She's nice." Then she went back to her inquisition script. "Did you get days off there?"

"Actually, yes, we pretended to be having some kind of normal work schedule after we dug in. We had shifts and all, but a day off was rare. You'd get a few good hours maybe twelve if you weren't interrupted by an alert or a drill or some dignitary assholes. When I left they were making arrangements for guys to take rest and relaxation breaks, "R&R" out of the area, someplace nice like Germany, or Greece, Budapest or someplace where you could get liquor and whores…" I hesitated to go on, ashamed.

"Ha! How are you supposed to fight without those?" She laughed, "How long were you over there?"

I thought about it a moment. It seemed now that I had spent my whole life in the sand. "Little less than a year, I think." I made a show of counting my fingers for her.

"You're funny…oh we're here!"

And she parked her shiny new car far away from the mall where it was certain not to be scratched by someone being careless with their door. I thought she was just a lot of white noise and found her revolting for a moment. I wanted to fuck her, though, so I'd stick with her while she was interested and make the most of it.

I kept thinking about what Eric said about "The Other." Eric appeared in the backseat, I caught a glimpse of him in the side mirror as I unbuckled my seatbelt. "She's going to try and kill you, did you know that?" Now my hallucination was losing his mind. I ignored him. "Don't listen to me then, I'd kill you myself if I could right now. I know you're going to fuck this slut–not a day after my sister. Fuck you, man."

We made our way across the parking lot, Eric stayed in the car, setting it ablaze. Rachael didn't seem to notice so I didn't worry her with it. She continued her relentless interrogation, "Are you going back?"

"Nah, I doubt it. I have some medical issues after the crash."

"Medical issues? Crash?"

"Yeah, I was with Eric when he died. We were shot down near Baquaba. I was the only survivor." She gasped and wrapped her arm inside mine and placed her opposite hand on top of my own.

"I can't imagine! How, my god–that's amazing to have survived. I'm so sorry. You seem fine, though. How badly were you hurt?"

I thought about it and the doctors' puzzlement over my lack of apparent serious injuries. It was a miracle. "Not very, I was lucky, my wounds were minor. They army called them "million-dollar injuries." Good enough for a Purple Heart and pension but no significant damage. I got a concussion, some bruises. But I've had more painful sunburns after a drunken weekend in New Jersey. Speaking of sunburns, I saw a sign for a waterfall nearby, do you know it?"

"Yes, we can lie out there on the rocks and get burnt. There is also a fun hangout spot I could show you sometime!"

She was quiet for a while, but squeezed my hand and pulled me close as we went inside. We got an Orange Julius, Rachael put some vodka in it from a flask she carried in her purse and we found a fitting room in a JC Penney to have sex in. I found some civilian clothes not borrowed from Mr. Salem's donation pile and Rachael got me back to the bar in plenty of time to drink and forget that I should regret what I had done. Then we went upstairs to do it all again.

Rachael offered me some cocaine but I was happy with the effect of my pills and the booze at the moment. She was gone in the morning but Eric was back, sitting on the floor of our sparsely-furnished apartment. I wondered if he would burn a hole in the floor, what might happen. Would he fall through and kill everyone below? I saw less and less of him as the days went by and I clung to a bottle as I ran out of pills.

I did notice some of the places he sat or stood had begun to show signs of warping from heat, or burn marks. Eric was becoming increasingly real. Manifestly able to affect the physical world, beyond the hallucinatory ways he did, like in the restaurant that first night. I mostly just languished there in the dive bar in my basement trying to wash him and myself away.

CHAPTER 5

REGRET

Emily found me there, maybe two or three weeks later. She entered through the back door of what had become my bar. She looked hopeful then disappointed. I thought she might cry. I looked around wondering if Eric was nearby and if she saw him. Of course he was there standing in hissing, crackling judgment of me. He tried to tell her about my recent activities.

"He was fucking Rachael this week, someone named Candice and drinking all his calories. He hasn't had a meal in several days now and is probably going to hang himself from a rafter in his dismal bachelor pad upstairs. He can't do it soon enough as I understand that's the only way I can rest. Would you help me kill him?" I don't think she could hear him. She looked ashamed and piteous all the same. She pulled my beret from her bag and thrust it toward me

"I wanted to bring this back to you. It wasn't easy finding you, I wasn't sure you were still in town." She left out the fact that there were a lot of bars to check. I felt a hole in the hat, a small slit in the crown of the wool felt. There was something crusty like blood or snot around the puncture.

"Thank you, but I don't need it, never liked it." She noticed my puzzlement over the state of it.

"I found it in the garden, I'm sorry some animal may have gotten to it..."

"It's alright, I don't need it." I threw it into a trashcan behind the bar. "You want a drink? The bars not open 'open' yet but I live here so...Charlie lets me just grab what I want and I settle up at the end of the week." Charlie nodded at the mention of his name from the other end of the bar where he was trying to load up his beef jerky machine.

"No thanks. I'm not usually a big drinker, those days were not—I'm sorry for how I was, what happened."

"For leaving me there or...? There's nothing to be sorry about. I get it." I lied. I didn't understand anything at all.

"Is there someplace we can talk?" She had something important to talk about so I led her upstairs hoping Rachael wasn't there or her clothes weren't

21

strewn about. She had become something of a regular visitor. Emily barely concealed shock at the appearance of my place and I felt very filthy, ashamed and then angry. I apologized for the mess and invited her to sit on a box that had been doing for a chair lately. I was grateful the stale ashtray bouquet was concealing any hint of Rachael's scent and that none of her belongings were out in the open. I asked her what was on her mind and she looked lost for a moment then asked if I was alright.

"Yeah, I'm just...the maid doesn't come by 'til Tuesday." I don't know why I tried a joke.

She looked lost for a moment, tilted her head and folded her hands in her lap. "I'm worried about you. I heard you were here and there was an army guy asking about you at the house the other day. The airport brought your luggage by the funeral home. I have it in my car. But I'm worried about you. You can't be planning on being like this for much longer, can you?"

Like this? What the fuck was she talking about? I was still healing from the hospital, the crash, what was I supposed to do? I was angry but dared not show it. I probably failed. Eric appeared behind her.

"I'm still—I don't have anywhere to go. I don't have a car, I don't have a job except cleaning up around the bar to cover my tab but I don't know what to do right now. I thought you..." I was crying now again. She got up and tried to comfort me with a touch. I pushed her away. "I don't know what I thought about us. I see you regret it, and I don't blame you, but I'll figure it out on my own."

"Do you still see him?" She didn't care about me but was obsessing over her dead brother. Now I was furious so I just laid it all out there.

"Yes, most days. He's right behind you now." I pointed at Eric. She turned to look and spoke directly to him, asking if he could hear her.

"Tell her I said yes." He hissed.

"Fuck no man, you're dead, I'm imagining you and I'm not going to be some kind of goddamn Ouija board for you two!" I grabbed a coat and slammed the door as I stormed out past her.

I went to the bar across the street and sat down, had two shots before she caught up to me. She was fighting back fresh tears as she pleaded with me to talk to her.

"I'm seeing someone else right now. Really I don't know if..." She interrupted me.

"I know, Rachael, she's a schoolmate, I know everything. She's barely 20, you know."

"So what?"

"She's into bad shit, she's not going to finish the term and I think she's heading for expulsion. She's trouble. You aren't her only friend who can get her a fix, you know."

That stung. I don't know why but it did. I pretended it didn't bother me. "So what, I wasn't looking to marry her. I don't even know how long I'm sticking around."

"I thought you wanted to go to college, have a life and be like him. Not waste your life in a stupor." That cut me deeply and I had no words but I saw Eric now again at the bar, this time setting a stool aflame with his ass. She cut me again. "He gave you his life! You said he died so you could...crawl inside a bottle and kill yourself. I wish you'd hurry it up because it's killing me to watch you do it so slowly. And if Eric can see you...how can you do that to him?" She wept freely but I tried to fight my own tears.

She was right. I caught a glimpse of myself in the mirror behind the bar. I looked a hundred years old. I was dying. I couldn't remember the last time I had real food, or saw daylight. She was about to slap me when I turned to her and said I was sorry. It wasn't a lie, and for it she embraced me again and held my head tight to her chest as I began to sob. The bartender told us to get lost and she took me to a friend's house where I slept for days.

CHAPTER 6

EAGLE

When I woke there was no booze to be found, but a host of new prescription bottles on a silver tray on an ottoman beside the bed I was resting in. There was an unfamiliar smell, fresh cooking, wafting in from a kitchen downstairs. There was an enormous wall of glass, great windows like some "A" frame millionaire hunting lodge with a breathtaking view of the local reservoir. I had an IV stuck in my arm and there was a machine monitoring my vitals. I worried what might have happened to me. What I might have done. I was cold, and I ached. Everything was stiff as I tried to raise myself out of bed but the sound of footsteps stopped me.

A tall, dark-haired woman entered. She wore turquoise and silver, a bead choker and her long hair in a simple ponytail. "I'm a friend of Emily's, you're a guest." She said with a smile.

"How long have I been out?"

"Three days, you've been here three days and long nights. You've been very sick and haven't been able to hold down food. That's what the needle in your arm is for."

"Who's paying for all this?" All of this looked expensive to me.

"Emily's loaded, you do know Emily, right?" She laughed softly as she looked at me wryly. She introduced herself as Eagle Elk, Eagle to her friends. It was her last name that she preferred to her own first name ever since she joined the Navy. I liked her immediately. "I was a nurse in the navy, now I'm a therapist by trade. I work at the campus health center and teach as an assistant while pretending to pursue my Ph.D." She didn't look old enough to buy beer legally but she had already lived two of my lifetimes. "And I'm married, mister, so don't get any ideas! My husband is the chef working so hard in the other room so...behave, you." She winked at me.

I wondered if she was going to show me her Nobel Prize that her grandkids presented to her at a special ceremony when I was still learning to ride my bike so many years ago.

"What happened to me?"

She looked at me pitifully for a moment. She sighed and broke it down for me honestly. "You, sir, are a budding alcoholic. You were having acute withdrawals and tremors. Emily said you weren't even a drinker before, during your last visit a year ago you refused alcohol but you've advanced quickly."

I nodded. It was painful but real. Eric appeared and sat down next to me setting the room ablaze. She must have noticed a change in me. Unlike Emily, she didn't seem to be able to locate Eric. Emily had located Eric the last time I had seen them together.

"You were on some kind of bender and apparently hell-bent on dying this time. Under pressure Rachael admitted to supplying you with amateur medications while stealing your army scripts…so I got in touch with the VA for you and got you some new meds. Emily is out looking for a proper apartment for you now and a proper doctor is coming to see you this afternoon. In the meantime, there is a Nokia charging in the office. Emily bought it for you so you can reach her, or me, whenever you need to."

I explained I didn't like those phones, I thought they were an annoying fad, that no one would want to be tethered to a leash like that willingly. She laughed and showed me a pager she still carried saying she had dropped it in the fish tank more than once. She went on to explain it wasn't optional, that the phone was a condition of not being sent to an inpatient facility.

"You said a proper doctor—you're not a doctor?"

"No, I'm not a medical student, either. I switched to psychology and I'm a therapist. I'm hoping to be your therapist, not to put too fine a point on it. I'm a specialist in post-traumatic stress and addiction. In nursing I was a psych nurse, my father was an addict, I'm an alcoholic, and have experienced, and worked through my own trauma. I think I can help you, if you'd let me."

How could I say no? I nodded.

"Good!" and breakfast arrived. Her husband was a towering giant, twice her age easily, very white, but no less jovial. He spoke easily, proudly explaining his dish, as he placed it before me with instructions for how to eat it properly. He kissed his wife and she shooed him away.

"He loves an audience, it's his defect. I think he wants to quit medicine to do one of those cooking shows on PBS."

"He's a doctor?"

Eagle nodded, "A neurologist to be exact. But we call him Paul. He teaches now, he suffered a stroke after a motorcycle accident that was not kind to him. He is still a top chef." She got up to excuse herself, "You should consider giving Emily a call to let her know you're awake now, more than any time before anyway. She was here for most of it helping me clean you up. But she finally had to leave. If I were you, mister, I'd plan on a long stay to get still more rest." She pointed out a bucket nearby in case I couldn't hold down the food and she vanished.

I devoured the plate, hardly stopping to taste anything then unhooked the medical equipment. I found my clothes in a familiar nearby green army duffle, dressed and went to explore. I found the office and the cell phone with a post-it note stuck to it with my name and a phone number I supposed belonged to the device. I picked it up and saw that it had "Emily" preprogrammed into the address book and called her. On the other side was a very-relieved-sounding Emily.

"God it's so good to hear you, you sound like yourself."

"Thanks, I feel worn a bit."

"Eagle said you'll feel terrible but over the next four months you'll feel better."

"Four months?"

"I'm sorry I wasn't there when you woke up, I was there as long as I could be but Mother, school–I can only hide for so long."

"It's okay, Eagle told me you were here all you could be. Thank you. And thanks for this phone."

"I'm sorry for what I said. I don't know what came over me. I really didn't mean it."

Then I started to remember. "No, you were, you are right. I'm sorry for being a mess and all."

"Just the same, I'll never do it again."

"No it's okay, really, I can't thank you enough for this–everything."

"I still really need to talk to you, it's important, so get rest and feel better soon, I don't want to try and do this over the phone."

She still wanted me to be an Ouija board for her and her brother. Why not? Maybe he'd stop trying to kill me. "Okay."

"Great, I'm going to risk my grade dropping and skip tomorrow and we can spend the whole day together, okay?"

"Sure." I was afraid to be with her a whole day, I don't know why. Then I lied, "I would love that." Later that day, Eric found me.

"The Other, it lives inside you. He torments me. He keeps the hurt in his hands. He makes the fires burn. He is you. He killed me. You killed me. You killed everyone on the bird that day."

CHAPTER 7

GUILT

I fell to the floor on the spot and wept. I saw the dead from the squad. The nameless pilots I didn't know, but they weren't real like Eric. They were just memories. When I recovered, I took the phone and my clothes and started walking towards town. Eric followed me, angrily pleading with me to return to the sanctuary of the super couple and their good intentions. I raged at him, gesturing wildly. I must have looked insane to the people driving past me on the highway. I shouted at him, he screamed at me, setting the roadside debris and dry grass alight.

Everything behind us burned. After a while, the sky was being choked with smoke and I struggled to understand how no one else could see what I was seeing, how it was not real to them. I coughed, gagging at the smoke when the wind changed or when I walked too slow and Eric, now a raging inferno, not a smoldering mess, tailed me by only an few paces. I saw more of my friends, now dead, in the ditches beside the road.

They were people I thought were still alive, or were when I was shot down. They were shot dead or blown to pieces now, burning or just broken in ways the living couldn't bend. They were all just wilted deflated lumps of people in that dull blood-rot color. You had to look twice to know you were looking at the dead. Our brains are trained to see dead like in a horror movie, but it wasn't like that. No film I had seen had captured the true look of the dead. Sadly the news lately and the internet had been doing just that, so the world was getting a crash course in identifying the really-real dead.

I found my way back to the bar and got comfortable inside a glass. I noticed my phone had some missed calls but I just ignored it as the battery drained a bit slower than the booze. I spotted Rachael and she took me upstairs where she opened a fresh bottle of vodka and we drank it, mixed at first, then straight and we slept together late into the morning after making love with the music up too loud.

I was ripped from a refreshingly pleasant, erotic dream by Rachael's elbow in my ribs.

"Babe, someone's in the apartment," she whispered and I stood to confront an attacker. Eric stood in the closet

"Who is it?"

"Emily. You were supposed to spend the day with her," he said without as much as a look in my direction. He just stared at the floor. Emily appeared at the beaded curtain that did for a door to my bedroom. She looked at me and I relaxed, she looked at the bed and who occupied it before issuing a grave threat.

"Get out, bitch! If I ever see you near him again, I will kill you." I was afraid for a second. I can't imagine what Rachael felt, but she gripped a sheet to herself and gathered up her things wordlessly, looking at me only once before obsequiously squeezing past Emily and out into the world. Then Emily turned her wrathful gaze to me. Gone was the joy and sadness, sorrow, pity or concern. "I don't know why…what are you doing?"

"I'm sorry." I don't know why I said that, I knew it was the last thing she wanted to hear.

"Fuck 'sorry!' Do you know how you worried my friends, how embarrassed I am? Can you even for a minute think about anything besides yourself and the fucking bleach blonde blow-up doll?" She didn't wait for an answer, "and you're clearly drinking again." She kicked an empty across the floor. "I don't know why I'm trying. Why I care." She looked around and tried not to look so exasperated. "Just get dressed, we're going to get you clean if it kills you." She headed out the door announcing, "I'll be in the car," as she slammed the door shut causing an empty to fall from some unseen perch. It was something I'd have to worry about later.

I rushed into some clothes, did my best to ignore the headache and sick feeling in my stomach, the tremors in my hands. I chewed some pills, and washed them down with something from a glass that looked like it might do the trick. Yup, it was vodka. I hurried down the stairs and out onto the street to the waiting car. I caught myself looking for Rachael, afraid for her.

CHAPTER 8

RECOVERY

Over a few meek protestations Emily drove me to a Lutheran church, led me arm-in-arm into the basement and I sat stone-faced through my first recovery group meeting. The judging eyes of the people there ignited fresh rage in me. But Eagle was there wearing a smile and Emily held my hand, her touch probably kept me calm enough not to black out and kill everyone in the room. Eric paced outside. I could see his feet through a glass block window at the street level above. I spoke to no one during the meeting. After the meeting following several failed attempts by Emily to introduce me to the people there, she gave up and led me back to the car. She spoke to Eagle for a few minutes and Eagle was nice enough to smile at me at least, though I was too ashamed to look at her.

"I have a craving, indulge me. If you do I promise it'll be worth your time, okay?" We went to get some frozen yogurt.

"I'm sorry for the Rachael mess. I don't know why I'm apologizing, really, you've been quite an ass and she's awful, she really is."

She was right. I didn't apologize, just kept my mouth full of fro-yo. Her demeanor had softened and I was glad for it. I thought to speak but she stopped me. "The meeting people gave me a schedule and a list of phone numbers for you. Keep it with you, okay? Try to talk to someone there. Eagle will help you, too, she completely understands. She was a train wreck herself once, she gets it."

I nodded, "Is that what you wanted to talk to me about?"

"Yes, but there is more." There is always more. She paused a moment and ordered her thoughts. I finished my yogurt and fished out the final, now frozen, gummy bear from the bottom of the cup. "I have to go away. I'm taking a semester abroad. It's my last chance to do it and Mother insists I do it, she's paying for it all, of course, so I really must."

"But you don't want to go?"

She took my hands in hers. "No, I really want to stay with you. Do you understand?"

I didn't and was honest about it for a change. "No, I don't. Not really, I thought you wanted me to be a radio for talking to your brother's ghost. You can see him, can't you?"

"No, I wish I could."

"No you don't."

"But I can feel him. I know he's almost always near you and I want to tell him so much…" She was fighting back tears. It was about him. "But more than that, I care about you deeply. I know it's silly but–I want desperately for you to be here when I get back. I can't bear to think you might be gone. I really am happy to see you, every time. Okay, not that last time. I was happy you were there and that you came with me for the meeting and fro-yo."

"He wants you to kill me." And the blood drained from her face. "He spent the first few days begging everyone around me to kill me. He thinks it's the only way he'll be free to rest. He said Rachael was going to kill me and I kept waiting for her to do it. A lot of days I want to die. I'm only sticking around hoping to be around you. Why can't I come with you?"

"There isn't anything for you where I'm going. Eagle is here, she helps me and I know she can help you. There is a recovery group, the VA hospital isn't far, and you can get your medications and help there. I was hoping to convince you to enroll, we have rolling enrollment. And you don't speak French, how are you going to get by in Paris?"

"She's not going to Paris." Eric wore the smile of the cat that ate the canary. He was pleased to reveal this little tidbit. He sought to upset me and I ignored him but set out to test this.

"Paris?"

She tap-danced, "I don't have all the particulars in a brochure or anything but I will have my phone and I'll get you an address as soon as I have one." I wondered if it was a lie, and why.

"You will be back?"

"Oh, yes, of course, yes." She seemed surprised by her own commitment but I decided to forget about it. She was helping me and all I could do was be grateful.

"I need to call those VA people. I'm knee deep in unopened mail from them."

"I saw." She frowned playfully. "I know all the horror stories; I saw that *Dateline* or whatever about it."

"The Walter Reed mess?" I guessed.

"Yes, that is embarrassing."

"In fifteen years no one will remember. It'll probably still be there pretending to be fixing whatever is wrong. But that's more the army than the VA. The VA did a thousand other horrible things to veterans, though. But I blame congress. Don't get me started on those bozos."

32

Eric snickered there standing close enough beside me that I could feel the heat from his burning flesh and smell the stink of it. "She changed the subject, you didn't even see it. Ah well, women have secrets it doesn't matter and I can't help you. I'm bound to you and can't very well follow her." I ignored him.

"Oh and because I don't like that place of yours, I got you a new place in town, close to the school but not over a bar." She reached into her bag and pulled out an envelope with an address printed on the front. "The keys are in there and all the paperwork you'll need. The first month's rent is paid, it's a little more than what you paid at the bar but you can manage. There is a second bedroom and you can find a roommate if you need to. That's where I expect to find you when I get home, okay? It's even furnished for you, no milk carton chairs." My heart sank. I was supposed to be looking after her for Eric but I was the one needing looked after.

Emily finished her sweet treat. "Let's get out of here." She smiled so that I pondered what it was she had in mind. Was she going to feed me to a shark or take me back to her place for another romp? I couldn't be sure and my normal high state of anxiety became nearly crippling. It's probably how I was surprised by the carjacker.

CHAPTER 9

ASSASSINS

We walked the half block to Emily's parked car. I offered her a camel but she said, "I quit." I turned away to light my cig in a cupped hand to shield it from the breeze. I opened the door for her and heard a distinct sound—gunmetal striking flesh and bone. My whole being exploded with electric fright, time stopped. I wheeled around to see Emily crumpling to the ground. There was a figure with a gun.

He was bringing a bright revolver to bear too slowly at this range to be sure of a win. He was brown and tattooed, in an oversized white shirt and baggy dark jeans. I leapt at him and he fired a shot, I saw the muzzle flash, but did not hear the shot before everything went black.

I found myself in a hospital operating room, standing next to Eric who was now comforting in his demeanor. His hand was on my back and he was thanking me again and again as we watched doctors pull a bullet from my chest. I asked him where Emily was and he said she was in a waiting area and safe. I went to the waiting area and there were two plainclothes detective types interviewing Emily with a little old lady whose hospital name tag identified her as a social worker. A frantic Mara was just arriving. I realized I was out of my body and took advantage of it; I took a swipe at the old lady just to get a rise out of Eric who laughed from behind me. Mara turned and stared right through me. "Can she see me, Eric?"

"No, no one can see us...we're like the ghosts from the *Christmas Carol* right now." Eric shrugged, doubting his own declaration for at least a moment.

Mara turned away and ranted at the police and Emily, scolding her for being in that part of town, for being with me. She ranted that I should be locked up or given the chair. Emily defended me. She said I had been shot but then grabbed the man and wrestled the gun away.

The cops asked Emily if she had seen how exactly I had taken the carjackers eyes, what manner of tool I had used to burn them out. She seemed completely perplexed. Then a suit entered.

Emily pleaded with the officers to tell her if I was in trouble and the officers said that the district attorney would decide my fate. Mara continued to rant and Emily shouted her down and cursed at her viciously. I hadn't realized there was friction between the two. The detectives said that since a man was killed on a public sidewalk in full view of the public that the DA would determine if charges were warranted or not. Emily defended me and decried the officers inference of murder. "It was self-defense, you assholes!" Then the suit produced a letter from his coat pocket and stepped between Emily and the cops. He handed the letter to the noisiest detective then leaned in and whispered to Emily. She nodded and looked satisfied as the detective read the form in disgust.

I felt the peaceful darkness, the thing Eric called "The Other" I realized I knew it now. In this semi-dead state I knew it was there and for the first time was conscious of it. I thought to make it take the cops. I wondered if I could. I tried. One of the officers seemed to briefly convulse, like he had been surprised by a sneeze and managed to hold it in. Then he seemed to be choking, I blacked out, my last thought a terrible dread that I had unleashed The Other and he would kill Emily.

There was an old crumpled man in horn-rimmed glasses and tweed sitting next to me reading a file when I awoke next. I was in my own body again. "Water, coffee?"

"Water, yes, thank you." I sat up and with a trembling hand, took a cup from the older fellow. "Thanks again."

"I see my presence is making you anxious, I am sorry. I'm Walter Ewing, the Assistant District Attorney for victims' advocacy. I'm just here to check a box on a form, you are in no legal jeopardy, the interview is only a formality and if you like, you may opt to end the interview and obtain counsel prior to making any statement."

I nodded, "Okay, what happened?" I honestly didn't remember.

"Do you wish to waive your right at this time?"

I looked for Eric, he nodded at me so I agreed, "Yes."

"Very well, the carjacker, he struck and injured Ms. Salem, then shot you, is that correct?"

"I remember hearing someone get hit but I don't remember if I was shot first or not."

"It's okay. There were some very credible witnesses there who reported that was what they saw. We got a statement from a state trooper getting some coffee across the street, a federal marshal escorting a prisoner to the courthouse near where you were parked and the pastor of the Anglican Church walking nearby. They all said they saw a woman on the ground when they turned to hear where the shot came from. The pastor saw Emily being struck and tried to warn you. He had the best view. The marshal moved away with his witness, and the trooper came running. He reported you on top of this fellow bleeding from a chest wound and squeezing the assailant's wrists until they were crushed."

I began to worry more now and he seemed to sense my apprehension.

"Did you crush this man's wrists?"

"I guess, I mean if that's what the cops saw, I guess, I don't remember. I have PTSD and when I get too stimulated sometimes, angry or scared I can black out I don't remember what happens. Someone has to tell me afterward." This seemed to confuse the fellow.

"Has no one else spoken to you about this yet at all?"

"No. Not that I remember."

He dug through his manila folder and let out an exasperated sigh. "I'm terribly sorry son. Do you have any questions for me?"

"Is Emily okay?"

"Oh yes, yes, and thank you. I, uh, I don't know how to tell you this but, I'm a friend of the Salem's. Arthur, Emily's grandfather was a good friend and mentor to me as a young man. His son, Emily's father, Bill, got me through college. After I struggled to work my way through pre-law, maintaining the grounds at the estate, he picked up the tab for me to finish at the middling law school I was able to gain acceptance to. My own father had recently died in prison then and I had no support or resources of my own. I was at the funeral. I can't imagine what it was like for you, how you are suffering now. I heard some of your nightmares here at your bedside waiting. What you said, at the service—that was very powerful. And yesterday, you saved Emily. Eric would be proud." He began to cry, took a handkerchief from his coat and wiped the tears away.

"Mara is an old woman, Emily is all that's left of that family and I want to personally thank you and shake your hand if I may." He offered his hand and I took it. He gently shook my hand. "Know in your heart, son, no matter what you might think in your head, that you are a hero, son."

"Are you okay?"

"Yes. Thank you. As I said I'm the assistant DA for victim advocacy, I'm here to help you get help if you need it. If you are okay for now and don't need anything, we can finish this procedural interview at a later time." He tapped on his business card on the bedside table. "You call anytime. My personal mobile and home phone numbers are on the back. Anything you need."

"I did have one more question."

"Of course."

"Who was the carjacker?"

Eric stepped in from the hallway. "He's a low-rent thug, a mentally defective cholo, with an I.Q. of maybe 60, a parolee awaiting deportation. He was apparently contracted to kill you. He's been cursing and muttering about it and trying to find the bitch that paid him. But he's quite confused and unable to adapt to being bound to you as he is now."

"Bound to me?"

"You killed him, you and The Other. Boiled his fucking eyes in their sockets, his brain was steamed by the blood you boiled. It was the same fire that killed me, the fire of The Other. It scared the fuck out of the medics and officers responding. He was still cooking, sizzling after you were led away."

"Excuse me?" Walter inquired in response to my question to Eric.

"I'm sorry, I was thinking something else, I missed his name."

"Oh, I don't have it, actually it seems left out of the file here. I actually don't have anything on him. I remember being told he was here illegally, a low-level career criminal and gang member. That's all I know. You need to rest and heal, we can talk later, I'll get that information ready for you, should've had it in the file, I am sorry. Goodnight, son."

I turned my attention back to Eric, "Where is the bastard?"

"He's in the bathroom, trying to find his eyes. You could ask him, he's quite talkative if you speak Spanish." Eric spoke Spanish, French, German and Serbo-Croatian; I barely spoke English, a victim of the public school system. Eric led the blind assassin from the bathroom so I could interrogate him. I learned nothing more than what Eric had already told me. He was looking for his eyes and wondering why in heaven he was blind. He didn't understand that he wasn't in Heaven and didn't believe he could be in Hell. I was becoming annoyed so I asked him who had paid him to kill me and he clammed up. I got out of the bed and tried to put the squeeze on him, but how do you menace a blind ghost?

"The Other, let The Other loose. You can use it to hurt him like it hurts me relentlessly." I tried. There was a vortex of flame and panicked Spanish pleading that gradually became fluent English.

"What do you know, he speaks English!" Eric laughed, "I guess it's just a matter of temperature gradients." We both laughed as the blind burning ghost gave up the location of his hidden stash and his address in town.

"Who paid you to shoot me?"

"It was my PO, man. She gave me $1,000 and said she'd lose my hot piss test that would put me back inside."

"Weren't you facing deportation?"

"For six years, if you don't go court, they don't look for you. I got deported twice."

"I'm glad you're dead."

"Stop the burning, man! Where are my eyes, why can't I see?" I used what little control I could exert over the darkness, The Other to leave the cholo suffering there. I turned up the heat and his screams were a lullaby sending me to sleep where I hid for the next couple of days.

CHAPTER 10

SUPERHERO

Eric knew town well enough to get me to the thug's home. We walked there and found the building which was once a large townhouse now divided into several tiny apartments. This third floor apartment was shared with at least three others. It was on the town's only notorious street, the part of town the junkies frequented and where the cops knew everyone's names. The front door was open and I let Eric reconnoiter the interior.

"The three junkies inside are passed out, half dead or dead. No problem." I went in, found the shoe box and several other caches of valuables and helped myself. There was less than $3,000. I shook my head and decided to take only a single hundred dollar bill with me. On the way out I looked around and felt like a superhero. I had at least one helpful ghost, and he was real. I asked Eric if he could take care of the place and he nodded, his flames brightened. "I'll wait for you to get home and order a pizza to establish and alibi."

I walked home. On the way I ordered a pizza using my Nokia. I beat the pizza guy and started digging through the mountain of VA mail I had been ignoring. I put in a call to Emily and left a message asking her to find me as soon as she had a chance. The pizza guy arrived with my pie and I gave him the hundred. He asked if I needed change, I closed the door. I heard sirens in the distance and smiled. I tried to think of a superhero name.

I called a number in the VA letter and confirmed an appointment there in a few days. The VA hospital was a thirty-minute drive from my place so I decided to buy a vehicle. I got a newspaper at the campus union building and one of those auto trader magazines and started looking. I headed back to the house and watched TV. Dean Koontz's *Phantoms* was on. It was just starting and I felt lucky to catch the beginning of a movie. The heroines were driving into town in a Jeep. I took it as a sign, made some popcorn, enjoyed the schlock fest and went Jeep shopping that evening.

I picked out a green one with a manual transmission and a soft top. I paid with a check, spending about half of my first enlistment and re-enlistment bonus that I had kept stashed for several years. Unlike most of my colleagues, I had not squandered mine the day I got it or lost it in a card game or to a stripper ex-girlfriend or get-rich-quick scheme. I went to find Emily the next day, annoyed that she had not returned my calls.

I drove to the family estate, and I asked Eric to check the house. "She's not there. I don't know where she is. Mother isn't there, either." That was odd. I headed by the school and no one had seen her. I remembered she was friends with Eagle and I went to the health center. Eagle was in session so I waited. The rainbow hair dye the student worker receptionist was sporting did not detract enough from her face to make me want to talk to her. When Eagle was done, she let her client leave before even greeting me.

She smiled in her unique wry manner, "Well, hello, young man, what brings you here today? My constant badgering voicemails, no doubt?"

"I didn't get any voicemails."

"Really?"

"What number did you call?"

She read me the wrong number from her cell phone call log. I gave her the right one and we laughed. "Well I guess I take back all those awful things I said about you when you didn't call me back." She had a gift for making me smile. "So what can I do for you today?"

"I'm looking for Emily."

"I haven't seen her since the day of the shooting. She called me and I met her at her mother's home."

"Was she okay? She's not calling me back."

"Well yes, she seemed fine, considering." She folded her arms leaned against the doorframe and gave it all a good think.

"Did you hear what happened?"

"Yes, someone tried to steal her car with a gun! Here, it's never happened here before."

"Well we were lucky the S.O.B. didn't have a driver's license, he would have driven by and probably killed us both."

"We?"

"Yes, I was with her."

"She didn't mention you were there."

"She didn't? Was her mom with her when you visited?"

"Mara? Yes. I think so. She was in and out with tea, scones. She explained that Emily was going out of state to stay with some relatives in Bar Harbor or Paris someplace like that." I must have let the hurt show. "Did you want to come in, sit down and talk? I don't have any more appointments today."

I surrendered a bit inside and it felt good. "Okay, yeah." I remembered what Emily said and how great Eagle had been to me before. Eagle offered me a cup of coffee from her Keurig machine and I accepted. She made small talk about the weather and the campus events while the coffee brewed for the two of us. When it was ready, she handed me my mug and sat down.

"So this is our first session, I'm so excited, sorry. I don't want to go through a lot of paperwork or official stuff right now. Let's just deal with what's on your mind and I'll get to the paperwork later on as we go along, would that be alright?"

"Yes, that's fine with me." I looked for Eric. He wasn't with me at the moment.

"Alright, what's on your mind?"

"I was expecting not to want to talk to you. I didn't talk at that recovery meeting Emily took me to. I don't want to talk there. Those old creepy people scare me. I don't think they like me either. I'm not ready to be a sad old retired fuck. But I'm getting desperate. I'm really sorry about running off the other day and I really appreciate what you did for me." She nodded and smiled then sipped her coffee. "I have PTSD and you know I have a drinking problem. But there are things I haven't told anyone. I'm supposed to see the VA doctors soon but I'm honestly afraid to tell the government." I took a sip of my coffee and sat back for a minute thinking about how to start and what to say.

"Go on, this is getting very interesting."

"I have hallucinations. But I'm not sure they are."

"Aural or visual or both?"

"Both for sure."

"Okay, both together or both types occurring separately?"

"I hear and see the things, they speak or crackle."

"Crackle?"

"Yeah, I thought I was seeing a ghost back in Germany. In the hospital there, I thought I was being haunted by my dead friend. He was angry and scary. He screamed at me and broke things, but they weren't really broken and he was on fire and just crazy."

"Okay, what did he scream at you?"

"He blamed me for killing him and he yelled at other people asking them to kill me. He asked me to make the hurt stop but we're okay now."

"We're okay?"

"Eric and I."

"Eric, the hallucination is named Eric? Emily's brother?"

"Yes, that's him. He hated me. On the flight here he tried to set the plane on fire to kill us all. Then after the carjacking we're best buds again."

"So it's the one personality that haunts you?"

"Well there were others I seen, like when I left your house. There were thousands of dead. It was like a waking nightmare. It made no sense. But Eric was there too. He set the roadside brush alight..." She interrupted me.

"The day you left, there was a huge wildfire on the reservoir lake drive, and you're saying you did that?"

"No, fucking Eric did that. Wait, are you telling me that was real?" Eagle turned to her computer and brought up an article from the local paper about the fire and showed me the date.

"That was the day you left. The police have been looking for the arsonist."

My body tensed. Fear and rage came up together. I struggled to keep it together. "You have to report me now?"

"Hell no, you are reporting symptoms of a disorder, hallucinations, not a crime that I'd have to report."

I wondered aloud, "What would you have to report?"

"Child or elder abuse, and murder or rape, I think…yes, that's right."

"I killed a guy, but it was self-defense, the DA said I was good to go there."

She nodded excitedly, "The carjacker yes, so you were there for that, did you want to talk about that?"

"The guy, the thug, was hired to kill me by his PO. I really need to know who his PO was. How do I find that out?"

"I don't know how you would find that out. Call the parole office maybe?"

"Maybe. I have the DA's number, I could ask him I suppose but when we talked he didn't even know the guy's name."

"The carjacker–you killed him, right? That's not a murder but we can certainly talk about it. It's very traumatic, murder or not."

"Yes, I got lucky, I guess I blacked out. I was shot and I got lucky the bullet bounced off a rib."

"Damn, that's incredible."

"Yeah, I got strangers trying to kill me. I kinda understood it in Iraq. I quickly discovered I didn't like it when people tried to kill me. I really thought those days were behind me. Then now, here at 'home' it happens again, I've only been here a short few weeks. And this guy told me he was hired to do it. So that person might try again. Someone out there still wants me dead."

"Right, the PO, how do you know the parole officer wants you dead?"

"The guy told me."

"Eric?"

"No, the carjacker, Eric translated until I tortured the guy and found out he can speak English." Eagle looked like she had heard all she could handle for a long while.

"I need to map this." She grabbed a note pad and starting diagraming out the relationships and characters in the story so far.

"Tortured the guy?"

"Yeah, I can hurt the ghosts, I was hurting Eric and didn't know it or how to stop it. It seems that when he stopped being angry with me, I stopped hurting him. He says there is another in here with me. Eric calls it 'The Other.' I just discovered what he meant. I just learned to sense it and control it a bit. When it comes on, I black out and people get hurt. I don't remember Eric dying except from nightmares and stories people told me, doctors, Eric himself and the intelligence guys. I don't remember the carjacker dying. I blacked out before I heard the shot. Then he was dead a moment later. I killed him."

"Your army training could account for that."

"Yeah, but the cops didn't see it that way. The kept asking Emily about a weapon I used to remove the guys eyes. Even his ghost doesn't have eyes."

"Ghost? The hallucinations, why do you call them ghosts?"

"I think that's what they are. They're actually ghosts. I thought Eric wasn't real—he didn't set the plane on fire no matter how hard he tried but he broke a mirror then did some other stuff and I can feel the heat from him now when he stands too close. The carjacker, he's a ghost. He told me some things I couldn't have known unless he was real."

"What was that?"

"He told me where he lived and where he kept the money he got for shooting me."

"How did you test that?"

"I went to the address he gave me and found the money. I took some to buy a pizza."

"Okay, before we run out of time. Let me see if I understand this. You see a dead friend regularly, and have conversations, even disagreements with him. He apparently can set things on fire and is now your friend again. There is a dead thief who told you his PO paid him to murder you, and who, as a hallucination, told you where he kept his loot and you went there and found it?"

"Yup."

"Do you know how dangerous that was?"

"Yes, I sent Eric in to investigate the scene first." I felt a weight lifted from me, getting this off my chest was liberating and I wanted to keep going.

"Eric went in first?"

"Yes, and he found no danger. Only then did I go in. I couldn't have found it without him, I don't know the town at all and Eric knew it enough to lead me to the dump on foot. I felt like a superhero. I could use Eric like X-ray vision."

"I want to explore this some more with you and I want to run some of this past a colleague of mine, my Ph.D. supervisor, is that okay?"

"Sure, I don't care."

Eagle made a follow-up appointment for me, I felt exhausted but very accomplished now. She test-called me first, though, to make sure she had my number correct. Satisfied she had the right number she shook my hand and thanked me for taking that first step in recovery. As I left she caught up to me in the lobby and handed me a leather bound book. "Start a journal, it's therapeutic and will help with recollecting some of this for our sessions. Write whenever you want, but at least once a day, and bring it back next week, okay?" I nodded in agreement.

Waiting for session two to start was torture. I thought I'd have to talk to the rainbow hairdo at the reception desk. She kept looking at me and I kept ignoring her. I read every pamphlet in the lobby, the old newspapers and the articles in the family magazines about how to get the most out of being at your kid's t-ball practice. I read a recipe for a goat cheese lasagna and gluten-free pizza crusts. I wanted to gnaw my arm off. Finally Eagle arrived, late.

"I'm sorry, I'm sorry." She rushed in with her hands full of bags and her coffee mug, "My chiropractor was backed up."

"Puns, really, Navy?" I think she liked her new nickname.

"A new low, I know." She dropped her keys and I picked them up for her before I stood from the lobby chair. "Can you open the door then, too, please?"

"Sure." I opened the door and she dashed in. I closed it as I entered and she threw her things onto the desk and started a Keurig for me, blew a few loose hairs from her face and plopped down dramatically in her overstuffed chair.

"Where were we? Ah, the initial paperwork and your journaling, how's that going?"

"I forgot it. But I don't need it. I think I have everything fresh in my mind."

"Okay so, you look well, how are you doing?"

"I'm good. I got moved into the new apartment that's not over a bar. After this I'm heading to the VA for some kind of intake thing."

"Great." The coffee was ready quickly. She hopped up and got it for me, handed it to me and plopped back down.

"Thank you. Anyway, I think I've got four or five days without a drink. The nightmares are still there, I still see my ghosts. The cholo has lost his mind. He just lies on the floor mewing and clawing at his face, muttering in Spanish. I don't feel bad for him at all. Is that bad?"

"Nah. F that guy, he tried to kill you. How's the chest wound?"

"That's healed up."

"Already, what are you, Wolverine?"

"Nah, that name is taken, but I been wondering what name to use for Eric and me—we're kind of a superhero team." I hope I hadn't told her about the burning of the crack house. I looked around for a minute and outside I saw Eric, apparently bored—he was trying to hit birds outside on a telephone wire with little balls of his own burning flesh that he hurled at them.

"When I shared the story with my supervisor he asked if I had heard about another suspicious fire." I continued to watch Eric, he had moved on to trying to set fire to a dumpster at the end of the parking lot. I really hoped he failed, and was relieved to see he wasn't trying very hard. He wandered off and there were no sirens. Eagle was aware that I had drifted away. "Hello?"

"I didn't do it!" It was technically not a lie.

"You didn't set the suspicious fire?" She asked with a knowing wink.

"Nope." I said a tad too cheerfully.

"Did Eric?"

"Maybe. I didn't actually see it happen."

"Okay. We'll come back to that. I don't care about fires. My concern is how you're doing. You seem like you're doing quite well, considering everything you've been through..."

"...And no doubt how Emily described my condition."

"You don't go more than a few minutes at a time without thinking about her do you? Independent of her descriptions of your condition, my observations in the days you were at my home, you were a complete teardown job. You were dying, now you're joking, full of color and you're not slouching in that chair. You love her, don't you?" I nodded. I think she might love me, too, but I didn't want to have cold water thrown on that fantasy so I kept it to myself. "I think she has some very strong feelings for you as well, my fine friend."

"Yeah, she got me that new apartment, got me to you, bought me that fro-yo."

"Always with the jokes."

I shrugged, "I deplore seriousness. I wasn't a great soldier. I was something of a mascot, really, a comedy relief specialist. I got promoted for making a colonel laugh, I think."

"So are you going to enroll? I know Emily had told me she expected you to."

"I might."

"You need to, that would make it easier for me to see you–the school picks up the tab for students."

"Oh, I don't have any insurance right now."

"Tricare? It's not important, I owe Emily a favor anyway, I work with you gratis but I have to squeeze you in between paid clients so the school doesn't hassle me. Sorry that got all technical, but while we're in that mode let me get you the paperwork." She handed me a pink clipboard with some forms and a pen. I started working on it while she yammered on about something ridiculous Paul had done the other day.

There was a knock at the door. Eagle apologized for the unprecedented interruption and chastised the rainbow-coifed receptionist through the cracked door. Then she turned to me and explained she had to end the session early. She promised to call me for a new appointment as soon as she could. I was disappointed and angry. I left the incomplete papers on the chair. I nearly didn't see the state trooper waiting in the lobby and almost ran into him. I was looking down, frightened and anxious about the surprise, but I caught his name on his badge, "Oldham," and I thought what a perfect name for a pig.

CHAPTER 11

BRITTNEY

I hopped in my Jeep and made the thirty-minute drive to the VA in twenty-five. The place was swarming with guys I should have felt like I belonged with, but I didn't. I don't like other veterans and I don't know why. I just haven't felt comfortable with them at all. I can't relate to them and it made no sense to me. I kept my head down and tried not to let anyone see how afraid of them I really was. I called Emily just to have something to do besides worry. I left a message when she didn't answer again.

I must have looked lost, a volunteer in a bright vest with the word "Volunteer" emblazoned on it bounced into my private space bubble and unleashed a beaming smile at me. She was a petite and delightfully awkward woman, about my age I guessed. She stood up tall as she could and her breasts were putting the vest's stitching and buttons to the test as she craned her neck up to look at me. She smelled of strawberry lip gloss and cheerfully declared, "I'm Brittney! Can I help you find something?" I couldn't help but smile. She had infected me immediately with her joyful outlook. I got lost in her eyes for a moment and she adjusted her glasses at me.

"What's your name, is that it on your jacket?" She pointed to my chest. I nodded. I was still wearing my old army field jacket with my name and rank on it. It seemed like it was appropriate considering this was a trip to the VA and it was a comfortable coat with pockets enough to hide a six-pack of beer. "I like it. Maybe you just need a cup of coffee or a friend?" She never dropped the smile.

I found myself wanting to kiss her. I shook my head to try and shake off her enchantment. "Coffee would be great, I'm early and I got time to kill."

"Great!" Brittney took my hand carefully, like I might bite or something and led me into the hospital and to the lobby Starbucks. I ordered my usual, peppermint mocha and asked her if I could get her something but she politely declined. I persisted and, to my delight, she changed her mind. "Alright, you talked me into it but you're gonna have to sit and talk to me now, you know!" I giggled and was immediately embarrassed but it didn't seem to faze her. I wanted to keep her in a bottle in my bedroom for those dark days when the ghosts surround me.

"I accept your terms."

She looked at me skeptically, "Terms, where are you from?"

"McKnightstown." She led me to a table and we sat down.

"Oh, how dreadful!"

"Yes it is."

She playfully slugged me across the table, "I'm kidding, I love that town, they have the best haunted houses at Halloween! I can't wait, my favorite radio station does ghost hunts there, they do these live remotes, it's awesome. Last year I won the contest to do the hunt with my favorite DJs. I was up too late and really dragging at work the next day."

"Work here?"

"No, I do this for fun. I have a regular job, but I volunteer to help here ever since my uncle got the Alzheimer's. I was helping him with an appointment here, help him get here and there and got mistook for a volunteer. I helped another old guy while my uncle was in with his doctor and next thing you know I'm here every Tuesday and the VFW gave me a scholarship for nursing school. Though I don't know if I want to be a nurse, I got a free ride. I'm a beautician." She shrugged and licked the caramel drizzle and whip cream off the top of her drink. "What about you?"

"Well I just got out of the army a few weeks ago. My friend died in a helicopter crash, everyone did. But I came here to bury him. I've been moping around hoping to figure life out. That's really about it. There isn't much more to me." Happiness left me, I felt deflated and depressed. She must have seen it and she came to the rescue immediately.

"Oh, there has to be more! What's your favorite color? What's your sign? So you're from Mckightston originally or just recently arrived?" I couldn't keep up.

"Well, it used to be green but the army kinda ruined that." She laughed and her eyes smiled at me brightly. "I don't know my sign, and I just recently arrived here. My best friend grew up here, though, and I was in foster housing my whole life, a ward of the state if you will, an orphan and troublemaker. The army was a step up for me, at least until 9/11 happened."

"Confession, I slept through that whole thing."

"What thing, 9/11?"

"Yeah, everyone remembers where they were that day and it's usually something cool. Not for me. I was in bed avoiding stuff, I had snoozed my alarm and not hung-over but like I was having a heavy flow day—sorry, I saw you cringe there. Sorry, and I was just drained. I skipped school. I was still in high school, I was a senior. I gave myself the day off. I had good grades and my parents left for work before I had to wake up so they never knew. I didn't know what happened until that afternoon. Over the next few days everyone else was like competing to be less degrees of separation from the attacks than the next person. Like, my dad was at The Pentagon–six months ago, with a tour group. Or I saw the World Trade Center in a movie once. It was the strangest contest. Everyone was losing their shit. My brother enlisted."

"Your brother, in the army?"

"Nah, he wasn't that tough, he went in the air force, got kicked out day two for bringing drugs and wetting his bed or something." I chortled embarrassingly and felt the sting of peppermint and coffee in my sinuses. "Oh god, I'm sorry, hon!"

"It's okay, I haven't had this much fun in a while! Thank you..."

"Brittney. Brittney, Brittney." She took a pen from her pocket and wrote her number on my hand with her name in cursive, "Brittney," a heart dotting the "i." "Now let's get you to your appointment before you choke on a marshmallow or something." I took the letter from my pocket and showed it to her. "That's the second floor, there is a big sign and a waiting room, you can't miss it but it's the second elevator bank, not the one next to the lobby. I'll get you there." She hopped up and took my hand with comfortable familiarity and I managed to keep up with her. She waved at me as the elevator doors closed and I smiled not knowing exactly what to do.

Upstairs I was able to find the clinic I needed and was able to get to where I needed to be with the help of the staff who were nothing like the nightmares I had heard about. Everyone was attentive, considerate and kind. The doctors were concerned and another volunteer got me across the campus to a hidden office where I got an ID card. Another volunteer helped me with a travel voucher so I could get reimbursed for mileage between my apartment and the hospital. I got extra meds and a new brace for my ankle which had been bugging me. I got new appointments and they gave me all of the information I needed on one sheet of paper I could stick to my refrigerator. When I was done I found my way back to the lobby and looked for Brittney. An older volunteer told me she had gone home for the day. I hopped in the Jeep and headed home. I wondered how long to wait before calling her.

I called Emily instead and left another message. I found a gas station where I could get a coffee, a burger and smoke a cigarette in peace. I waited for Emily to call me back. When I had finished a couple of cigarettes, a coffee and my food I called Brittney. She answered groggily, "Hello?" I felt like an idiot. "Hello-o?"

"Hi! Sorry if I woke you."

"Oh, you didn't wait three days! Are you crazy? What kind of girl do you think I am?"

"I'm sorry." I was about to hang up but I heard her laughing even as I stared at the phone away from my ear.

"Oh god, it's fine, silly. I was just having a little cat nap. I was avoiding making dinner."

"I just had a burger."

"You called to tell me that?"

"Well no, but–"

"Wanna do something?"

"Yes?" I wondered if that was the right answer and if it was possible to do anything right, or if that would be ill-received.

"There is a movie I wanna see, you're gonna take me okay? And since you already ate your dinner I'm only going to make you buy me popcorn and snow caps."

"Deal?" I guessed.

"Okay I like the theatre off exit 84 they have my movie at 8, okay?"

"Okay, meet you there or?"

"You could come get me now, or I could get cleaned up, do my hair, shower? Do you like dirty Brittney or clean Brittney?"

"Is there a wrong answer?"

"Not really."

"I'll take a chance on dirty Brittney. What movie are we seeing?" I heard her snicker on the other side.

"Perfect, the *Butterfly Effect*." She gave me the address for her apartment complex and told me to call when I got there and she'd appear in a cloud of smoke. I laughed and rushed home for a quick change and refresh. Eric was trying to read a newspaper in my new chair. It kept falling apart on him like it was tossed in a bonfire. He cursed and then stared at me. I chased burning embers around the apartment and put them out where I found them.

"What the fuck, bro?!"

"Sorry, bored. I thought 'well, I can turn the heat up, maybe I can turn it off,' now that you're not torturing me."

"I don't have time for this." I rushed to my closet and changed, brushed my teeth and ran a comb through my hair. I walked through a quick mist of some body spray, threw my pills in my pocket and dashed out.

"Where you going?"

"Got a date."

"With who?"

"It doesn't matter."

"Brittney?"

How did he know? "Who's Brittney?"

"I don't know, but she wrote her name and number on your hand."

"She's just a friend I'm meeting."

"You don't have any 'just friends' you have sex with every girl you meet lately, you bastard."

"I didn't bang Eagle."

"Yet."

"Not now, don't you have some squirrels to BBQ or something?"

"Why didn't I think of that? But, yeah, I can't sleep, I can't eat and I can't even read a newspaper."

"I could leave the TV on for you if you like." I fumbled with the remote. I hadn't learned how to use it yet and Eric kept trying to give me advice on which button did what. I managed to figure it out and we found ESPN.

"Thank my sister for me when you get a chance."

"I would if I could reach her. She won't answer my calls."

"I could pop over to the house and see if she is there."

"You can do that?"

"Well, yeah, I thought I told you I could do that."

"I don't remember a lot of stuff. I still got that post-concussive syndrome, you know?"

"Don't blame the crash. You're just a dumbass. I don't wanna miss this game if I don't have to, give her a call."

I thought it couldn't hurt anything. I called Emily and there was no answer. I left the usual message. "Call me when you get a chance, would love to hear your voice, you." Before I pushed the little red button, Eric shouted into the phone.

"Thanks for the cable. I got the Phillies game tonight, thanks!" Then I finished the message.

"Eric says to thank you for the cable at the apartment. just call me, okay?" She knows I'm crazy, she wasn't calling me anyway, maybe that would get a response.

Eric got himself comfortable in the new chair, which was already showing signs of wear from the heat that bled into the apartment. I thought that this winter, we would save a ton on heating. I hopped into the Jeep and tore off south to meet...looked at my hand. "Brittney," yeah, "Brittney."

I found the apartment without any trouble. I dialed the phone number still on my hand and she didn't answer. At least not the way a conventional human being would. Brittney came bounding out of nowhere and with the excitement of a child discovering an unattended cupcake, reached into the Jeep and threw her arms around me. She kissed my cheek and said, "Hi! What took you so long?"

"What? My place is thirty minutes away." She giggled and skipped around to the other side of the Jeep and climbed in. She was wearing a delightfully immodest skirt and an ironic t-shirt with an anime character on it that I didn't recognize in an exaggerated pose yelling something in Japanese. Her hair was worn down but perfectly polished without a single strand out of place, like she had just left a salon and was ready for her wedding march. She had heels on her feet that tied on like gladiator sandals. Her toes each had its own custom paint job, one had a Hello Kitty, and another had a flower, a unicorn head. She caught me trying to figure out what was painted on her toe nails in the dying light and she leaned over and kissed me again. I thought to tell her to stop but didn't. She grabbed the Jeep dashboard "oh shit handle" and said, "Drive too fast!"

"Where? I don't know where I'm going."

"Well I don't drive stick so…" and she proceeded to give me directions and off we went.

CHAPTER 12

PICKLES

I hadn't ventured into a crowded place again since the out-of-body experience at the hospital. Things had changed then, but I hadn't yet realized how much. I knew I could now sense and control The Other to some degree, I could lessen Eric's suffering, leaving him bored and irritated but he could learn to live with boredom. I had not yet realized what kind of danger I was in. I didn't know how much things had changed, it seemed like I had been gone years. Going into public like that was dangerous. It was a mistake. I realized it as I pulled in to the parking lot.

The scene was chaos and terror took me. I felt sweat and was glad for the breeze whisking through the doorless, topless Jeep cabin. I saw Brittney scanning the parking lot for a good spot and she pointed, pretending not to notice I was in a full panic. The metal halide lights in the parking lot were just coming on and made the glitter in her otherwise subtle eye shadow sparkle. That somehow brought me some small measure of calm. Something to cling to besides the fear, the steering wheel I thought I would crush in my white knuckle grip.

We got to a parking spot. Brittney had assumed a calm demeanor, perhaps sensing what I needed. She jumped down from the Jeep and appeared at my side before I could get the keys out. She took my hand and I climbed down. She wrapped me up tight with her arm in mine like Emily did the morning of the funeral. She took my hand in hers like she did at the hospital. I steadied myself up like the armored personnel carrier ramp was about to drop exposing my team to gunfire. I took a few steps and she spoke softly so only I could hear her.

Brittney observed, "The sunset is amazing!" But I was only looking at her, she sparkled like a new day. "We have plenty of time so let's not get run over trying to get across this parking lot." There was so much noise I could barely think. We got to the edge of the mall, where the cars were no longer a threat. The theatre façade towered above an open court full of shops and restaurants. There were people all around us. I could hardly track them all.

There were awkward teenagers run amok and unsupervised tweens trying to look cool. There was a mom changing a diaper hoping none of the drunk childless winos she was with would stop thinking she was cool. A dad chased a toddler that rushed towards the empty fountain. There were cigarette butts stuck in bubble gum at the bike rack, but no bikes. I saw thirty-seven cents lying in the fountain as we passed it. Some of the restaurants featured open-patio seating and there were drunks enjoying the baseball and bowling on a dozen TVs hung all over. There were torches burning and demons feasting on pieces of souls strewn about.

Some of the living were being devoured and didn't seem to know it. The demons saw me and scurried away or hid behind one another, or an innocent. Some of the living looked at me and saw a threat too. Some of them were demons or had no ghost of their own, they were empty, something was wrong. I feared those as much as the ghosts I first saw. She shook me as we got to the line.

"Hey, are you okay? Where are you right now?" I wondered how many broken men she had known.

"I'm right here, just, uh, taking it all in, ya know, I never been here before or seen such an expensive-looking mall. I never seen some of the stores you have here."

"This place is fancy, and new. I never shop here but I work here. My salon is just around the corner there." She pointed west past the panda kitchen and an Irish eatery, "Shennanigans" or something.

"You wanna grab a pint before the movie?"

"No!" She made a sideways frumpy face at me.

"Okay!" I put a hand up in surrender.

"Sorry, I have been trying to see a movie for a while is all. So okay, two weeks ago, the guy I was dating met me for a movie and he had a few drinks before. I met him at the Shennanigans over there. We drank right through the show I wanted to see and went to a later one. I got my blue raspberry slushy and sat down and he had a cherry one. He poured booze into his then passed out during the trailers. I think he wet himself, too, and I just left him there. And I really would love to see at least some of this movie and be able to see you again. I'm not talking to that sleepy drunk fella anymore."

She made me laugh and forget everything happening around me. The ringing in my ears was gone, the crunching of bone and souls being gnawed or ground to dust by the demons around me, they all disappeared as I laughed and looked at her smiling eyes. I focused on her and she put two fingers on my chin to hold my focus there a moment longer than I planned. I felt a tear forming; it was a mix of laughter and longing filling it. Her smile softened, losing its aggression and she turned her chin up and offered a kiss, her fingers guiding my chin down to her. I joined her in a gentle kiss.

Then she hugged me with her usual exuberance and let out a relieved sigh. "There, now that's out of the way, our first kiss-kiss." She turned to the ticket window, we had reached the head of the line and I didn't even notice the pizza-faced kid waiting patiently behind the bulletproof window. "Two for the *Butterfly Effect*, please." She couldn't conceal her own excitement. I paid the guy and we went in and split up, heading to our respective washrooms before reuniting with joined hands in the popcorn line.

Inside the auditorium, numbered three, we found the seats she wanted. "I didn't wear my dork glasses so I need to sit at just the right spot, so thank you for going in early and sitting through the whole starting bit with me. Otherwise we'd be stuck someplace I couldn't see and I'd wanna cry."

"No problem." I tried to get comfortable and she pushed the armrest between us out of the way and scooted up close, pressing against me.

"Not gonna lie, I usually finish my popcorn before the movie even starts, like my dad used to take me to the movies when I was little and if I didn't chomp it down I might not get any. He ate like he didn't know where his next meal was coming from."

People began streaming in, and fear, a chilling anxiety returned. I had already found the exits but now had to calculate times to climb over people as I planned an escape. I lost her voice in the noise but she kept trying. She mixed in her favorite candies and munched away. I found some pills in my jacket pocket and hoped she didn't notice me chewing them. The film started before I had reached a snapping point. The darkness was comforting. I felt safe if only for a moment. She kissed my cheek as the movie started. I didn't make it to the end.

The dark music and themes of the *Butterfly Effect* unhinged me. The main character suffering black outs and lurking fears of death and trying to remember things from a journal hit too close to home. One of the demons out front had followed me into the dark and sat beside me. It wasn't like the others, it wasn't afraid of me, I think it sensed an easy meal. I grabbed my coat and climbed out over someone and stumble-crawled halfway to an exit before I could find my feet.

I broke out into the back alley, it was dark but the parking lot lights murdered the beauty of the stars above. There was nothing to see but a dumpster and a lonely stray cat. I was shaking violently. I found more pills and chewed them, swallowing with fear, as voices of the dead entered my head. Anger and accusations filled my ears, shame and guilt filled my chest and I was drowning, I couldn't breathe. I collapsed into a heap, into darkness.

Something rough on my nose woke me, there was a tiny kitten, leading a half-starved litter of strays watching me from behind their brave brother. He was licking my nose and I heard the door to the theatre close. The kittens scattered, except for the brave one. I heard Brittney gasp. "The fuck, are you okay?" She knelt beside me to help me up. A pill bottle rolled away from my hand with all hope of hiding what was wrong with me. With strength I wouldn't have suspected she hoisted me up onto her shoulder. "C'mon, hon, let's getcha home!" She got me to the Jeep and tossed me into the back seat with the help of a passerby. She reached into my pants for my wallet and pulled my license out. "Is this the right address?"

I shook my head, "No." I told her what I thought was the right address and she found my keys in the other pocket. She started the Jeep and drove, I fell asleep. I felt her nudging me awake. We were at a gas station near the apartment. She looked worried but still glowed. "What happened?"

"I'm really not sure. The movie kinda freaked you out a bit, I'm sorry, we should have seen *Shrek 2*."

"It's hardly your fault I freaked out."

"Those pills, I hope you didn't take too many of them. There weren't any left."

"Nah, I got more inside the house. I thought you couldn't drive stick."

"A story for another time, hon. You want something from inside?" She had finished gassing the Jeep up and was putting the nozzle back.

"I'd like to go in and see about finding something, yes." I heard a tiny meow from the front seat.

"Oh, he followed us. Sorry, you're a dad now." I looked at the scruffy kitten and scooped him up into my oversized pocket and went into the convenience store. I looked at myself in the restroom mirror. I had aged a dozen years today. I looked worn. I tried to wash it off but could not. I shopped and found coffee, a tin of meat for the cat and some ibuprofen for the headache. Brittney had a roll of Spree candy and an energy drink when I found her at the register. She gently stroked my arm in reassurance and it brought me back to center where I needed to be. I was coming back and smiled at her, the only thing I could manage to show my appreciation. Then I realized I had no idea how to get her home.

"How are we getting you home?"

She shrugged it off. "I'll call a friend to pick me up, I have those. Some of them suck but it isn't late and a few of them might even be slumming it here and could use a D.D., it's Friday night." She smiled back.

"Let me get that." I paid for our stuff.

"You took a lot of those pills. Let me finish the drive home, okay? You still look groggy." She repeated the address I had given her back to me. It was Emily's so I gave Brittney the right address and pointed in the general direction. I noticed as I climbed into the front seat and opened the tin for the kitten that my phone had a dozen missed calls and voicemails. "That thing was exploding ever since we left the theatre." I listened to the voicemails before we drove off. We watched the kitten scarf down the food, swallowing whole mouthfuls at a time. The tearful pleading of Emily on the voicemail was loud enough Brittney could hear. Sadness marred her face and she ventured, "Girlfriend?"

"No. She's just a friend Eric's sister." It was a lie and also true. I held on to the truth hoping she wouldn't hear the lie.

"It's okay, it's none of my business." She shook off sadness as regret and shame tried to find a purchase on her beautiful face. She wiped them away and pulled her dork glasses out of her purse. She found her smile and turned to me, "Hang on to your butt, hon! We'll get you home to your worried 'friend.'" I buckled up and snatched up the kitten that was licking his chops, satisfied and happy with a full belly.

When we reached the apartment, Emily was standing outside in a long coat, a closed umbrella hanging from the crook of her elbow. She looked affright. Mascara streaked, hair tangled and she seemed to be shivering, though it wasn't particularly cool. Brittney parked in a space short of Emily. She seemed to know everything in that moment. She handed me back my keys, sighed through a smile and climbed down. I should have said something, anything but didn't.

"I'll get home fine, don't worry, hon." There was heartbreak in her voice, wounds reopened. Regret filled my heart.

"Thank you." I called after her and climbed out. I rushed to Emily with the kitten in one hand. Emily saw Brittney but ignored her, her eruption centered on her worry about me, anger at me not answering her calls. I got defensive, had I not called her a thousand times without a reply? We argued in the street, I imagined Brittney's smirk as she no doubt heard us, and there was no way to mistake our relationship even from that distance. I didn't understand our relationship but I'm sure any woman who heard the fight would. We managed to agree to take it inside.

"Where is Eric?" She demanded as she shed her coat and umbrella. I made a show of looking around.

"He's not here right now."

"Call him, I know you can!" She could not know this I told myself, but quickly made an attempt. I called out to him and reached down into the darkness. He was not there though something else stirred.

"I took a lot of pills earlier. I had a freak out, an episode at a movie theater." She was growing increasingly frustrated.

"Who was that? She your date for the movie, some girl you met on the internet or something?"

I lied. "No, I met her at the VA. She's a volunteer there. I ran into her at the movie and she saw me freak out and helped me out."

"Why can't you be honest with me? She's Brittney, right? Like on your hand?" She was near exhausted. She wept uncontrollably. "Are you fucking her." It wasn't really a question. She was saying she knew I was fucking her or wanted to, and that's all that mattered. But I could lie again.

"No."

She collapsed into the chair. The baseball game was a doubleheader. It was still dragging on. I hate baseball. Emily opened her phone and turned off the TV. "Just because I can't see him right now doesn't mean he wasn't watching that, I had that on for him."

"Listen." She played the voicemail on speaker. I heard the call I made to her before I left to meet Brittney and there was Eric's voice plain as day thanking her for the cable so he could watch the game. "He's here, you can't keep him to yourself, you know! He's *my* brother!" She threw her phone at me and it shattered on my face, cutting my eyebrow. I started to black out as blood ran into my eye. I was blind from the sting, the minor pain. It was enough to wake The Other. Horror swallowed me, I was about to kill her but I loved her. I fought my way back to light and took myself out. With the last moment of self will left to me, I smashed my head into the kitchen counter and fell unconscious into a dark place.

When I awoke she was still a mess. Someone had stitched me up, I was dizzy and my vision was foggy. Emily was clutching pieces of her phone. I was in a hospital bed. "Where's the cat?"

"He's in my purse chewing on my scrunchy."

"It's okay, as long as he's alright."

"What's his name?"

"I was leaning towards Pickles. I just found him. He rescued me with Brittney, the girl who drove me home, from the alley behind the movies."

"That's a strange name for a cat." She looked at me with my bandaged and stitched head then retreated from that, "Pickles it is." She handed me the kitten. He seemed happy to see me, I was glad for it. Emily hadn't yet shown any desire to be close and I feared I had lost Brittney forever too.

"Why are we in the hospital?"

"You hit your head, really, really hard. You're gonna have to wear a collar, you cracked a neck vertebrae or something, the doctors said."

"Fuck. This sounds expensive."

"They said it's gratis. The VA will handle your after care." I heard rain outside on the roof it was terrible. That explained Emily's outfit.

"I left my top down."

"You should watch the weather forecast sometime." Her attempt at levity annoyed me but I smiled. She mistook my annoyance for pain and offered me a button. "The doctors said to press this if it hurts." I did, if only to see what it did and to avoid Eric appearing to startle me and precipitate further injury. I felt a little lightheaded and the warm purring of Pickles resting against my hand comforted me as I drifted into a peaceful dream.

CHAPTER 13

ABSENCE

When I awoke Emily was gone. I was home again with no idea how. Little Pickles was sitting in the window staring at some birds outside. Eric stood in the kitchen kicking the cholo. It seemed to amuse him so I didn't interrupt him. There was a letter on the nightstand. Eric's fingers had smudged the envelope. I imagine he tried to read it. I opened it. It was from Emily.

My Beloved,

I wish I didn't have to leave you like this. I can't get out of this and am already late to arrive and will have to beg forgiveness to stay enrolled. There is a home nurse scheduled to visit you, please cooperate with her. I made an appointment for you with our admissions office. The time and date are enclosed on the counselor's card included herein. I'm sorry for what I said that night. I hope you can forgive me. I never made my feelings or expectations clear to you, and I was careless with your feelings when I threw myself at you for my own comfort. I took advantage of you then expected you to honor an unspoken commitment to me in return. It was terribly selfish and childish of me. Please know that I am very sorry, but I have no regrets except for losing my temper with you. No one else can understand what I am going through right now like you can. Even Mother, who should share the pain we know, is only full of anger and hatred. She has no sympathy for either of us. I am still desperate to tell you some very important things and I hope that when I return, you are still willing to receive me. If you hear little from me, know my heart is with you. Please, if you see Eric again, tell him I miss him, I love him and I pray he finds rest. If he can talk to me as he did on the phone, perhaps he can try to speak to Mother too. Maybe he can reach her and help her through her grieving process which seems arrested beyond hope of relief. Don't fail to call that Brittney and thank her for both of us, for bringing you home safe. Don't pass up a good thing either. Life is too short for that, joy too precious a commodity. There seems so little of it left in the world right now. War took another man from our town as I'm writing this. I heard, too, that they're going to start calling back men who have come home already. Please, if they try to call you back, run away. Don't be a brave fool. Find me and I'll hide you in Canada or someplace safe from the army.

Always yours,

Emily

I found the card in the envelope and I had several days before I had to worry. I felt my neck, it was stiff but healed. I knew it was healed. Like the bullet hole in my chest, wounds vanished quickly since I gained The Other. If I hadn't struck my head so hard I probably wouldn't have any problems with my concussion anymore either. Relief washed over me as I rose painlessly from the bed. Pickles dutifully reported to my side and sat at attention. I reached down and hoisted him up pressing him to my face. I had managed to mend things with Emily, Eric had stopped bothering me and I was feeling stronger than in a long time. I had Emily's blessing to pursue Brittney and I would be able to do it without guilt. I looked for the bathroom, then my pants and went out to find something to drink.

I saw missed calls from Brittney in my phone and listened to the voicemails before calling her. It had been three days and each day she left a message asking me to let her know how things went with the girlfriend and to assure me she got home safe and wanted to know if I would be able to meet her for coffee or something again. I called her and I got lucky, she picked up.

"God, I'm so happy I got you on the first try!"

"Nope, no god here, just Brittney, Bitch. Is that you, hon? What happened? I started to worry! Now you wait three days? You got this whole dating phone etiquette mucked up."

"Yeah, I do everything wrong. Look, I wanted to thank you—not just for driving me home but for caring to check on me afterward. Emily wanted me to thank you too. She is normally the kindest person."

"It's okay I've had worse dates, believe it or not."

"So what are we doing here? You want to meet up or just wanted to leave it at that?"

"I want to see you again."

"Okay but you have to explain this whole Emily thing. I don't want to get murdered here by your wife."

"She's not my wife!"

"I hardly know that right now do I?" I realized she was joking. I joined her in the laughter I heard from the other side. "Look, I'm off in an hour, as soon as I get this bridezilla's highlights done and, honestly, I need a drink. Can you meet me someplace safe and comfortable for you?"

"Yeah, Kildare's on the square you know it?"

"Yup. I'll be there in about two hours, if dirty Brittney is okay."

"It's the one I know and love."

"Gay." We giggled, she had a gift. "See you then, hon, bye, bye, bye!" I pounded a few quick shots and headed home.

"Sis left a kit for Pickles in the second bedroom. There is a bunch of goodies, cat box and all that rubbish. I can't seem to catch the little fucker so I guess we have a cat now. Remember all the strays in Iraq? Everyone was adopting critters over there, made the damn colonel nuts."

"Yup, I recall. I saw on the news guys were starting to bring some of them back home now too. In any case, young Pickles is here to stay." And the little creature appeared as if on cue and I picked him up for a scratch. I investigated the back room and saw the basket of goodies including a flea dip with a note instructing me to give him another bath to be sure today. So I washed the oddly-cooperative Pickles, again, dried him off, played with him a bit, fed him with some treats I found in the basket and hopped in the shower.

I got back to the bar late and spied Brittney looking impatient in the parking lot. She was about to call someone on her phone when I whistled to her. She stood on her tip toes, smiled and waved when she saw me.

"Hi, sorry I'm late, Pickles needed a bath..."

"You kept him? Aw, you big softy. Can I visit him later?"

"If this goes the way I hope, yes."

"You have cable?"

"Yes."

"Cheesy movies?"

"Probably." Though I knew baseball was on again for Eric.

"Popcorn?"

"Yup, and Cheetos."

"Puffs or those wrinkled gnarly shriveled up ones?"

"Puffs."

"Okay, let's split an app here, have two pints and then take a six-pack back to your place for popcorn and cheesiness!"

"Deal, come let me buy you an apology drink."

"You owe me more than that! No, I'm kidding, let's get inside before the rain comes back."

"My Jeep seats are still damp from the last time." We shared a quiet pint and some laughter. We made fun of the decorations in the bar and the strange couples there, pretending to read their lips and doing silly voices in voiceovers of their conversations. It started to hurt to laugh. We got a six-pack to go when we finished making the other people uncomfortable and we headed back to my apartment.

During the stupid movie, between spare laughs, I did my best to explain the Emily situation, even going so far as showing Brittney the letter. "To be perfectly honest I think I love her but I don't understand her and what she wants from me. She keeps saying there is something important to tell me and we keep screwing up the chance to talk."

"You guys had sex?"

"The day of the funeral, I think she just wanted to feel alive. I saw some shrink explain it in a movie, and it's apparently a common way to react to death or something?"

"Lazy writers, I never heard of that."

"Well, we did it the next time we were together too. But that was it. It was clearly impulsive and I think she regretted it so I didn't think we were going anywhere." I didn't want to share about Rachael.

"You found another girl? You dog."

How did she know that, is she psychic? "Well, she found me, really. I was reeling from Emily leaving me there."

"Emily left you where?"

"At her cottage, I had a nightmare and it scared her or upset her. I was seeing her brother and I guess I talked in my dream…"

"It's okay, I can tell it's upsetting, but another girl found you?" and I thought of the last time I saw Rachael and chuckled a bit.

"Yeah, you were right to be cautious. When Emily found out about the other girl, she politely cautioned me about her. She gently suggested I not see her anymore."

"Can we just name her?"

"Rachael. Her name is Rachael. Haven't seen her in a while, last time I saw her, Emily found her here and told her to get out and if she saw her again, she'd kill her."

"Damn. Damn. She's outta town, right?"

"Yup."

"Would you rub my feet? I'm on 'em all day and if jealous ex or whatever is gonna stab me in my sleep, I'd like a foot massage first."

"You plan on staying the night?"

"Depends how good the foot massage goes." She turned and put her feet in my lap. I did my best but had to admit it was my first time.

"Mmm, do you have any lotion?"

"I doubt it."

"It's okay, you're doing fine."

"I wanted to ask you how long it takes to do that with your nails."

"Do what?"

"All the little custom paintings: Hello Kitty, the unicorn, the happy face with the bullet hole."

"Pft, those are stickers. I put like two coats of clear on top to seal 'em. If I try to paint details on my toes it's like I got Parkinson's, it's impossible. So, stickers, shortcut, win! Mmm don't stop."

Eric appeared, "I can't lie, I like her." He startled me and I excused myself for a moment to fetch some pills to wash him away. When I returned to Brittney, she had moved to the bed.

"It's more comfortable here, come finish my feet." She patted the bed next to her. I joined her and she turned out the light.

In the morning she woke me with a kiss, several, and unselfishly gave still more pleasure. She asked me to take her for waffles. I watched the cat climb down a curtain and suggested, "Maybe a shower first?"

"Only if you come help me!" She sang her proposition as she danced towards the bathroom.

"I accept your terms." She laughed at that. I think I was growing on her. After that, we were dressing and I noticed my phone blinking a voicemail alert. It was Emily.

"I'm at Charles de Gaulle, got a message from the home nurse. She said no one answered the door yesterday. Are you okay? God this call is like $45 a second. Please just call me, I'm worried."

I took Brittney to her car left at Kildare's on the square and I followed her to the waffle place I had never know was there. It was a greasy spoon out halfway to Gettysburg on some highway through the twilight zone. We made small talk but it was awkward, I was out of my element and though the food was good I was distracted. She picked up on it right away but didn't let it show that it bothered her.

"Sorry if I seem off, new place, I think I forgot my meds last night and this morning."

She put her hand on mine. "It's okay, I get it. You been through a lot, you talked a lot in your sleep and you couldn't have got much rest."

"Oh god, what did I say?"

"You talked to The Other and asked him to leave you alone. You talked to Eric but he ignored you and kept yelling at cholo to shut the fuck up. And you were asking for Rachael. Then it got weird."

I shrunk inside myself, my shoulders contracted and I felt smaller, "I'm sorry."

"Nah, it's okay. When you relived the crash and dove under the bed, you woke me up screaming and scared the shit out of the cat but I didn't mind. I held you in a ball on the floor for a few minutes and got you some water and got you back into bed. You really don't remember?"

"Nope, I'm sorry."

"Stop apologizing. I know the war screws with your mind. My uncle had the TSPD. I get it. Regular boys are way more screwed up. At least you earned your crazy."

"PTSD."

"Right, what did I say?"

"Don't worry about it." I left a twenty on the table and we went back to our cars. She embraced me and we kissed hello, we kissed stay with me and we kissed goodbye.

The last thing she said was, "Call me, hon."

I nodded and watched her climb into her car and drive away. We waved and smiled and I got into my Jeep. I drove towards the reservoir. I wanted to hike a trailhead I read about in the paper the other day that went to a waterfall. The trail wasn't far from me, just over the border into Maryland and the reservoir road had a dirt service route that was a shortcut. I headed that way eager to enjoy a bone-jarring ride on that pitted service trail. I never made it.

CHAPTER 14

GUN

I noticed a silver unmarked Crown Victoria behind me. It flashed internal mounted blue lights and pulled me over. I went into the glove box for my paperwork and got my wallet out. The cop got out of her car. I thought she was a guy at first. She was tall, heavy and pear-shaped with a belly overhang and a crew cut. Her face had liver-spotted jowls and was stuck in a scowl. Her suit was sharkskin and ill-fitted to her, as if it was cut for a smaller man and had no means to accommodate even an as unfortunately misshapen a woman as her. I saw the badge on her belt and she had a gun out. The dark stirred, I felt a great restlessness inside and I nearly blacked out as she approached. Fear was taking me at the sight of that gun. I dropped the papers and reached for my pills. I didn't have them. There was just an empty tin of cat food.

The cop pointed the gun at me and I threw my hands up and turned to look at her, "Whoa, you got the wrong guy, I didn't do anything!"

"Get out—slowly, bitch."

I complied. "Okay, but you gotta put the gun down."

"It won't be your problem much longer, son." The darkness was screaming at me. "Walk that way," she pointed with the gun to the roadside, "over the guard rail and into the weeds." I walked and she followed closely with some difficulty, I could hear her grunting, huffing and puffing. "Alright, that's far enough, any last words?"

Rage answered. "Yes, you're not going to survive this if you don't walk away now!" She cocked her head to one side slightly, in disbelief, tightened her aim with a smirk. I saw the muzzle flash but never heard or felt the shot.

The darkness took me. I wanted it to take over. Unlike many times before there were no innocents in danger here, just Frankenbitch and me. She was going to die. I was ready for it, holding it down until that last moment. It didn't disappoint. When I was conscious again, when I could see, I was in the Jeep, bleeding some but alive.

The Other had driven into a parking lot for a small neighborhood park, in a town I didn't know. There was a jungle gym and soccer moms with strollers and minivans. There were ducks, a pond and weeping willows. I could see the darkness didn't know how to park. The Jeep was diagonal across two spaces. I saw a bathroom and a water fountain nearby. My abdomen burned, I was shot, but the wound was small. A couple of stiches would fix it, I might be able to do it alone and avoid the emergency room and questions about the bullet.

I saw the gun. It was on the floor of the passenger side. It had blood on it. There was blood on a lot of stuff. This wasn't good, it would attract attention, the wrong kind. I picked up the gun. The barrel was still warm to the touch. I ejected the magazine, four rounds. No brass in the Jeep, it wasn't fired here. The chamber still had a round in it, making five total rounds. I put the safety on and locked it in the glove box. It was a nickel-finished colt model 1911 in .45 ACP.

That single shot should have been lethal at less than 50 yards. The entry wounds are small, but there should be an exit wound the size of Nebraska. I checked myself again. I put my finger in the wound and felt the slug. It was just beneath the surface. It stung like hell but I dug it out in the bathroom with my Jeep key. I wrapped my belly with paper towels and buttoned my shirt up over it. I threw on a hoodie I found in the back seat. I used some paper towels to clean off the slippery wet blood, though by now much of it was drying quickly. I threw the paper towels into a nearby litter bin and drove towards McKnightstown.

I found Gettysburg first and went to Walmart. I got duct tape and closed the wound in the bathroom. I got more medical supplies, fresh clothes without blood and a Red Bull. I heard sirens tearing off towards the reservoir road where someone must have found the dead Frankenbitch.

I went to the liquor store, got three bottles of scotch and drove through Wendy's. I took my lunch home and drank half a bottle before I got there. When I got to the apartment, Frankenbitch was standing there at the bottom of the stairs with a look of horror plastered on her face. She backed away from me and fell to her knees. She begged me to release her and apologized for what happened. I ignored her and made my way upstairs.

Blood had begun to seep out of me again, making my keys slippery as I trembled towards the lock. There was so much blood, the tape had failed. I managed to get inside but collapsed in the doorway. Eric was there, he had been watching from the window. He took the phone from my pocket and melted the 9, 1 and send buttons. He was babbling that he saw her show up and felt the dark, it was hurting them all, and then I passed out.

I awoke to the all-too-familiar hospital antiseptic smell, the sounds of vital signs monitoring equipment, doctors and nurses muttering beyond my curtain. I wanted to throw up. I worried about Pickles. Was he okay? I never called Emily back. Where was my phone? I was weak and in pain. Ears ringing, head pounding like a NYE hang over. I waited. Eric showed up and I was actually glad to see him.

"Pickles?"

"He's fine, sleeping like a baby in a window. The home visit nurse showed up just after you did. When the ambulance got there the kitten ran and hid. She saw him and got him some food and played with him."

"What about the cops?"

"No cops. They either didn't find the dead woman or recognize your wound as being from a bullet. The doctors are puzzled but haven't alerted the cops. You're in the clear for the moment I would guess. But you got an admissions appointment tomorrow. I hope you don't miss that, and your phone was blowing up, I think my sis was calling in a panic. The home nurse called her and well, there you have it. It might snow tomorrow. Freak weather system everyone in the hospital waiting area is freaking out about. Did you know there are ghosts in the morgue? Fun fact, this hospital, no shit—is super haunted."

"You're nuts."

"You can get rid of me anytime you want."

"I can't be a superhero without you."

"If you start wearing leotards and a cape, I'll find a way to kill ya myself."

"Did you dial the phone?"

"You saw that? Yes, I'm getting stronger. I can mess with real world stuff now, scared myself the other day I accidentally killed a butterfly that got too close to me while I was trying to turn some road sand into glass."

"You and your hobbies."

"You gonna see Brittney again?"

"Try and stop me, oh and, I saw her first."

"Don't forget Rachael is still out here and she's going to try and kill you too."

"Why didn't you warn me about the cop?"

"I didn't know about the cop. I'm a ghost, I'm not psychic." This conversation stopped making sense to me just in time. A doctor came in and asked how I was doing. He didn't care.

"Can you tell me what happened? Bad puncture, managed to put a big enough hole in you that you almost fell out. About three pints did."

"I have black outs. I don't remember."

"Were you driving like that?"

"Like what? Bleeding?"

"Black out drunk."

"No, I wasn't drunk I have PTSD and dissociative episodes."

"Your BAC was very elevated."

"I got hurt before that, I remember taping the wound shut then getting the booze. I went home and used some to kill the pain." The doctor let out an exasperated sigh.

"That looks like a bullet wound, a close range entry wound but no bullet or exit wound. Do you remember anything about it at all?"

"No. I was having a nightmare, or day-mare, and blacked out afraid of something, maybe a vulture or a plane I don't know. Oh, I ran with scissors, what do you care?"

"Well, you're stitched up and we've replaced your blood at taxpayer expense…" I noticed his coat said VA on it, "You can go home anytime you feel up to it. I see you have a therapy appoint here next week, I'm going to include my notes for your counseling staff so they can work with you and your addiction. I hope you get the help you need. The booze is going to kill you. You need to stop and I'm done. Thank you for your service, young man." Then the doctor left. Maybe he did care. A nurse came in with a stack of folded laundry.

"I got all your stuff clean for you, Sergeant. I hope you'll choose to stay another day, the doc said you could."

"No, thank you." She unhooked the needles and monitors. I noticed a huge diamond on her finger.

She said, "It's fake, I married one of you guys and you guys are broke. I have a soft spot for you rugged boy scouts with clean-shaven faces." She finished cleaning the tape goo from a few stubborn spots, using some rubbing alcohol. When she was finished she wished me luck and warned me to be careful around sharp objects. I thanked her and got dressed. I went out to the Starbucks in the lobby. I spied Brittney looking like a ray of sunshine and hope, sparkling for visitors as she gave them directions. Eric followed me.

"You need a ride, dude."

"Yes I do." Eric followed my eyes to her.

"Not what I meant, you bag of dicks."

I approached her, now keenly aware that I hadn't brushed my teeth for I couldn't remember how many days. "Eric, how long was I in there?"

"Overnight." She heard me and turned, beaming.

She approached excited but not leaping onto me. "Hon, you came back!"

"Hi!" I tried to talk without exhaling and she made a face.

"Did you eat little Pickles?" She held her nose. "What the hell, hon?"

"Sorry I was in the ER overnight." Her face crumpled into despair and concern.

"But why what happened?"

"Can you keep a secret?"

"No. I do hair, which is like being a therapist or a priest."

"Sarcasm? So not you."

"Irony is more my thing. Sarcasm is mean."

"I need a ride home, what time do you get done here?"

"I'm a volunteer, I leave when I'm bored. I can take you as soon as you find a peppermint patty or an Altoid." She made me laugh. I was with her for less than a minute, after stumbling in terrible pain from the emergency room, she had me laughing, causing still more excruciating pain. I winced and she stepped closer and touched my belly causing still more shooting pain.

"Oh god, I'm so sorry, hon!" She rocked back on her heels and started taking her vest off. It looked new, I guessed her breasts had defeated the last one and I wondered how long this one would last. The top button stitching already looked worn and it couldn't be more than a few days old.

She told the volunteer coordinator behind the information desk that she had to leave early, girl problem, and he looked down and raised his hands in surrender. "Say no more. Thank you, Ms. Brittney." We were off to the employee parking lot. I started to cramp and I had to stop. She looked at me as I curled over into a stoop. She told me to wait here, she'd get the car. I thanked her and sat on a nearby bench.

"She's a keeper. I think you should marry that one. I mean, my sis likes you but I mean, she's way outta your league and this girl is funny."

"Emily's funny."

Eric just looked at me, frowned and set some ants on fire. "You like fucking her, she's not funny. She's terminally unfunny."

"You grew up with her. You got a slightly different take."

"Yeah, I have known her my whole life. I know all her secrets. You can't make her into something she's not just cuz she gave you some attention and…well, fuck, I don't care. I just want to finish dying. I'm stuck here, fuck your relationships. But this girl…"

"You know all her secrets? Like desires and stuff? Perfect gift ideas? Her birthday is coming up isn't it?"

"Die ants! Muahaha!"

"Focus."

"Fuck you, man. I'm busy. Go have sex, she's pulling up now. Ten bucks she offers you a handy on the way home."

"C'mon, man, that's not fair."

Brittney pushed her passenger door open from inside the car, "Get in, hon!" A nearby vet helped me up and to the car. He could see I was in pain and struggling. "Hand job express is leaving the station, get those pants off, boy!" Eric laughed from the backseat. I tried to ignore him.

"Wow, no smile? I'm not funny without my vest am I?"

"No, you're funny. I was trying to weather some pain."

"Ah, so what happened?"

"I got shot." I didn't have the energy to lie.

Eric was furious, "Asshole, you made her a witness now!"

Brittney turned to me and looked at the road, then back to me, obviously frightened. "Shot, like with a gun?"

"Yup."

"I didn't see anything about a shooting in the news."

"How are you so funny…why are you so sweet?"

"Well here's how I see it. You can't get too much in your own head or take shit so damn serious. If you do, you end up not so happy. Just be grateful you have what you do. There are others out there that have it worse. No matter what's going on. So who shot you?"

"Would you believe a cop?"

Eric grumbled at me, "She wasn't a cop, she was the cholo's PO c'mon man. Even I figured that out." Brittney pulled over and put the car in park.

"A cop shot you?"

"A probation or parole officer. The cholo's PO."

"Who's the cholo? I feel like I'm missing something. Like a lot of something."

"Ya, I didn't want to drag you into my insane world but that's the tip of the iceberg. I'm sorry to have scared you."

"No, it's okay I think I have worse secrets, but why? Why did this PO try to shoot you and do I want to know who the cholo is?"

I turned to Eric in the back seat. "Can you show her something you can do?"

"Huh? Me? Don't drag me into this. I want my $10 by the way."

"Please, Eric." Brittney watched me talk to the empty backseat.

"Fuck. I hate this shit man. Okay, but you're gonna do something for me later. I want a favor."

"Anything, I need to show Brittney I'm not batshit crazy."

"Too late…but okay, pull out a cigarette."

I reached for them and pulled the pack from my pocket. "No, not in this car, I don't need secondhand wrinkles!"

"Sorry," I got out of the car. "Watch this. Okay, Eric, go ahead." He lit the cigarette for me with his fingertip, cringing as he did so. Brittney just stared in disbelief. "That's not a bar trick to pick up chicks either. That's Eric, the friend I buried. He's a ghost, and he follows me everywhere."

"Was he in the apartment when we…?" I nodded. "Did he watch or was he polite and sit in the other room?"

"I didn't watch. That's the last thing I wanna see."

"He says he didn't watch–he doesn't want to see me on the job."

"Can you thank him for me?"

"You're welcome."

"He says you're welcome."

"Okay so why did you get shot and why wasn't it on the news? How are you walking?"

"Well, when I black out, my ghost, the 'Other,' a dark entity that lives inside since the crash. It takes over and it's highly resistant to injury, at least from the other haunted folks with demons inside them. I heal incredibly fast too. This is the second time in as many months that I've been shot. Last one was a chest wound. You saw the scar."

"That was a recent gun shot? It looked ten years old, like it was mostly gone."

"Yup."

"Wait, make him light something else."

"Got some paper?"

She dug around in the car producing a fast food brown paper bag, "Here!"

"Eric, if you please." He looked very annoyed now. He snatched the bag from me.

"Parlor tricks, really? You're taking me to a skin bar after this." I nodded. He squeezed the bag and his body burnt brightly for a moment. The bag ignited and evaporated leaving behind the scent of the stale fries that were stuck in the bottom of it.

"Damn. Do you know what you can do with this?"

"Yes, I'm beginning to figure it out. At first he could only warm things a bit, crack a mirror. Then he could ignite dry grass and paper, if given time. Now he is like a blowtorch when he wants to be."

"Okay I'm jealous. I want a superpower ghost sidekick." Eric doubled over in laughter. When he recovered, he told me again that I should marry her. "Get back in the car, hon, I'll get you home. You tell me everything."

"I accept your terms." I don't know why but I did. I told her about the crash, the funeral, the time with Emily and my relationship with Rachael. The cholo and how that happened. The ghosts I see in different places, the nightmares. I told Brittney about the rages that unleashed the darkness, "The Other." I told her about the therapist, Eagle, trying to help me, the day-mares of dead friends on the roadsides. I told her about the PO and the carjacking. As I got home I saw my phone still lying on the floor. The battery was dead so I put in on the charger and noticed the appointment card on the refrigerator. I was late. I fed Pickles and asked Brittney if she would stay a while with him and she agreed to entertain the kitten while I went off to see if I couldn't get to talk to this admissions counselor.

CHAPTER 15

SECRETS

I got to the office and the counselor agreed to see me. My case was simple enough and in a few minutes my application paperwork was completed. I paid by a debit card swipe and was on my way. I noticed the international studies office was empty so I stepped in there. A student worker asked if she could help me and I asked her if she could help me get my girlfriend's mailing address, she's studying abroad in France.

"What's her name?"

"Emily Salem." Tap-tap went the keyboard.

"Nope, she's not actively enrolled, seems she took the semester off, she's not abroad." Panic sweat. Terror, shame, betrayal filled me. Eric was right, she lied. I remembered Eagle, too, thought Emily was going to Bar Harbor perhaps, though she wasn't sure. A shadow of doubt challenged reality, but the reality was that she had lied. Whether it was Bar Harbor or Paris, she lied to me. "Women have secrets," Eric warned. I apologized for bothering the girl and disappeared. I ran to Eagle's office. She was gone for the day so I ran home to call her. When I arrived Brittney was enjoying a game of hide under the cardboard box with Pickles. I think she was having more fun than the cat.

"How'd it go?"

"Awesome, I'm basically enrolled. Army transcripts will take a few days to transmit but I'm basically in since I have that GI bill money and they want it."

"You look flushed. Oh my god, your stomach!" She pointed at my belly, I was bleeding, I had dashed from place to place and my panic tensed my muscles so that they tore the stitches open. She took me back to the emergency room and they repaired the stitches and got me some sedatives as my heart rate and blood pressure were dangerously elevated. Brittney held my hand through all of it and I let sleep take me.

I was happy to see I was in my own bed when I awoke. Brittney was in the kitchen and Eric was talking to Frankenbitch near the recliner. I heard little of the whispered conversation but figured if there was anything urgent, Eric would alert me. I had to piss so I got up to go. I was dizzy and I fell, The

Other stirred angrily and I was afraid of him again, there was no reason I could see for him to be alert. Brittney heard me stumble and curse, she came running. I had caught myself and thanked her for her help, letting her get me to the bathroom. I was naked and wondered why she felt it was necessary to strip me.

Eric said, "Because you pissed yourself." Then he returned to his own conversation.

"You can read my mind now?"

"I have always been able to hear your noisy thoughts. We're bound. I think that's my superpower. Leslie here's telling me the secret names to drop at the skin bar to get in free. She told me which dancers will give a little extra on the side after the club closes. Not that you need to know that. You got three girls in town already."

"You forgot Candice, and what are you gonna do in the champagne room, do they have ghosts in there?"

"Candice left town, she graduated you were an accidental one night 'cuz she thought you looked like that actor."

"She was super high."

"Yup, only way you gonna land a hottie like that."

"I banged your sister."

"Eww, she's my sis, she isn't allowed to be hot."

"I got pictures."

"Man, I burn yo house down."

Brittney called in her singing voice from the bedroom, just on the other side of the bathroom door, "I can hear you, who the fuck is Candice?" Eric vanished in a cackling puff of smoke. I washed my hands and came out to face her. "I really don't care. I'm already surprised how comfortable I am with you talking to a ghost and being able to make sense of what is being said. I need to go back to regular land now and get home because I don't have any girl things I need and it's that kind of day." She leaned in and kissed me tugging at my lip for a second and smiling at me when she let go. "Dinner is ready, it's just mac 'n cheese and hot dogs but it's hot. You gonna be okay if I leave you alone tonight?"

"I'm gonna be lonely."

"Don't hump the cat. I have to work tomorrow. If shit gets real bad you call me. I'll take off. But don't make a habit of making me miss work. Especially when I'm having my period and don't feel like fucking so much."

"How long was I out this time?"

"Just about two hours. You just had an odd electrolyte imbalance, the bleed wasn't bad. They only had to give you a little saline and I got this orange juice for you at the 7/11. It's in the fridge."

"Thank you again, I owe you one."

"That's two or is that three now?"

"It's anything you want."

"Okay well I'm getting out of here before Emily gets angry and shows up. Ever since your phone got a charge it's been blowing up on the counter where you left it plugged in."

"Thank you, Brittney."

"Wuv you, hon. Okay, bye, bye, bye!" She blew me a kiss from the kitchen, danced through the door and down the stairs. Pickles chased a moth she let in and I watched him for a good few minutes before the phone beeped. Yet another voicemail I would ignore. I didn't want to talk to her. But I needed to call Eagle. I dialed her number from the card on the refrigerator.

"Hello?"

"Hey, Navy."

"Hey pain in the ass…Emily is harshing my serenity with voicemail, emails and possibly even carrier pigeons. You need to call her."

"I don't want to talk to her, but I need to see you."

"Oh yes, I called, too, left you a message about an appointment opening I had this afternoon. You missed that. I'm off tomorrow. Can you come by the home office?"

"Yeah, sure. Can you tell Emily I'm okay?"

"I don't know that. Are you?"

"Yeah, I'm fine."

"Okay I'll call her for you this one time. But tomorrow I want an explanation. Don't forget your journal."

"Deal, I'll throw it in the Jeep right now." I hung up remembering I hadn't written anything in there yet but meant to after seeing that film. I've been on a conveyor belt pulling me along through crazy for I can't remember how long now. All of it since seeing that film, I needed to write things down just to be sure I could remember things for my therapist. I found the journal, checked the cat's food supply then sat down to write.

Monday I think. I hate Mondays. I hate most days. I don't know how to do this. Am I writing to myself or to the journal? I'm afraid. I should be happy. The woman that wanted me dead is gone. The cholo she sent after me is gone. There is a beautiful, vibrant young woman who adores me. Emily cares about me, even if she's lying to me. I should forgive her. I lie to her almost all the time. I'm a terrible person for that. She paid for this apartment and the furniture and I fucked B. on pretty much all of it. Except the tv and one of the nightstands. Eric and I are getting along as well as can be expected. I should be safe now from anyone else trying to kill me. So why am I still miserable? Are my meds wrong?

I started crying without knowing why. I chewed some pills and played with the cat. I ate the whole pot of mac 'n cheese. I ate two hot dogs and a bunch of Cheetos. I looked for my booze but it was all gone. I found some ginger ale and the orange juice Brittney had bought. I drank half of that and got a stomach ache. I went to bed and woke up to nightmares under my bed, behind the couch and chewed too many pills to find sleep.

I travelled to Eagle's home on the lake and Paul waved in greeting when I arrived, he was walking away from the house with two enormous Samoyeds on leashes. Eagle came out on the loft balcony above the driveway and waved at me. "The door's open, come on up." I nodded and made my way inside. She shouted, "Bring up coffee, the machine up here is busted." I stopped in the kitchen, found two large mugs and filled them with the drip brewed in the Mr. Coffee on the kitchen counter. I brought the coffee up with the journal in my teeth.

She opened the office door and rushed to grab the coffee. "You can't seriously be getting drool on that handmade leather book!"

I took the book from my mouth, "Sorry, I wasn't thinking."

"It's okay, I'm just happy to see you again. I'm so sorry for what happened last time."

"Not your fault. It was the government. Screw those guys."

"What's happening with you? Did you write in the book?"

"Yeah, f them guys, I'm–just look in the book. I'm exhausted. I was at the hospital last night with an electrolyte imbalance after suffering a mystery wound, bleeding out and waking up in the emergency room."

"Whoa, back that way up. When did I see you last? You were just getting into your new apartment and getting along with your ghosts. What happened since then?"

"Where do I start? I got a kitten, met a new girl who is actually really funny, cute and into me, so she must be crazy. I had a freak out at a movie theatre. Learned Eric can now read my mind and light cigarettes for me."

"I'd love to see that."

"Okay, now or…"

"Let's do that at the end. Go on, I'm actually following this."

"Okay I was in Maryland, to take this girl Brittney to a movie. It was the *Butterfly Effect* at that big fancy open air mall."

"I know the one. They have the best Mediterranean place there."

"Sure, have you seen the *Butterfly Effect*?"

"No, Paul doesn't believe in going to the movies, he waits for them to come to cable or VHS."

"They still make VHS tapes?"

"No, so I'll probably never see *Shrek 2*."

"Well I haven't seen it, either. About halfway through the movie I freaked out. It was dark, and the music, the guy being lost in black outs and the journal to remember stuff. A demon, one that I saw outside in the plaza, chewing on a junkie, followed me inside and sat next to me. I think it was going to eat me. I fled. Brittney took me home to safety with the kitten, Pickles, who helped wake me up."

"Pickles, demon chewing on a guy?"

"Why does everyone say it like that when I tell them the kitten's name?" Eagle shrugged. She looked at the journal.

"One page? Wow, I'm overwhelmed. Can you get me another cup while I go ahead and read this?"

"Sure. I gotta pee anyway, it was a long drive today."

When I came back from the kitchen downstairs she was making her own notes on her legal pad.

"I just want to congratulate you. That one page was real. Wow, like I'm really impressed. Yes, I'm concerned but it gives us something to work with beyond these vibrant hallucinations you deal with almost every day. What medications are you on?" I detailed the list. I didn't know all the dosages, so she guessed and asked me what other combinations I had been on. I told her that it's been the same since the hospital in Germany. The VA doctor only upped the dosages recently. "Sounds right for those bastards."

"They seemed nice, actually."

"They're nice sure, but they can smile while feeding you to an alligator. They don't care really. They're paid by the hour in that system. They have policy guidance to work in and really don't doctor much. D.C. tells them to push X med, they push that one. It's often just for a study. The drugs you're on are not indicated for PTSD. It's off-label use, and those drugs are poorly understood. The FDA rushed them all through the approval process with kickbacks. I have literature and recent studies about the SSRI's and benzos that would make your head explode. Those things are no less dangerous and unpredictable than methamphetamines."

"But they make the ghosts disappear."

"Great, but your ghost, he's your friend now, right?"

"Yes."

"How do you feel when he's gone?"

I thought about it. "The last time Eric was gone I was worried, scared."

"There you go. The drugs aren't preventing these hallucinations, just disrupting them and this disruption is causing you still more emotional stress."

"I never thought of it that way."

"I'd like to look for a different doctor for you, maybe a neuro-feedback practitioner. I'd like to try EMDR with you—it's a, I'll explain that." She handed me a pamphlet. "It's a drug-free intervention. There might be some reason to be on some drugs, maybe, but I think if you find some honesty and sobriety, you can minimize the other trauma's impact day to day."

It made sense, "Okay let's try that."

"Great, but before we do any of that, why haven't you talked to Emily, really?"

"I don't know."

She threw a hacky sack at me. "That's bullshit. It's right here in your own writing." She held up my journal, "You don't feel adequate. She's too good for you. She gave you all this stuff and you lie to her all the time. You don't deserve her so you decide to get angry at her. That's so much easier, isn't it?"

"I don't know."

"Can we call her right after this and get this straight with her?"

"Did you talk to her last night?"

"Yes. She was able to sleep, finally. She almost got on a plane to come back here, you know, ruining her school, costing thousands and…"

"She's not enrolled."

"Say what?"

"She lied to you, too. She's not in France, or not in school there."

"How do you know?"

"The girl at the international studies office told me she was on a break."

Eagle looked positively perplexed and then annoyed. "Well it's a good thing then this isn't her session."

"Eric says it's okay for women to have secrets."

"Do you believe that?"

"After spending a little time with Brittney, I'm okay with it. Some things I don't want to know."

"Tell me more about her, your relationship."

"She is a ray of light, joyous and captivating. Somehow world weary beyond pretentions, she's honest and hopeful. She's caring to a fault. Passionate, generous and likes waffles. She is funny as hell."

"How's the sex?"

"Amazing."

"So why don't you like her?"

"I might love her, what do you mean?"

"You have reservations about her. Why, are you afraid of something?"

"She likes me, so she must be crazy."

"Yeah, so see what you're doing here? Sabotaging all chances at happiness?"

"No, I don't."

"Okay, you lie to Emily even though you know she can tell, right? She's told me you point blank lie to her, like you know it's gonna hurt her and eventually drive her away. You keep Brittney at a distance. You haven't told her how you feel; you decide on your own she must be crazy even though she sounds perfectly awesome. You go after Rachael with complete abandon knowing she's terrible for you—you don't have any fear of being tied to her, she is in and out of your life like she is out of so many. And you know she'll make the other girls think twice about commitment. Emily threatened to kill her, right?"

"How did you know that? I never told you that."

"Paranoid much? Medication side-effects," she shook her head. "Emily told me, she asked me for feedback on it. I see her, too, you know, professionally."

"How do I love both girls?"

"You don't. You might love Brittney, I don't know. But you—how well do you think you know Emily?"

"I don't know, Eric says not very."

"She's kind of an idealized set of expectations for you. She represents a romanticized notion. You have mom issues. She's been deeply ill emotionally the whole time you've known her. She is trapped in a deep, heavily-medicated grief cycle."

"She's on medications too?"

"She mostly self-medicates, glug glug, you know? But when you first met her, what was happening?"

"Her gramma died."

"And the next visit? Her dad's wake, Eric's funeral...have you been around her not in the company of death?"

I thought hard and long. "No."

"There you go. You know vulnerable and frightened, intoxicated desperate and bad-decision-making Emily."

"Fuck. But she's taking such good care of me."

"Yeah, I can't explain that. I'd have dropped you a while ago. The whole Rachael two strikes, that's enough for me."

"So what the fuck am I supposed to do?"

"Stop thinking about you and what you want. Get into those recovery meetings and meet people, help people and see how that can help you. Don't make any big decisions right now."

"Like what?"

"Don't propose to any of these girls, don't move any in, it's like the same thing, don't move to another town or take any big trips. Just get centered, give it a year."

"Wait, I just enrolled and got a cat."

"College is good, and a kitty isn't a dog. They pretty much handle themselves. And our time is up. I hear Paul back with Thor and Akira so I have to take them to the groomers."

"When can I see you again?"

"Next week, you wanna come here or try EMDR in my office on Wednesday?"

"Wednesday."

"Done, 10 am."

"Thanks, Navy."

She smiled. "One more thing, school has a long weekend next Thursday thru the following Tuesday. Special events in town, classed are cancelled. My uncle teaches at M.U. in New England, he also won the lottery twice, is a Jeopardy champion and has a lovely ranch of sorts. He holds a retreat there most weekends. Usually he's hosting M.U. faculty, select grad students or celebrity authors and the like, but I'm going up next weekend. I bet you'd love it and get a lot out of it. Get away from all this for a nice happy weekend. I'll drive if you don't mine riding with the mutts. And if you can keep a secret, it's an unusual...arrangement."

"Is there a cost? It sounds great!"

"No cost, he's loaded, he can't spend his money fast enough now that he's sober."

"Is everyone sober now?"

"You aren't."

"Ouch."

"Oh, yeah, no booze at the retreat, okay? So pack warm clothes, it's high altitude and near ski spots, so it's cold even if it's not snowing."

"Okay, I'll pack a coat and extra socks."

"Great, I'll give you all the details at Wednesday's session, 10 o'clock, right?"

"Okay, I'll see you there."

CHAPTER 16

RELEASE

I drove home and saw a sign for the waterfall I never got to visit. I spotted the shortcut trail and turned down the rutted path and put the Jeep in "four wheel high." I was soon covered with a fine dust and my cabin and upholstery suffered the same fate. Eric appeared. "Holy balls, this is not safe!"

"Dude, I just wanna go the waterfall. Please, no revelations. I've had way too much drama lately. Please."

"You don't wanna hear about Leslie?"

"Frankenbitch the PO? No. Not unless she's got yet-another assassin out to get me."

"She didn't say as much, no. But I think she knows more than she's letting on, I can't motivate her to talk like you can." I'd have to bring "The Other" in to torment her. I didn't have it in my heart now to do that, even to her. I just wanted to be left alone a while. The talk of a retreat made me crave just that, a retreat. I couldn't wait a week, I needed an escape now.

"Tomorrow, okay?"

"Thanks. You want to be alone?"

"Please."

"Alright, you have had a rough week. I'll humor you. But the skin bar is calling."

"Can't you go without me?"

"I can't apparently, I did try."

"How come you can enter a church but not a skin bar without me?"

"I wasn't in a church. You mean the funeral home? A priest there doesn't make it a church."

"Can you enter a church?"

"I don't know. Let's try later."

"Sounds like fun. For now, please fuck off, Boss."

"Carry on, Sergeant."

I made my way to the waterfalls, only getting lost once. I found the trailhead, managed the easy hike and forgot the world for a while. As dusk approached, a ranger alerted me to the gates being closed soon and the real possibility I would be stranded here. I made my way with the ranger to the parking lot and there found Eric burning holes in my Jeep's rag top and Rachael sitting on the hood. Eric whispered, "She's here to kill you, dumbass." Paranoid delusions, I told myself. He vanished with some pills I chewed and quickly swallowed.

She was a welcome sight. It seemed I hadn't seen her in a long while. Sure I had Brittney now but Rachael had a broken trashiness that meant she didn't care if I respected her in the morning and I wasn't such a terrible monster that I could do any more damage to her trash fire life. She was risk-free uncomplicated fun. She produced a bottle of Jack Daniels as I got close enough to touch her. She smiled and I put my hands on her knees. "I thought Vodka was your drink."

"You said clear liquors are for housewives on diets or something. And I remember you like scotch." Jack Daniels wasn't scotch but I wasn't going to correct her. She leaned forward for a kiss and I obliged her. She tugged at my lip a second and I thought of Brittney.

"How did you find me?"

"I remembered you saying you wanted to hike here, and I was out riding around with Jeanine, we saw you go this way and we came to see if we could find you. She wanted to meet you. I tried calling but you didn't answer your phone and Jeanine had to go so I stayed here, figured you'd have to come back to the Jeep eventually!"

"That phone is garbage, when I need it, it's out of charge. When I call people, they don't answer. And when people call me, it's always someone I really don't wanna talk to at that moment."

She giggled. "You wanna party or what?"

"Is Jeanine coming back?"

"Would you like that? I can call her…"

"Nah, you're more than I can handle alone, if I had to juggle two women, I'd be in real trouble."

"You have no idea." She spread her thighs apart wider scooting her hips forward to press herself against me.

"Your place? I don't want any repeats of the last visit."

"Actually, you didn't grow up around here, you never been to the spot, have you?"

"No, what's that about?"

She wrapped her arms around me and kissed me again, "This." She kissed me deeper then said, "It's not far, you drive I'll point, okay?"

The ranger meandered closer and chided us about alcohol in the park and we expedited our departure.

We drove only a few minutes and pulled over near a deer carcass on a narrow shoulder with a dented guardrail. She grabbed a blanket out of the back of the Jeep and handed it to me. She led me into the woods along a narrow but well-worn, trash-strewn trail. I began to feel sleepy. I hoped I could shake that off. The trail went up and winded around large boulders covered with faded graffiti. I thought I could hear the falls for a moment, but just then the ringing in my ears rose to a crescendo. Annoying buzzing insects disappeared. As we came around a bend, I saw the first ghost.

A teenager in vintage 1970s attire, she had one of those big afros and noticed me right away. She seemed to try and speak and came hurrying towards me, but I couldn't hear her. I reached inside, The Other stirred and I touched her forehead, releasing her into a faint pillar of light that appeared for a blink. I was wide awake now.

Rachael tugged at me to hurry me along and around another bend I saw a large clearing ahead, the trail descended into the broad dirt clearing. There was a fire pit ringed with stones and several of the trees on the perimeter were blackened or painted.

I stopped at the peak of the ridge with a good view of the clearing. I tried to count the ghosts here. They seemed to flee Rachael as she bounded into the clearing. When she reached the edge of the fire pit she put her bag down and opened the J.D. bottle and took a swig. She beckoned to me but I was counting the ghosts, there were more than a dozen. They hadn't noticed me but they were fleeing her. I wondered why, I came into the clearing calling to Eric, and trying to gain the attention of the nearest specter.

Rachael didn't seem to notice or care. She took another sip and put the bottle down, then pulled her top over her head exposing her breasts. I sleepwalked towards her and felt a deep pain as I stepped past one of the black painted trees. The ghosts now reappeared at the perimeter and watched. They seemed terribly afraid of us, or something. I didn't feel "The Other" trying to lash out, I wondered if there was something more.

Rachael whistled loudly. "I'm over here, baby." She opened the button on her shorts and shimmied out of them.

"Can't you see them?" I pointed to the ghosts. She looked around and pretended not to be able to see them. Now I was alarmed and took a step back. This brought about a distinct change in Rachael's demeanor. Gone was her beguiling smile and relaxed seductive swaying.

She pulled a large dagger from her bag and lunged at me in a smooth, swift motion suggesting mastery. The rage came up but seemed stuck in my gut. The ringing in my ears exploded and made it hard to keep my eyes open. She sliced my arm open as I swept it to the side to block her attack from striking my vitals. I kicked her knee out and shoved her away. She went sprawling into the grass beyond the clearing. I summoned the darkness but it only stirred deeply. I called it again! It tried to lash out but could not reach beyond my own skin that began to burn inside.

Rachael leapt up hissing and calling to her own demonic ally but there was no apparent response. I spun my head rapidly to each side searching for another attacker, the ghosts pointed to Rachael and seemed to shout warnings. It was a trick, damn she was wily! She had recovered her knife and I decided I had had enough. I didn't wait for her next attack. I rushed at her putting fist in hand, making a battering ram of my elbow. I launched myself inside her swing with all my weight driving my strike. The dagger plunged into my back along the right shoulder blade at a glancing angle. It deflected away causing only a superficial wound, I hoped.

I crashed my elbow, trailing blood from her first slash, into her septum blinding her and spraying blood everywhere. Her nose and part of her upper jaw was broken. She fell back and let go of the knife. I stepped out of the clearing, onto the grass and I slipped on blood or dew. I was out of the clearing and I felt the darkness finally respond. It came up from inside and surrounded me in an instant. I slept.

When I was aware again, it was near dark. Rachael was broken into three main pieces but parts of her were flung haphazardly everywhere. Blood, gore and offal hung from tree branches and rocks. Blood pooled in grassy depressions. It looked like cannibals had attacked her then changed their mind about eating any of their kill. I vomited violently at the sight of one I loved so, ruined by my hand. Her once beautiful face seemed to have been scraped off against a sharp rock and it hung limply like a discarded rag, her eyelids open wide, with only blood-smeared granite where her eyes should be. They were nowhere to be seen.

I grabbed the bottle she had left in the clearing. The ghosts came and clawed at me, begging now audibly for release. I drank deeply from the bottle until I couldn't taste vomit and blood. That took near half the bottle. I cried.

I thought to ask the ghosts the myriad questions that each such encounter had raised but felt it cruel somehow. Some of these poor fellows seemed to have been waiting a half-century or more for release. I counted more than twenty before I stopped trying to keep track of them. I continued to weep, some were young children. I drank the rest of the bottle and thought to escape only to get more booze. Then as I rummaged through Rachael's bag, Eric appeared.

"This is a crime scene, stop touching shit, fucktard." He was right. I looked around. My boot prints—my DNA was everywhere.

"I'm fucked. They're gonna give me the chair. There is no way I tear a girl up like that and get away with self-defense."

"Yeah, look at this fucking mess, god, I've never seen anything like that. How did you do this?"

"I didn't, there is no fucking way! It looks like a damn dinosaur got her!"

"I'm fucking glad it's getting dark and I can hardly see shit." Eric wept too.

"I gotta get outta here, I need an alibi. And I'm bleeding."

"Those wounds are not healing fast enough, hold still."

Eric came at me before I could brace myself for it. He slapped his hands down onto the wounds and my skin sizzled. I wailed in pain and thought I would pass out again. I felt the darkness stirring and begged Eric to stop. He backed away and the blood loss stopped. I didn't know how to explain those burns but I was glad the bleeding had stopped at least. Those wounds, the burns, caused by a ghost not a bullet or a knife, I expected would heal fast. I could feel and see them healing very quickly and found courage in this.

"I got this bro. Get home. Clean off the blood with that blanket so you don't get pulled over. And get the fuck home. We gotta burn those clothes, bag 'em for me, we'll take 'em someplace and torch 'em, okay?" Eric began to burn brightly. "Yes, I can do this. I will burn this whole side of the mountain. You aren't going to take the fall for this."

"You didn't see it happen then, did you?"

"Thank God, no. I never want to see anything like that, like this again. Please, next time just boil their damn eyes like the cholo."

"I hope there is never a next time."

"There will be. But I hope I'm gone then. Now run, you fool!"

I struggled to navigate the trail in the dying light. It was dark before I was halfway back to the road. I slid into a draw and had to guess at a way out from there. I got lucky and happened upon the road and was able to guess the direction back to the Jeep. I got in and drove straight home using unlit secondary roads so my appearance wouldn't be noticed.

I got home and got cleaned up. I got a shower and bagged my clothes. I waited for Eric to finish his work. I would not summon him before the clearing was cleansed. I watched the news and sure enough a wildfire at a local youth gathering spot burned over a hundred acres before it was contained. A few unoccupied structures were destroyed but there were no reported injuries as of the time of the broadcast.

I could stop shaking with fear and dreading that at any moment the swat team would burst into the apartment. Pickles came begging for a bite, chewing on my toe. I scooped him up and put him on the kitchen counter. I opened a tin of meat and pushed it in front of him. He meowed as if to ask me, "you want to split this or can I have the whole thing?" I scratched his head and told him he could have the whole thing. I was talking to a cat. I was completely mad now.

CHAPTER 17

BACON

In the morning, Eric was kicking at the bag of stuff to burn and said, "Just throw it in the complex dumpster and do it now, the truck is coming." This I did. Then after I was satisfied it was all gone, having watched the garbage truck empty the dumpster and drive out of sight, I sat down and started reading my mail pile which I was only just starting to put a dent in.

"Thanks, Boss. That was ah…"

"Stop, I really don't, I don't wanna talk about it, I don't wanna think about it. Okay? I need a break. I mean, we should maybe split up a while. I don't know how much more of this I can handle. If you and my sister didn't still need me to cover for you, I'd really like you to release me like those others."

"What if it sends you to Hell?"

"Nothing could be worse than this existence."

I sorted the bills from the mystery mail first and started writing checks to pay the bills then worked through the mystery mail. The first mystery letter turned out to be a stop-loss letter I had dreaded. The Army had switched from unit-based stop-loss to going after personnel based on specialty. It ordered me to report for a physical but I had already missed the date. I threw it away and kept going through the mystery mail. Most of it was garbage, coupons for having recently moved, junk mail disguised smartly as something important and a tax form from the local tax collector. I threw it all away and decided to take Eric to the skin bar, he'd been asking lately and I didn't see a good reason to deny him a distraction.

"Sensations," the tall sign in front of the tiny roadside club read. The parking lot was mostly empty. Looked like enough cars for the staff if the dancers walked to work, unlikely. Eric told me a code word for the doorman and it worked. He waved me in without a cover charge. There weren't any customers and there was some music but no dancers. There were two skanks in glitter and bikinis doing cocaine at a small table in a dark corner. The bartender told me the kitchen wasn't open yet, the cook was late. The DJ was asleep in his booth. One of the skanks noticed me and the other ran off in fright. Eric nudged me. "Skank number two saw me, that's why she ran off."

"Other people can see you now?"

"She's like the second or third."

"I hate learning more about this, especially being the last one to know all the time." Skank one looked ten years younger at ten paces than she did up close and as she got even closer, well–could have passed for my grandmother. She went to embrace me but I put my hand out to stop her. "I'm just looking for a drink and some directions." Her face turned uglier and hostile.

"The gay bar is on queen street, homo." She turned about and shuffled off.

"I didn't know they had a gay bar, Eric."

"We don't, do we?"

"We should totally go, see what kind of disaster that is."

"You gonna talk to yourself all night or can I pour you a drink…" the bartender interrupted.

"My hangover wants a gin and tonic."

The bartender smiled. "Sure." In a flash, my tonic with a splash of gin was ready. "Seven."

"Can you get herpes from a dirty glass?" He just stared at me.

I plopped down a ten and threw the drink back. A man with a shot gun came out from the back with skank number two. He looked around and then started chewing the stripper out. She kept pointing and frantically gesturing towards Eric. The man slapped her and Eric got annoyed. "That's not her fault. I should fuck that guy up."

"Can you?"

"Blow, I don't need you involved if I do."

"Suits me, I didn't want to visit this slit trench anyway." I drove off. I don't know what happened there and decided never to ask him.

When I got home there was a box outside. The return address was a post office box in Vermont. Inside were four electronic recording devices of an unusual design. There was a card inside with a machine printed message.

My Beloved,
Please keep at least one of these with you always, when you speak to my brother these may pick up his voice. Please ask him to get Mother a message and I would love to hear from him as well.
Thank you.

XOXO
Emily

I put one on in the kitchen where Eric often stands and plugged it in. I loaded batteries into the others as the instructions read and put one in my hoodie pocket. I put one in the bedroom and left one on the table next to the recliner Eric had been trying to ruin.

I found my phone. I called Emily, no answer. I left another message, this time telling her I got the gift and that I would do everything I could to get Eric to talk to Mara. I called Eagle at the office, Rainbow Hair confirmed my appointment and finally I called Brittney and left a message hoping it wasn't too late to plan a get together sometime soon. I played with Pickles and fell asleep on the kitchen floor.

I woke up in time to make my therapy appointment. I was on my way to my there when my phone rang. I accidentally answered it. "This is Corporal Oldham, Pennsylvania state patrol. Who am I speaking with?" I told him he got the right guy. "Good, I need to talk, do you have time this morning?"

"No. I have a doctor appointment then I'm leaving town for a long weekend."

"How about this afternoon? I only need a few minutes."

"No. Sorry. How about I call you when I get back Tuesday?"

I could sense frustration in his response. "Okay, can you be at the barracks at 9 am on Tuesday?"

I hated this guy, I could smell the chew on his breath through the phone, and I was pretty sure he knew I hated him. "If I'm back in town that early, I don't have all the details about my schedule yet."

"Alright, Tuesday, 9 am. Do you know where the barracks are?"

I lied. "Yes." I didn't care. I had no intention of going.

At Eagle's, Oldham was sitting in his car out front. He was reading a porno and spitting tobacco goo into an empty Mountain Dew bottle. He didn't think I could see what he was reading but the images reflected off one of his windows. I chuckled and I think he hated that I was having a laugh, knowing it was at his expense somehow. I don't know where the chutzpah to torment a living cop came from. Before the crash, I'd go out of my way to avoid these guys or annoying them. Too many of them knew my name to begin with.

When I entered Eagle's office, she put her finger to her lip to shush me. She put on some music and brewed some coffee.

She tried to look calm. She handed me coffee and finally spoke quietly. "Do you have your journal?"

"Yes?"

"Good. Let me see it." She shook her head back and forth. I held on to it. "Oh, very good."

She crossed the room, gently took my arm in her hand and whispered, "What the fuck?"

I was in trouble. I had broken my only friend. I wanted to fall into the usual chair. "Seriously, what the fuck–look at you. What is going on? Your bullshit is giving me freaking PTSD." She slumped down into her chair. She looked beyond exasperated and desperate to be anywhere else. I apologized and she let out a long sigh. "No, I'm sorry. That was not professional. We should start over…but before we do, you saw the cop, right? You know why he was here?"

I nodded. Of course I knew. I asked her if she could tell me about it.

"No. I can't tell you about it. I could lose my board certification."

"It's okay, I know he was asking about me."

"Not knowing is going to bother you, isn't it?"

"Hell yeah, my paranoia is through the roof already." I felt like this was a mistake to try and talk to her anymore.

"You know I'm an Indian and how I feel about the government and that as a professional I have to make an effort to remove barriers to your treatment and health. If not knowing is going to hurt our chances of success here–and I honestly don't like our chances right now, the least I can do is give you a comforting lie."

I felt an eyebrow lift in speculation and disbelief. What the hell kind of joke was this? "Sure, let's try that."

"Okay so, since I can't tell you the truth about the conversation with the nice officer, let me make up a fun story and we can pretend that it was the truth and move on with therapy."

I nodded. She pointed to a tape recorder hidden in a tissue box and went on.

"The police officer wasn't here to ask me about your apartment that burnt down."

"That wasn't my apartment, that was the junkies'."

"Right, I know that, shut up. They don't think you had anything to do with another officer that's gone missing or a missing student. They didn't ask to illegally access your files and my notes. The officer only wanted to assure me that his concern was for your health and safety and that of the rest of the students and staff here. Even though they are apparently willing to jeopardize your health by clumsily making visits to this safe place and threatening us with violence and force by their mere presence."

"They don't think I did any of it?" She held up her finger and asked if I wanted a cup of coffee now. "Yes coffee, please."

She asked superficial questions about the weather, how I liked my current accommodations, how journaling was going, if I had yet found the courage to speak at the alcoholic meetings then apologized profusely for spilling my coffee into the tape recorder. "That's wrecked, how sad." She tossed the dripping device into the garbage after making sure she stopped it.

She got serious. "Are WE good?"

"Yes." I was trying not to laugh. I didn't know she was a subversive.

"Good, did you want coffee for real?"

I nodded and she made each of us a cup. She told me she was glad for that and apologized again for the government's ham-handed attempts to exploit the therapeutic relationship. She asked me to start at the beginning since she felt like she had missed a lot of the original story, and I had held back a lot. I drank my coffee and I told her what I found this morning and that Eric had been with me since the hospital in Germany.

Eagle was genuinely curious now about the ghosts, where before she dismissed them as symptoms she now wanted to know everything about them. She was interested in how Eric seemed to know things I didn't and even concealed things from me I ought to know. The appearance of the Leslie ghost intrigued her. Leslie's silence puzzled us both. I told her they wanted to kill me. Even Eric wanted to, tried to–in the hospital in Germany. He tried to set the plane on fire on the way home and had caused a dozen false fire alarms at the apartment building when I wasn't there and today had melted the tile in my kitchenette. She asked to see the tiles and we took the unusual step of leaving and I took her to my place.

At the apartment she turned white when she saw the foot prints in the floor and touched them. She looked at me with bewildered shock and back at the floor. I know she wondered how I had done this and knew it was impossible. We sat and she asked me about my plans for the break. I shrugged. I had been planning on attending that retreat with her.

"You have been through a lot, just being new to this environment unhinges many ordinary students without your exceptional experiences." I thought that was some euphemism, "exceptional experiences" indeed. "I think you would enjoy and benefit greatly from attending the retreat this weekend, the one we talked about last session."

I nodded. "That's precisely what I was hoping to do. You were going to give me details about it today."

"I forgot, the cop got me flustered. Okay well tonight, after work meet me at the office, 4:30, we'll go get the dogs and my bags and off we go, okay?"

"Perfect. I need a nap now the whole cop thing's got me freaked out."

"Okay, well let's call today's session complete then. I'm going to use the rest of my free time to talk to the director about this cop bullshit."

"I know an assistant district attorney."

"Really?"

"Yeah, Ewing, Walter Ewing. He's the victim advocate guy."

Eagle pulled Oldham's card from her pocket and handed it to me. "Call Walter, he's a stand up fellow. Tell him this trooper is harassing you and what he tried to do today with that tape recorder bullshit."

I agreed and called the office number on the card. A secretary answered and patched me through. Walter was happy to hear from me and agreed to meet in twenty minutes for lunch at Kildare's on the square. Eagle gave me a "thumbs up" and a satisfied grin then headed back to her office. I played with the cat a few minutes on the couch before heading into town.

I met Mr. Ewing at Kildare's it was too early for booze, even for me. I ordered one of the daily varieties of baked mac 'n cheese available and Walter ordered two pints with pastrami on rye.

"I'm glad you called me, I was beginning to worry something might be wrong. I recall my office leaving a couple of voicemails for you."

"I'm sorry if I worried you, sir."

"It's just Walter. And I wasn't worried, it's alright, I just wanted to get this paperwork off my desk and make sure you were getting the support you deserved. So you can imagine my shock at hearing one of the officers involved in your heroic carjacking incident was harassing you. Would you care to detail it all for me?"

"Sure, thanks for meeting with me on such short notice."

"You're my top priority right now. Police impropriety is my pet peeve. I abhor bad cops." He looked around and whispered, "Most of them are bad, too, believe you me."

I was shocked at his stark admission and my lack of a poker face made it plain to see. It wasn't that I thought cops were good people, just I didn't expect someone in his position to readily offer such a cynical, if honest assessment. "I went to a therapy session and learned from my therapist that he threatened her to gain her cooperation in surreptitiously recording a treatment session. He was parked out there surveilling me and was accessing my files without a writ or warrant whichever is the right one."

"Neither is appropriate in this case, a judge wouldn't issue a warrant to search a victim's medical records and the state patrol isn't the office responsible here, it's my office. The trooper is beyond out of line. Do you want me to take a written statement and make this a formal inquiry or would you like me to handle this quicker and off paper for you?"

"I don't want any more attention drawn to me. There has been too much crazy bullshit going on."

Walter drained his first pint and asked for a third as he started into the second. "You sure you don't want one?"

"Nah, I would love one but it's early."

He looked at his watch. "It's afternoon have one, on me."

Fuck, I thought. "I'm trying the A.A. thing right now. I'm supposed to be."

"I'm sorry. That sounds terrible."

"What do you mean, how awful the people and their stories are?"

"Life is short. I tried it once, and it was just a complete disaster. Everyone was miserable and sad and just hanging on for dear life so excited they didn't drink today. They used their power to catastrophize anything to tell themselves one drink would kill them. It's catastrophizing when that was one of the kinds of crazy defects they wanted to eliminate. It's all so nonsensical and sometimes paradoxical, annoyingly manipulative of the weak minded. It's smoke and mirrors, mind games. I'd rather just have a few pints."

"Don't you need to get back to the office?"

"No, I'll make a call from my cell on my way home. I live in a modest bachelor's apartment here in town. No big family digs in the suburbs. I'm a confirmed bachelor and wouldn't have it any other way. I don't even own a car. I have a driver for work stuff and I can get anything I need delivered."

"Alright fuck it. I'll have a pint."

"Two more for my friend over here, please!"

Our buxom server brought our drinks with a smile and our food arrived a moment later, brought by a diminutive, proud, excitedly gay fellow of comical appearance with an even funnier name on a plastic tag, "TREY," it read. I couldn't help but laugh out loud at that. He set the tray on a stand with a flourish and the server put our plates before us, ignoring the joke she didn't get and asking if we needed anything else before departing.

"Hot sauce," I said, sending her on her way to the server station. I turned my attention back to my friend Walter. "Is there something else going on I'm missing?"

"Not that I know of, and I would know. I have the file in my satchel here did you still need the assailant's information?"

"No, I don't need to know anything else about him, really. I was just curious about his condition. I heard he was burned somehow. And I remember you told me his wrists were crushed."

He looked at me a moment and washed down a bite with more beer. "Well the coroner's report was perplexing. I admit I thought it odd, I read it twice." He pulled the report from his leather messenger bag and put in on the table facing me. It was one of those black and white line drawings of a person with marks where the injuries were. If showed and X through each wrist and both eyes with lines to text around the body diagram in medical terms I couldn't quite translate. Walter explained in greater detail.

"So his wrists were melted mush, extremely strange, more than just broken. That's what those medical terms mean. His eyes there, his ocular cavities showed evidence of chemical burns, like someone had poured acid in them but there were lacerations too. See those words there—something had steamed his eyes and they burst, it looks like his blood did that work. As for the chemical, they haven't figured out what that was. His blood work is still out, for all we know he had antifreeze and every drug known to man in his system."

"Why isn't his name on there?"

"He was a 'John Doe' or 'Juan Doe' when he was being processed."

"What about his rap sheet? I heard he had a bunch of priors and was awaiting deportation."

"Oh, yeah, the feds' incompetence is enough to make you drink." He ordered another. "The guy was deported twice, once for aggravated sexual assault of a minor. The feds can't make up their mind what to do with guys like this it seems. From month to month policy changes and even when they try to do this right, they screw it up. Guys like this are all over the country though, if you knew, it would make you gray. You were in the army, you know all about that right, bad government?"

"Yup." I tossed back another, grateful I could also walk home from here.

"How was that?"

"You a veteran?"

"No. I have flat feet."

"Well you didn't miss much. I wouldn't recommend it or do it again. The army is stupid when it doesn't have to be and lies when it makes more sense to tell the truth. It consistently finds ways to make the simple impossible and the most basic thing, like peeling potatoes or driving trucks, into nuclear physics. It's beyond stupid. They need a new word to describe it."

"I would suggest congress perhaps."

"Ha, those fucktards. I don't know who's worse, them, the U.N. or the damn news jackals."

"Dirty Laundry."

"Yup."

"Well I've got a date this evening and I need to get myself together for that and get a few things done around the ole homestead before the place is condemned." He paid the check and handed me a form from his file. "Here is a simple statement form if you want to fill in what's left on there. The basics are already filled in for you. So I can put this in the archives. Just drop it by when you have a chance, you know the address, right?"

"Yup." He put a cash tip on the table.

He got up to leave. "Do remember me to Emily and her mother when next you see them."

I lied. "Of course I will, Walter."

"Thank you my friend."

CHAPTER 18

RETREAT

I lingered to finish my beer. I had no date that evening. I went to the bar and ordered another drink and called Brittney, she didn't answer. I told her voicemail recording that I was going out of town for the long weekend. I tried to call Emily again and she didn't answer. I didn't bother leaving another message. I decided to leave the phone at the apartment. I went to an A.A. meeting and then returned to Kildare's for a couple of shots before meeting Eagle.

We loaded her very large dogs, the Samoyeds Akira and Thor, into her ancient blue Subaru covered in subversive bumper stickers and scratches. One read, "You can trust the government, ask an Indian." Amongst the many I had seen before was another that proclaimed, "Yossarian Lives!" I had to ask about that, I'd never heard of Yossarian and she complained, "No one reads anymore." She helped me load my bag. "Yossarian is the mysteriously fated protagonist in a favorite book, *Catch-22* by Heller."

"Never heard of it."

"Odd, it's the subversives' bible, anyway—I didn't really like it that much. I liked the guy being an immigrant and that perspective. I liked the illustration of the absurdity of the bureaucratic war machine, of war itself but it was also in places pedantic and sexist."

"Which war was it?"

"Not yours, the second world war, I think, the guys flew B-25 bombers."

"World War Two, then, yes. It was a different time, movies from then are probably pretty sexist too."

"Yes, but this took it a step further perhaps than the John Wayne movies of the time even, and those were filmed back then. This was a look back and I felt Heller kinda went out of his way to spit on the women in the story. If you read it you might get it."

"Do you have a copy?"

"One. You can't have it. See I don't like that book so much as the person who it reminds me of."

"Is this a story I get to hear?"

"Yeah, I'm gonna share it with you but—you aren't allowed to, okay?"

"Sure, I can't wait now."

"Okay so I had a crush in the Navy, the guy was a pilot and he was reading it. He left it in my apartment the last time I saw him. It's the only thing I have of his. God, that was years ago and the book still smells like his hands. So I keep it in my nightstand. I read it every once in a while. I don't know what the scent is but it's mechanical and chemical and strength. I'm babbling."

"No, please do go on."

"Well, that's about it. I love the smell of that stupid book. One day it's going to fall apart and I'll have nothing."

"What happened to the pilot?"

"He got 'emergency sortied' out with his radar intercept officer to replace a sick crew. The ship was in a hot zone and was crippled by some terrible GI infection. So he went out there and I guess maintenance had suffered with all the sickness, that's the navy's story. He crashed over Northern Iraq."

"I'm sorry."

"Thank you, it's okay. I later found out that he was married. I was just a pit stop for him. I met his wife at his funeral. Awkward, right? Yeah. Little while ago, in the whole campaign to attack Iraq this time around, they had declassified the fact that he was shot down. Something like twenty two Navy crews lost over there enforcing no-fly zones since the first gulf war."

"Still, that sucks."

"I never should have joined, I just wanted off the reservation. I wanted, you know, college and skills I could bring back to the nation. I haven't been back much. I'm a terrible Indian. The worst part is I was really hung up on him even after meeting his wife. I pretended he wasn't dead. I fell asleep holding the book every night for months. I kept thinking I would rock his world when he came back for it. You know what a psychotic is?"

I hoped she wasn't going to tell me. "No."

"It's someone more neurotic than your doctor. I don't think there is anything about you and what's going on with you that's more screwed up than what's happening in my damn head every day."

"Thank you, I think."

"Don't mention it, especially to Paul, God love him. If you tell him about my book I'll cut you."

"Yes, ma'am."

We sat in silence for a minute. Then she pulled into a rest stop to let the dogs run a few minutes and to stretch our own legs.

"How did you meet Paul?"

"He was a supervisor in the hospital at Portsmouth. He was a director, I think, whatever, and he collected nurses. I was hung up on my pilot and so I was a real challenge for him. I drove him nuts being exotic of appearance and I played hard to get. He tried for months to get me to have a drink with him, go to a movie, anything. He tried all kinds of stuff. One day, he was putting together a team to go out on a humanitarian assistance mission. I volunteered since it wasn't a combat zone. It was like a Caribbean hurricane or something." She was lost in thought staring into memory.

"We all got geared up to go, flight suits and all that, which no one looks good in, maybe me. But anyway that smell, the pilot fingers? He had it when we got off the plane and walked out on to the carrier flight deck. I was shaken and ill owing to the bone-jarring ride and tripped going down the plane's ramp. Paul caught me, awkwardly. He caught a boob and my face. But I smelled my pilot and we had sex in one of the exam rooms in sick bay fifteen minutes later. I told him he'd have to marry me then and he agreed. We've been together ever since. My career ended. Apparently the women in my chain of command, one being an ex of his, didn't take kindly to me winning the Paul prize."

"He agreed to marry you after one…session?" She nodded slowly.

"Damn. I don't think I've had anyone like that good."

"You never know, Army." We got back into the Subaru.

"Paul had a stroke a few years ago, he's mostly recovered now but it's been a long tough slog. He, uh, can't perform anymore."

"So you two haven't?"

"We do, but we have to get creative, lots of toys. And this conversation is probably not a good one to have with your therapist." I laughed at her abrupt reserve.

"Right, what would the board say?"

"It's okay, though, he's good to me, I love him and we're great together. We hit rock bottom together got through it, even though he had to do time. And we got sober together, even though I feel like I fought him every step of the way. It was his stroke I think that finally did it for me. I never drank again after that."

"How long have you been sober?"

"I drank the night we crashed, but the next day in the hospital I did have some then, too, never mind. He was there about a week. Then he had the stroke. The doctors told me what was going to be involved in his recovery and I asked God how I was going to do it. He said nothing. I asked God to help me…" She started to cry and sniffled. She pointed to the glove box. I found tissues there and handed her one. "Thank you." She took a deep breath and continued. "And God said, 'Okay, I made you a fucking nurse.' And I swear that's what God said."

"Only the Navy god would curse." She laughed into her snotty tissue. I handed her another.

"Thanks, Army, it's hard—it's been six years. The first two were the worst. I know you're struggling, you still haven't decided you've had your last drink, but maybe you did. You know we don't drink at these retreats, right?"

"Yeah, I think you told me that. So I drank a bunch before I came to see you."

"I know, I can smell it a good long way off and this is a small car. I can only smell scotch and dog farts right now." I remembered now that the Heller book, I had heard about it once and seen it next to its sequel in the library once.

"Did you read the *Catch-22* sequel?"

"There's a sequel?"

"I think so. I'm gonna take you word, though, that Yossarian lives. Bumper stickers don't lie, do they?"

She laughed. "Nope, never. I put that there in case his ghost would see me driving around he'd know that was me somehow and he'd follow me home."

I reached down deep and felt a writhing mass of hatred. Eric appeared in the backseat. "Damn, you think I'll scare the dogs?"

"I just hope you don't set 'em on fire."

"Woof!" Eric barked and the dogs barked a reply in unison.

Eagle wiped her face then looked in the back, the dogs were separated and there was room enough between them for a man. "Are you talking to your ghost? Is he here?"

Why lie? "Yeah. I called him up."

"Why, we wanted to get away from all of that, didn't we?"

"I was going to ask him about your friend. Is that too much?"

"No, what do you mean, like he can find him?"

"Yeah, I was going to ask him about maybe doing that. He sees ghosts I don't and does things I don't understand. He has his own adventures I find out about later."

"I don't know. I really...okay, you find out if he can do it and don't tell me right now. I don't want to know just yet. I can't ask you to do this really. This is crazy."

"I thought you therapists didn't use the C and N words."

"I'm an unconventional sort, progress not perfection."

Eric grumbled. "Okay, I'm not right here, and I don't think that it's a good idea for me to disturb a resting spirit."

"He's resting?" I wondered how he could rest if his remains weren't recovered.

"I'm guessing."

"He was shot down in Iraq, he's probably still out there someplace unrecovered like that guy..."

"Scott, Scott Speicher." Eagle finished my sentence and wept anew, he wasn't her pilot but he was famously a symbol of men fighting and dying that

98

America didn't care about. He was forgotten and left there while we kept going to the mall. He was a symbol for anonymous service forgotten, a stain on our national honor. Her man was even less well remembered.

Eric looked at her. "I hate to see a girl cry, I'll see what I can do. I can travel to Iraq, I died there I have a strong connection and can manifest there. But it isn't instant, I still have to travel. It only takes a few hours, I think. I've been back twice, by accident the first time. You were having a flashback and called me from there. I thought you were there. Anyway, I don't understand exactly how it works. I'll go but don't summon me for a while, okay?"

"Thanks, Eric." Eagle joined me in that sentiment looking in her rear view mirror through watering eyes.

"You want me to drive a while?"

"Please?" We didn't speak anymore except for an occasional "turn here" or "turn there" and the dogs filled in the space Eric recently occupied. Akira put his fat head onto the center console and lazily licked at his mother's elbow for attention.

The rest of the ride was long and the careworn seats in the antique Subaru let you feel the antique shocks fail over the antique winding back roads Eagle seemed to prefer. At each brief stop for the dogs or for coffee, I creaked and ached and stretched. I searched for the dead I had been seeing for so long. There was no one. We went further and further into the mountains up past Pottsville, coal country and into New York and beyond. Our last leg took us through a winding foothills and a misty cool fog. It was like driving into a Lovecraft anthology. We talked again, about the misty peaks and Lovecraft. She was surprised I had read any of his works. I liked surprising her.

When we got to the site, the ground was covered in snow that had already been packed with neat little trails plowed and marked with stakes and rope guidelines where appropriate. The lake she had told me of was frozen, a pair of hockey goal nets were already out there waiting. I had expected kayaks and fishing boats. I think she read the palpable disappointment on my face but ignored it. There were several cars parked nearby with a good day's worth of fresh snow entombing them. A grizzly man was repairing a snowmobile nearby wearing only a pair of pair of flip flops and overalls and his own thick coat of coarse hair that grew thickly from his ears down to his knuckles. He briefly acknowledged us with a wave and resumed his work.

Eagle motioned for me to follow her to the house, a massive log cabin which could easily be a hotel and then the dogs exploded from the back seat and tore off into the snow, porpoise-like as they made their own tunnels through the fresh powder. I've never seen such joy in any creature before. I was hypnotized for a moment and Eagle caught me. "They'll be fine. As soon as the grill is fired up, they'll be back." I stopped at the threshold, shaking. I was gripped with terror and Eagle reminded me to use a mindfulness trick and that this place, though new, was safe and full of healing energy. "There is no threat here, no danger—only love and rest."

Eric opened the door and laughed. "I always hated her, damn hippie tree hugger. Get in or you'll freeze to death." I pushed myself to go in after Eagle and wondered who had really opened the door. I quickly forgot about that and surveyed the room inside. There were a dozen people in the room of all size and description. They were in good spirits and seemed to be at ease in a way I never could be. They could not have been strangers, and indeed some of them may have been related. I saw at least one couple and in another room beyond I could hear still more voices.

"There are more than two dozen people here, I should have told you that—I hope it's not going to stress you any," Eagle whispered.

"Nah, nothing to worry about." I shook my head and continued to watch the strangers who took no notice of us. Eagle tugged at my elbow and directed my attention to a nearby stair. Eagle described the taking of the heads of elk and moose that adorned the cabin. She told me the name of the bear at the end of the hall atop the stair and how she had killed it as a young girl.

I could barely hear her through the ever-present ringing that was near violent levels. It was maddening to me and I became aware that I was grimacing as if injured. Eagle also noticed and inquired about what I was "experiencing" right now.

"Just a damn headache, the tinnitus and I'm probably dehydrated."

She led me to what she said was her favorite suite at the end of the hall and gave me a tour of the three rooms within.

The bathroom was big, bigger than my first apartment. The commode had its own room away from the school-bus-length vanity with two sinks. There was a bidet in the commode room and the bathtub was the size of a lap pool. There was a decorative water feature and a small gas fireplace to warm the room. You could park two Jeeps in the empty space between it all. The bedroom was smaller but still large and very inviting with ample pillows, furs, throws and a bar trolley fully stocked with non-alcoholic beverages. The living room had its own fireplace and a sliding door leading to a deck connected to the adjacent suite.

There were no electronics and the only sign of modern convenience were the sparse electrical lights and a tea service complete with an electric kettle concealed in a console behind a plaid sectional sofa. There were hundreds of books on three tall floor-to-ceiling built-in bookshelves. I could live in this space forever, I thought. Eagle smiled, pleased that her selection of a room for me was satisfactory.

"This is a safe place; no matter what you can always retreat here. The other guests know the rules—no one is allowed to enter another guest's room without invitation, so no one will come and bother you unless you bring them in yourself." I nodded to indicate my understanding. "Can you feel safe here?" I nodded again. "Great, I'm very happy. Now for the other rules, they're quite simple. First, as you know, you may not enter any other guest's suite without invitation. I invite you to bother me anytime. I'm across the hall, okay? I'm more staff than a guest, so the rule doesn't apply to me. I'm supposed to be reasonably available to you." She looked at my pocket that was wiggling.

"What's that?" She pointed to the pocket where Pickles was sleeping. I gently coaxed him out and the sleepy kitten drew Eagle close with an "aaaaw." "Has he been in there this whole time?"

"Yup."

"Amazing, he's so calm."

"Not once he finds those curtains."

"Okay, do you have supplies for him?"

"Yup I got litter and a box and all in my luggage."

"Okay, food—there is a kitchen, you saw that and the dining room coming in. There are regular meals prepared by the staff except on Sunday when we will cook together. Those who care to participate, anyway. While meal hours are set, you are free to help yourself to anything and to prepare anything you like. Roast a whole turkey to make a sandwich if you like. As I said before, there is no alcohol and no drugs permitted, however, medications are allowed but you must keep them in your room or in your possession at all times, it's a safety rule. If you see unattended medication—do not, for any reason touch it. Contact a staff member, I'll introduce you..."

I had tuned her out a long time ago. I was gazing into the frozen mist over the frozen lake between two frozen hills that bracketed this frozen oasis. I felt myself melting into a comfortable puddle. I put Pickles on the bed and he stomped around and explored a bit before curling up and going back to sleep. Eagle prattled on about I don't know what. Eventually she seemed happy and I nodded so she'd leave me alone. She hugged me which was awkward and unexpected and left, promising to introduce me to the team when I was ready. She said, "You'll smell when dinner is near ready and will hear the dogs barking anyway." I nodded.

I unpacked supplies for Pickles, a Tupperware litter box filled before we left. I filled a platter with Perrier from the bar trolley. I opened a tin of his favorite chow and he sprung to life and attacked his meal. I waited for him to finish then introduced him to his box and water. I went outside for a walk.

I wandered a trail and got lost in the grandeur of my surroundings. I half-expected I might encounter a Shoggoth out here. Then I heard the most sorrowful laments. I smelled Rachael's perfume and thought, the damn Shoggoth is imitating my dead girlfriend as they did their creators. That was an impossible thing, but as I pondered the reality I was living, it seemed comforting to face a Shoggoth. Rachael appeared. She was her beautiful self, as she was just before I smashed her face in. She was naked except for her boots and she wrapped herself around me begging forgiveness and sobbing miserably.

"How did you find me this time?" I asked her.

"Eric."

"Why did you try and kill me?"

"Why did you kill me? You could have fought the demon but you killed me instead."

"I'm sorry, I didn't know that. I don't know how this works."

"I wish I didn't."

No. She's a hallucination, I told myself. I'm alone out here, Eric hadn't mentioned her. She's not real. Why would she appear naked except it's how I like her best and last remembered her? "You're not real. You're like the Shoggoth. You're a lie, a figment of my imagination." I looked for pills in my pocket and chewed a handful.

She released me from her bear hug and turned ugly and broken, into a charcoal briquette stick figure only about half her mass with tiny twiggy fingers and beady red cigarette cherries for eyes. This form a clue to what The Other had done to her soul perhaps, for it did not manifestly represent the remains I recalled at the clearing. A crack below the eyes hissed at me. "I'm real as I was at the spot and I can still finish you off! I came to apologize to you, asshole!" She raked a twiggy claw across my face, scratching my eyebrow. I spun away in defense and crashed down into knee deep snow. I turned to find her and raised a hand to defend myself. The Other stirred and she returned to her beautiful form and backed away.

"Why?"

"Why what, baby? Why do we hurt the ones we love?" She cried, "Yeah, I wanted you. I still do. But you're hurting me. You have to stop please, release me!"

"I want answers first."

"Anything, just–I'm sorry. I'm so sorry."

"I'm listening but why are you still naked?"

She pulled a parka on from nowhere and slipped into a pair of snow pants, adjusted a hat and goggles, put her arm out around a snowboard and pulled a scarf away from her face. "Better?" She smiled. Her tears vanished and she walked to a log on the trails edge and sat, inviting me to join her. I tapped on the snowboard. It was real enough, until it vanished.

"What do you want to know?"

"Well why did you try to kill me?"

"My mother told me she was a witch when I was eleven, shortly after my gramma's funeral. She was trained by gramma to host an ancient and powerful demon and its collection of souls from which it draws strength and could use to activate certain powers. I didn't believe her but she started to show me and said one day, when her body failed, I would have to host the creature and I had to be trained to do it. I watched how she collected souls and learned what Mother and her friends did with them. I asked her if she was happy and she said no. She was terrified of the family secret, the demon. She had nightmares and struggled with it. Especially hard for her was watching her mother kill her father and harvest his soul. She said I would learn to live with it."

"But you rebelled."

"Yup. I did everything wrong. I polluted my body with drugs and booze. I let my grades slip. I shot heroin, anything to make my body uninviting for it. I thought Mother might have another kid and let the demon take her. She tried, but failed. She had paid for the artificial insemination and if failed to take each time."

"She can't adopt?"

"No, all magic is about the blood somehow, like with vampires. I don't have all the mechanics but I know a bit."

"Okay, what else do I need to know?"

"Well…Mom tried to kill you because the guy she sent to do it failed, after the group failed. The group tried to kill you using a group spell. Some kind of hellfire that is too much for any one or even a few of them to do alone. As a group they tried to kill you. They missed, or hadn't yet realized what you are. Any of the solo killing powers they have are too slow or short range, can't cross all that water or something."

"Okay, it took a bunch of witches to fail, I've killed one, right?" She nodded. "But you said they didn't realize what I am, what am I?"

"You are a host too. But you host a different beast, not a demonic or infernal creature. Maybe not an angel either. If it is an angel, it's the scum bag low-life bounty hunter. The one the others don't invite to cocktail parties. The kind they wonder about his loyalty. Yeah. But I think he's more a cosmic balancer. The witches are okay if they don't break the rules but these have been doing just that for centuries. The balancer appears like a natural consequence. It pushes back where they attempt to manifest their wills. It mostly sleeps, like it's hung-over, passive, tired. A sleeper they call 'em sometimes. Until confronted with a malicious intent manifesting magic. Then it springs into action, usually with overkill. It has like, a three, seven or tenfold rule."

"I've heard of that in like the Ouija board movies and some other witch stories."

"Those are awful. Anyway, your particular angel or balancer they had a name for–The Judge, that's his type, and he has a specific name, like Bob or Jim, you know, something in German I can't remember but it means something like 'Witch Hammer.' But they mostly just say judge when describing your kind of beasty."

"When they discuss it?"

"They don't know it's you yet. My demon never realized it. It told the group that it was killed by you, physically killed. It was fast and the demon went immediately to me. I was in the shower. And I died then, really. Once it took over, in its rage, it would never let go. I was too weak of spirit to resist it. Mom and the others, they can be like you, independent of it for sometimes whole days or weeks. But mostly, they just let the demons run their lives and ride along watching from the back seat."

"It woke The Other, it didn't see it?"

"No, that's one of the rules. The judges are invisible. They're seen only in the revelation of the law. Once those laws are broken, you lost your chance to see the correction, the consequence might take a while but it comes and it's certain. Once it realized you were The Judge, it was too late."

"Why do the other ghosts react differently to me?"

"Some are old enough to have learned what you are. They're not bound to a demon so they can see you. Some gifted humans can even see you, or see you very differently. To Melissa, you look like The Judge. She's never seen you the man, only you the monster. She's one of us, Lisa's daughter. I don't think she's resisting the preparation to host a demon, she wants it. Lisa wants to kill you. She's next assigned to do it. She will probably succeed if you don't have help."

"Your demon, why didn't it escape when I killed you like it escaped when your mother was killed?"

"You killed me, it devoured the demon, hiding inside—it had no place to go. It was going to slip away when I died. It would be taken out of our world if my blood ran cold. It could pass to my child, I had a little boy but...the demon was cut off from him by baptismal. My baby was adopted by religious people so the demon had nowhere to go. There is no way to hide from an angry judge."

"You said I didn't have to kill you."

"No, you didn't. You had knocked me senseless. When you broke my face, out of the clearing you could have separated me from the demon but you didn't know how, I shouldn't be mad at you. You obviously have no experience or you would have known I was possessed or infected as soon as you saw me on your Jeep, you'd have seen all the others too."

"I'm sorry." I don't know why I apologized.

"It's alright, I'm sorry I was so mad at you about that. It's just my whole life basically has been a living hell. I meet someone who can save me from it and oops you killed me. It's been really tough to accept."

"What about the church's power?"

"Rubbish. Mostly it's useless. Baptism is a sure ward for innocents, but that defense is gone when carnal knowledge is gained—sex or murder, certain other sins break it too."

"Why can't Eric enter the church?"

"You have to promise to release me if I tell you this, like I want released first."

"You'll disappear!"

"No, I could but I don't want to. I want to stay with you. I know how to stay for a good long time, like the other haunting type ghosts who linger here for centuries. I'll stay with you."

I don't know why I believed her or trusted her but I decided to, I could destroy her I thought if she tried to hurt me again, The Other could anyway. It wasn't stirring, and my tinnitus was silent. I touched her forehead and reached inside with love and let her go. She vanished and I jumped to my feet cursing and she reappeared snickering.

"I'm fucking with you, baby. I only got one chance at that prank." I was embarrassed and relieved. I smiled at her and sat back down. She kissed me. "Thank you, Lover, I don't hurt anymore and I am free, I can do so much now."

"So what about Eric, what do you know?"

"Well, he is Mara's son. So he has a mark, born of her after the demon possessed her, he is also of him."

"So the demons can't go in a church?"

"Only a few where the spirit is strong and true, surprisingly few churches are so protected. But it works in reverse, too, your judge couldn't manifest against me in the clearing sanctified to our dark master."

"So Eric is marked? He's part demon?"

"Basically."

"Where did I get my creature?"

"I don't know. How long have you had it?"

"I never had any kind of magic anything until the crash. That was probably the first time I noticed it."

"Your parent hosting it probably watched over you. Using ghosts and light magic, she saw you in danger and killed herself, sending The Judge to live in you, making you basically invincible. Your kind and mine differ dramatically in how they die. Our kind: murder, disease or…magical screw up and demonic sacrifice. Your kind dies only by their own hand, or by offending their judge, angering a god—which usually looks like a tragic accident. We're warned to always alert the coven about a new acquaintance whose parent died by suicide."

I hung my head and cried. I was responsible for yet another death. It was becoming too much. Now I would never know my true parents. I had always thought there was time to find them one day.

"I'm sorry, baby. I shouldn't have said it like that. I have a shit filter. You never knew your parents, right? You were an orphan, abandoned at a hospital?"

I wept and she waited, trying to touch me to comfort me but she was cold and dead. I missed her and I suffered more for it. "You said they discussed me, though, my judge the 'Witch Hammer' but, they didn't know I host him?"

"That's right. They taught me about your kind, I know some things. They fear you generally, your type, since the Salem incident. You're like the boogie man or Freddy Krueger to witches."

"Those women were innocent in Salem."

"True-ish. Where there is smoke, there is fire. One of your hosts got a bit overzealous learning his purpose and mission and misinterpreting a lot of bad teachings, carried things a bit too far. The final straw was when he angered the Massachusetts Territory Governor. One of the judge's minions accused the governor's wife. But it was a close call. Close enough the whole bunch of the real witches fled the territory when William Penn made space available here in his woods."

"Seems like an odd coincidence Emily's family name is 'Salem'"

"Yeah, the folks that founded this town founded it as New Salem, the McKnights and Salems are both fake names. All the founders were witches. The Salem's made up the name to conceal their identities they left behind. I don't know why they chose that, some kind of joke or to be ironic? I don't know."

"It doesn't matter."

"Over time a lot of the demons spread out to improve their hunting prospects and network of influence. But the judges are out there, and winning."

"I'm glad they're losing, I don't want them to be thought of favorably as underdogs...where is your loyalty? How does Mara fit in?"

"I hate them, baby. They took all my dreams when I was only a little girl. There were no more tomorrows for me when the demon took up residence. You know why I had a son? One of them cunts had one of her men impregnate me when I was fifteen. So they could have a healthy host to replace me. That's how they handled my rebellion. He raped me over and over for weeks until they knew I was pregnant. They sent me to the house in Bar Harbor to do it. I kept getting into trouble and the child services folks took the baby."

"That's horrible, I'm so sorry."

"Yeah, so I'm loyal to revenge. I had a glimmer of hope, one second when I realized you were The Judge when we were in the clearing but I didn't have a chance to try and fight the demon's control—your elbow smash took my focus. I had almost clawed my way back into the driver's seat. I had for just a second, a chance to be free and be yours." Now she fought back tears. I held her and she took comfort, thanking me.

"So, Mara..."

"Mara is the boss. She is the oldest and most powerful of the bunch. She directed the attack against you, the hellfire. They didn't miss, that kind of power has a large strike area it doesn't discriminate and the timing isn't always perfect. They chanted and danced for some nine hours before it finally kicked. I had to participate. It was awful, the waiting. I was sick to my stomach when we I heard that it worked and some people died far away. When we found out who it was, most of the witches were angry. Mara was so angry she blamed the group and killed two of them."

"There were other murders in town before I got here then?"

"No, the two just went to the Bar Harbor house for a retreat then were quietly put to death there, the witch and her daughter–inheritor. The rest hoped that would satisfy Mara but avoided her until the funeral weeks later. My mom was then moved up to the number two spot. Mara tried to kill you again, on her own but failed. She tried even to take your plane down but it was too much for her."

"Eric tried that, he couldn't do it."

"If she had half a brain she would have realized you were the dread creature and run away. She was blinded by her rage. She is an angry spirit, full of hate. She's quite mad honestly, in my humble opinion."

"This is all mad if you ask me."

She sat up and nodded. "Can I kiss you, baby?"

"Why not?" She leaned in and kissed me on the cheek, turned my lips toward her and kissed me again. She was able to manifest warmth. Her pencil thin lips excited me as they always had. My delicious trash fire was back.

"I wish we could do more. Maybe we can one day."

"So what happens if Mara finds out–she doesn't know who I am, right?"

"She doesn't, she should but she doesn't. If she finds out she might stop at nothing to end you, burn down the whole town. But there isn't any known way I was taught to stop a judge, certainly not you, the king of the judges. She'd have to seek a truce or run." I thought of Emily then. I looked for Eric. My pills were still keeping him away.

"My pills don't work on you, why?"

"We have a different bond. It's not tied to the same chemical parts in your melon. Certain medications have magical effects, which can vary some from person to person depending on your own maladies or gifts. Our bond is sexual, much harder to block. The pills you are on make our bond stronger. So when Eric can't come, I'm lively and you can't get rid of me. When you don't take the pills, he can come and I fall away, or have to struggle to manifest. I'm also trained and have knowledge. I've been preparing to work with a demon for near a decade."

"Eric wasn't trained?"

"No, the witches prefer to use their daughters, often sacrificing their sons."

"No, not…"

She nodded, "Yes they murder their babies for power. The male is a weaker host. It's not the right energy or something. Though something happened to Emily, you know."

Then my heart stopped. Emily was trained then, she is a witch. Rage and denial rose in a flood and my ears rang, my brain burned, my vision narrowed. I saw red halos and The Other stirred deep inside me. It angrily thrashed about–like it had just learned that Emily was its next meal. I was paralyzed by the horror of it. I thought to kill myself right then and there to protect her.

"What about Emily?"

"She's been groomed since her gramma died like I was. She wasn't a little girl so she dealt with it worse than I did. Her mother is the head of the group. She was trapped and she knew it. She did rebel as violently as I did, for a bit. She reluctantly trained but something went wrong. Nobody knows when she goes away she's going to the Bar Harbor house. Whatever is wrong with Emily, they're trying to deal with it there. I haven't been back there since I died. But I know where it is."

"So what's that got to do with Eric?"

"That's why Mara is so angry. A short while after her gramma died, Emily had her issue, whatever that is and we were told Eric would be the one. When he re-enlisted we learned together he would die there. So she tried to stop him with all the magic she had, but his will is too strong. He was also in grace, like his father, a devout catholic, so her spells couldn't penetrate to influence him. He never lost his protections of baptism and taking communion and all until the desert when he neglected his spiritual condition."

"Eric was a virgin?"

"Yes, as far as I know."

"He should have been safe from the hellfire, and he was, I think, until by his own actions he sacrificed himself. Your judge saw the mark on him, the mark his mother put there and thought that he was Mara trying to kill you. The Judge reacted, killing him brutally, not caring if he was the source of the hellfire or not. It was a simple and tragic case of misidentification. Your judge could just as easily have saved you both, but like I said, they're lazy dirtballs. They are brutally-efficient killing machines. They usually only have to strike once and they aren't thinkers."

"It took several swats to get you."

"And I'm proud of that. I gave it a workout like it ain't had in more than a hundred years."

"How many witches are there now?"

"There were twenty, the two families. Now there are less than six."

"How many are there in this group I have to kill?"

"You don't have to."

"Yes, you're right, but my judge might see it different. I don't want to and I won't try. Hell, I might run away or kill myself."

"If you want to kill yourself, let me teach you how not to cross first. I want to be with you, baby."

"So killing myself is okay?"

"It is easier than my plan. To take the girl you like and move in to her."

"You can do that?"

"I can possess a weaker spirit."

"I don't expect Brittney would fit that bill."

"You underestimate me."

"I'm not comfortable talking about this, her like that."

"Then kill yourself after I teach you how to be like me and we can be together forever!" She beamed at me like Brittney would when I showed up late for a date. This was too much. My head spun. I felt I might part completely from my reason, my mind evaporating. I ended the conversation and walked away.

"Baby?"

"I can't. Not now, we'll talk later."

"Oh, okay, baby."

My eye had bled the whole time we talked. That wasn't why I was dizzy but it couldn't have been helping. I pressed a mitten into it and trudged back to the lodge.

CHAPTER 19

PREDATORS

I stumbled in, bleeding slightly but I wasn't overly concerned, scalp and head wounds bled impressively but were usually minor. This was no exception, and I had learned that ghost wounds healed fast. A guest noticed me enter with blood dripping and went to alert a staffer who found me upstairs cleaning up in my room. The jerk-off staffer knocked and I told him to fuck off through the closed door. I watched the wound heal in the mirror and played with Pickles until I smelled dinner and heard the dogs barking. I looked around for Eric and instead spotted *Catch-22* on the bookshelf.

I pulled it down and flipped through it. It appeared new and unread. The distinctive cover with the marionette-like image of a man on the cover sucked me in. I started scanning it and took it with me to dinner. Eagle smiled and winked at me when she saw the distinctive cover. I read the foreword and placed it on the table beside me as folks began to join us there.

At dinner I met Eagle's uncle, a squat dark fellow with a face like a bulldog. She told me his name and I talked to him a moment but heard nothing over the ringing in my ears. I was still thinking only of suicide and poor Emily. Our host talked with his hands which made me tense, hands kill. The Other stirred at him. He was jovial, kind and touchy. I hated him. I resented the strangers around us, the other guests at the dinner table in the greenhouse like dining room on the south side of the house. I thought about bringing The Other up and making him murder everyone, surely they were all guilty of something worth punishing.

There were four dogs, not including Akira and Thor, awaiting scraps from our host. Eagle's beasts sat on either side of their mom with their characteristic comic smiles. They seemed completely oblivious to the meal before us. I wondered if they had some secret knowledge that the food was a prank and so they weren't interested in it. They may have thought we were fools for eating it. I noticed they had what looked like blood on their muzzles and asked Eagle about it.

111

"They killed something out there, probably a vole or maybe a fox. They probably ate the whole thing and Thor will be annoyingly gassy later, Akira will cough up some random part, a foot or a nose, then we'll know what they killed."

"I hope it wasn't the neighbor's cat!" Another guest joked and there were waves of laughter. I smiled nervously and made small talk sparingly, preferring to keep my mouth full and to limit my conversation to answering direct questions only. To their credit, none of the reprehensible strangers bothered me about it. I hated everyone and shrank into my shoulders. I got smaller and smaller until I fit within the boundaries of my chair back until Eagle provided me an out to excuse myself and return to my suite.

I fell asleep in my clothes curled up on the bed with Pickles and his laser toy. When I wiped away sleep, the clock said it was too damn early. I went onto the balcony and Pickles followed dutifully. I wondered if he was part dog. He didn't ignore me like most cats did their people. I found Eagle there stretching on her adjoining balcony. I tried not to be noticed noticing her but her form in pre-dawn light in a strange yoga stretch was hypnotizing. She straightened up and turned.

"I thought I heard your sliding door."

"Cold enough for you?" Smooth, I thought to myself. It didn't matter.

She sauntered over to me and asked if she could see my hands. I shrugged. She picked them up, put them together, raising them to her face, she inhaled slightly, closing her eyes and smiling. "You had that smell the first time I saw you, you still have it." I was aroused. I told myself I was dreaming. But she placed my hands on her face and I felt warmth and her perspiration, her pulse. Her heart was racing and mine quickened to catch up. She led my hands to her breasts and then down to her hips and leaned in to kiss me. Her lips were full and soft, but I preferred my trash fire and her thin delicate kiss.

She kissed me again and tasted me, I didn't recognize her taste but it was silky and smooth and lightly sweet. She pushed me backward gently towards my own room and then onto my bed. I tried to speak but she shushed me and took a cloth napkin from the table sending silverware clattering everywhere. She folded the napkin into a strip and tied it around my eyes.

"If you don't see this, it didn't happen. Lay down, Army."

I lay back, keenly aware of the cold air coming in, contrasted against her touch. She took my pants and I felt a chill that caused the monster inside to stir. I felt it roll back over, uninterested in her, into slumber and I felt safe.

The chill air made her furnace-like touch the only thing that mattered in the world. The rest of it melted away inside her embrace. She pressed herself down on me and rocked her hips as she kissed and bit me. She held my hands behind my head sometimes resting her head in one of them. She panted out another's name. I couldn't care less. She lingered afterward, keeping us coupled. She laid there until our racing hearts were resting and the chill began to penetrate us both. "Leave it on until I'm gone."

"Okay." She gently kissed me as she slid off and again as she stood. "Thank you," she whispered. I heard her close the sliding door and I waited another minute before removing the blindfold. Pickles was clinging to the valance above the sliding door. He had a great view of the whole thing. I got a shower and puzzled over her scent and flavor. Eric appeared. I got Pickles down and gave him a scratch and opened some food for him.

"No luck, it's a big country. There are a lot of dead guys there. If I can get some more information, maybe I can find him in ten years." I told Eric the name I heard during our encounter. "It smells like sex in here…you didn't? I've known you what, ten years, since your last stint in juvie? You had one date the whole time. She threw up on you and you made her walk home from the barracks. Now, you're irresistible to women, what the fuck?"

"I think it's the ghosts. I got like Old Spice haunted guy scent."

"You know it's pretty classically stupid and common to bang your therapist, right? It's a big no-no. Did you like me opening the door? Did you notice she didn't notice?"

"I'm curious about how animals react or don't react to you. Pickles avoids you, right?"

"Yeah, I can't catch him."

"But the dogs don't even see you."

"Nope, they moved away from me in the car but otherwise they're very calm—maybe not the best sample. Her dogs are like military trained or something. I'm new at this ghost thing."

"New? You've been dead for months now. I figure you'd have it all figured out by now."

"Well, fuck me if I'm a slow learner. It's not like I'm in a hurry, as far as I know, I can't rest until you die. I'd kill you but, well I tried. And I decided I like you now and I don't wanna. I don't think I can. Some kinda rule."

"Rules?"

"I don't know what you'd call it, a treatise, rule, law of ghost-dom. I'm not Beetlejuice. I didn't get a fucking manual. I got a face full of burning fuel and some messed up memories."

"I love that movie. So wait there are rules, you're learning, okay like we know you can fuck up smoke detectors, melt tiles in my floor and you burnt a house down. You seem to be getting good at this, like Beetlejuice."

"Please don't start calling me that."

"Wait if I say your name three times, do you become real?"

"Maybe try it in a mirror like Bloody Mary or the Candyman." I went into the bathroom and tried it. Nothing happened. "Did you use my middle name? Try the whole thing."

"Wait a tic, hang on. Have you seen the damn junkies?"

"No, I haven't seen the junkies."

"I ain't seen 'em either. But we killed them."

"Yeah, I reckon they were unable to escape the burning ruin of their crack house whilst so high they were completely incapacitated."

"Oxygen burglars."

"Yup, wastes of skin."

"But why haven't we seen 'em, everyone else we killed you've seen."

"Yeah, we're all trapped, tied to you somehow. The PO, me, the blind Costa Rican."

"He's from Costa Rica?"

"Yeah, every brown person isn't from Mexico."

"Ouch."

"Sorry, death makes me a bitch. We been talking, his English is better than yours, frankly. He has a sister who has been looking for news of him. I completely forgot but he asked me to ask you to pass a message to her."

That seemed beyond insane. I'm not the fucking ghost whisperer. "Hell no. The bastard tried to kill me."

"Funny, the cops called it a failed carjacking attempt. If he knew how to drive, you'd have been killed in a drive-by and I'd be free. Not gonna lie, at that point I was still rooting for the Mexican."

"I thought you said he was Costa Rican…"

"…for fuck's sake, man, Mexican is just easier to say."

"Well I'm not writing his sister a letter to explain a message from beyond the grave, fuck that bullshit." My mind drifted back to the junkies. "So why don't we see them? Is it that they died while I wasn't in a black out? I blacked out when all those other people died. I should get a notebook and start tracking these experiments in case I forget something that does and doesn't work."

"Did you see Rachael yet?"

"Yes, she was batshit crazy and tried to hug me then scratched at my face. I think she tried to take my eye." I wasn't ready to confront him with the rest of what she had told me. I don't think he knew and I feared his reaction.

"Not her fault. I saw her on my way back, she was down in the yard there talking to her mom, you know, Frankenbitch? It turns out the demon in that bitch was passed down to Rachael. Rachael is that giant beast's daughter."

"These ghosts, they're inherited?"

"Yup. But you knew that didn't you?"

"Yeah, she told me on the trail last night."

"Dodged a bullet not marrying that one. So when you killed Leslie, the haunting spirit, ghost whatever you want to call it…"

"…I like haunts, let's call 'em haunts."

"I smell bacon." I looked outside, the sun was now up and I heard the other guests stirring. The dogs were out and making a racket. I chewed some pills and hopped into the shower. "You just gonna do me like that?"

I swallowed the pills and ignored him as he faded away. I made sure Pickles was safe before I went down for bacon. I heard a group of the campers was going for a hike after breakfast and Eagle convinced me to join them.

"Are we going to have a session?"

"Therapy?"

"What else would I mean?"

She tried not to be seen snickering behind her oversized coffee mug. "We got a few days' time to work with, let's plan something for after the hike." We both laughed and no one else at breakfast could have guessed what was so funny.

We walked together with her dogs beside us in guard mode. I saw something stir on the lake as the trail brought us close to the water's edge. I asked her if I could have a moment.

"By all means, I'll watch from here in case you fall in."

I left the trail and fought through the deep snow until I slid onto the lake ice.

"That's a really bad idea, I don't know if it's thick enough for that yet."

I could see something moving but it seemed to be trapped under the ice. I ventured further out onto the ice. The dogs barked a warning. Eagle called to me shouting something I couldn't hear over the ringing in my ears. I had learned to interpret the ringing as a warning. I saw a face under the ice. It was a woman's face! She was frantically pounding on the ice. I ran to her and pounded too. I began calling for help, Eric could solve this but wouldn't come. The pills kept him away, maybe The Other? I reached down and nothing. I called to Leslie, nothing. I called Rachael and she appeared beside me.

"Help me break the ice!" I pounded at it with my fists. It was cracking, cracking under me.

"You will die, baby."

"I don't care!" I kept pounding. Rachael shrank into her charred and broken form and burned hot, stomping on the ice and together we broke through. She vanished as I fell into the freezing water. I felt pierced by knives and the rage awoke inside. The dogs were there swimming beside me, Thor was trying to pull me up by my pants, I couldn't swim. I fought the rage, if it hurt Eagle or the dogs, I couldn't live with that. The trapped person was tugging at me, too, pulling me back to the surface and towards shore.

She was a ghost. How did I miss that? Eagle pulled me up from the water I fought going into the dark knowing it might kill her to defend me. I tried to get away from her and stumbled back into the depths as I lost my footing in frantic shivering and thrashing. Rachael kissed me and stilled the rage. "Look at me! Let go, it won't kill her, just look at me and breathe, baby!" I stopped struggling and stared into her.

She vanished and I slipped into oblivion. When I came to I was wrapped in an emergency blanket, a shiny silver burrito in a sea of concerned fellow campers. They muttered as they constructed a hasty litter to carry me back. I felt terribly ashamed for not learning anyone's names or being friendly at all to any of them. It didn't look like I had hurt anyone. I was grateful for that. Trusting Rachael was the right thing to do.

Back at the house I was loaded into a warm bath and a hot drink was brought. They turned up the heat in my suite and before long I was well on my way to recovery. I missed Rachael, I summoned Eric. He didn't respond. The drowning girl was there. She asked for the same thing Rachael did and apologized for nearly killing me. I said, "That's okay." I released her with a touch and a thought. She was gone and I missed her too.

Eagle helped me to bed and a tray of food was brought up for me. She helped me eat, my muscles weren't all responding normally yet. I wasn't healing as fast as I had expected.

"What happened?"

"There was a girl, trapped under the ice."

"I didn't see anyone, are you sure?"

"She was a ghost. I should have realized it. My meds make me stupid. I chewed a bunch just before we went out." Pickles became aware that I was awake and climbed up the bed and curled up beside me with a meow to alert me to his presence so I wouldn't roll over on him. He chewed on my hand then fell asleep.

"You can't always tell the difference?"

"Not anymore. I guess my brain treats them just like other normal living people now that I've been dealing with them for so long."

"I can't wait to get you into the sweat lodge."

"The what?"

"Didn't I mention this before?"

"No, maybe. I don't remember so well sometimes."

"Have you used a sauna in a spa?"

"Yes."

"It's very much like that, though the true lodges aren't a part of our tribe's tradition—it was adopted from the Lakota, I think. We use it for cleansing and healing in much the same manner. There are songs and rituals but you can get a good benefit from a good sweat in the sauna. In this case, though, we'll have a pseudo-religious experience, kind of pop spirituality of a brand popular with the elite and celebs my uncle likes to rub elbows with. I'll apologize now for the cheesiness of it all."

"Would it be possible not to do it with the others?"

"I'm not authorized to lead a lodge. It takes years of training or a lot of money."

"Your uncle is trained?"

"You don't like him?"

"No."

"Me neither, but this place, wow."

"So can we do it alone like a half-assed version?"

"Sure there is a sauna in the basement gym. I can get the tea we can fire up the sauna and turn out the lights it's basically the same thing. Instead of chants we can have music, I bet it would work."

I scarfed down the hot food and felt my strength returning. "Let's go now."

"I need to change. You just wear a robe, okay? And bring a towel from the bathroom. I'll be back for you in a minute. Are you sure you don't want to do the drum circle with the friendly hippies who helped rescue you instead?"

"I do probably owe them some thanks but I want to see what happens with this sweat."

"Yes, so you might see your ghosts or other things and learn something about them and your purpose, all of that or nothing happens. Hopefully you don't die."

"Die?"

"People have died in a sweat not done right."

"Damn. Here?"

"No, oh no. Not here. I just thought I should tell you. If you feel like you're having distress let me know right away and we'll get the hell out of there, okay?"

"Deal."

"Okay, so now I'll go change."

She skipped with excitement and I thought again of Brittney and how I was betraying her. I thought of Emily and wondered about the voice recorder that was in my hoodie. It was probably ruined in the lake. I searched for it and found it. It was still working. I played it back and heard the drowning girl thanking me in the bath tub for letting her go. It caught her screaming at the lake as I fell through the ice and even captured the confrontation with Rachael. I got ready to go to the spa and sweat. It would feel great after being frozen half to death. Eagle came back, knocking before letting herself in and she handed me the special tea.

"Do I want to know what's in it?"

"Nope. There is honey, I'll tell you that much." I took a sip; it tasted like warm diarrhea with a hint of sweetness. Eagle cautioned me to sip it and I had to—it was hot, and tasted like shit.

"Can I play for you a recording?"

Her eyes widened, "You didn't!"

"No, not that," I waved a hand and sipped the tea. I put it down and picked up the recorder. "Emily had given me a number of these after she heard Eric on a voicemail I had left her. I was supposed to be taping him for her but I seem to have missed him each time."

"Emily heard Eric?"

"Yes, she was very upset about it that evening."

"So what's on this one?"

"I had it with me in my hoodie when I was out on the morning walk and got attacked by Rachael. Her voice is here and the girl I saw in the lake, she was in the bathroom with us when I was soaking in the tub. She talked, her voice is here too. I want you to hear it so I know I'm not crazy. Will you let me play it for you?"

"Sure, but what if we're both crazy?"

"Hadn't thought of that. Well, let's find out then." I started the playback. The voices were all there as I had heard before. Eagle asked me to play them over and over again. She nodded and seemed to understand what they were saying as well as I did.

"So Rachael was very angry and the drowning girl was really here." I nodded. Eagle fell back onto the bed. "This can't be real."

"Why not?"

"Has Eric found him? I must know, please."

"He hasn't said and I won't be able to see him for a while, the drugs keep him at bay."

"But they don't work on Rachael or the other ghost."

"I don't understand it either. Eric says it's not like *Beetlejuice*, there isn't a manual."

"This is all too much. Do you have another recorder?"

"At the house."

"How did that survive the lake incident?"

"I didn't believe it, either. I don't know how this survived the lake, made in America." We finished our tea and headed to the sauna with our towels sporting our robes and sandals. Her uncle spotted us and looked disapprovingly at us before his weathered visage cracked into a smile. We made our way to the basement fitness area, it was empty as one might expect. We had the whole place to ourselves.

"The actual lodge is outside, it's covered right now and I don't even know if it'll work in the bad cold we've got. So I'm glad we're doing this version. It should still work." She turned on the music and fired up the sauna. We got comfortable, she turned the lights down and we relaxed for a good fifteen minutes listening to soothing music. "I'm going to turn off the lights now, are you ready?"

"Mhm."

"Okay, how are you feeling?"

"Like a sweaty cloud."

"Pft." She smiled and it was the last thing I saw as the lights died. A moment later I felt her lips on me and my towel tossed aside. This time after she was done, she sat beside me. In the dark I lost all sense of time. The meds, whatever was in the tea, the sex and the heat took me deep into the world of my ghosts. I saw The Other.

In the darkness, he was a writhing mass of muscular tendrils at the edge of sight. I could only barely see his edges as he wrapped himself around the others that appeared. Leslie, Rachael, Eric and the cholo. Rachael was able to escape him and step away while the others remained bound. There were still more I didn't recognize. They were demons, not ghosts. The demons were crushed and broken, lifeless in The Other's grasp. Rachael whispered to Eagle's space in the dark. I didn't hear what Rachael said but Eagle fled from the sauna. Light poured in and broke the vision.

My ghosts were gone. I made my way to the suite and heard Eagle weeping in her room. Shame and guilt flooded me like I had awoken from a black out drunk not knowing what I might have done the night before. I thought to knock but decided she might do better alone. I went to my own room and dressed, drank some juice and played with Pickles. I decided to nap.

I woke two days later. I went down to the kitchen and Eagle's uncle asked me if I would need a ride.

"What do you mean? Where's Eagle?"

"She was in tears when she came out of the sauna. What happened?"

"She had a bad vision." I lied perfectly. It was all too easy.

"Well she left and said she wasn't coming back. I asked her what to do with you and she said to drown the murderer in the lake. I don't know what she meant but well if you don't have someone who can come and get you, I can take you to the train station."

Rage threatened to unhinge me again. I thought to burn this whole hedonistically evil shit show to the ground. I was about to but Pickles meowed. I heard him upstairs at the door I had not secured. The dogs did too. They rushed that way and I summoned Eric who burst into flame at the foot of the stair, halting the rushing hounds in their tracks. Eric looked to me and threatened, "Don't make me do it."

Seething, I spat fury filled words at him. "I can make the fire." I stalked up to my kitten. I packed him into my coat, bagged my things and made my way out the front door with the copy of *Catch-22* I wanted to finish. "I'll walk. Fuck you very much." Eric kept the hounds away from me and Pickles until I got outside and then he followed me.

"What was that all about?"

"I wish I knew. I was hoping you could tell me. Those hounds saw you or your fire and reacted."

"Well I was in the sauna, never got to finish my Iraq work. Thanks for not making me burn the place down."

"What did Rachael say to her?"

"Rachael told her you murdered her, and how, and where. She said you killed her mother and me and the crack heads. She said you might kill her."

"That would be upsetting to hear. Where did Eagle go?"

"She went to the spot to find Rachael's remains."

"Did she?"

"She did."

"Fuck. Anything else I need to know?"

"Yeah, you missed your turn if you're going to the highway and then the train station."

"Fuck." I backtracked to the turn I missed and walked the half mile to the highway.

"You keep on using that word, I do not think it means what you think it means."

"Nice. Leave the jokes to Brittney. She's the funny one."

"I can be funny."

"Funny looking."

"Ha fucking ha, ass."

CHAPTER 20

SARAH

I got home two days later. I had to wait for a train. I found a bottle and a place to hole up and wait. In Harrisburg I found a place to get drunk and eventually got a bus to McKnightstown. I fed little Pickles and played with him. He was oblivious to the turmoil I was experiencing. He was full of curious joy and played without care or worry. I envied him.

I began opening and reading my mail. I didn't get accepted to the college. It was recommended I try the community college first. I balled up the letter and threw it for the kitten. He chased it about for a bit to my delight. His bouncing and rolling around was always at least momentarily cheering. I found a bottle I had hid earlier and emptied it.

I called Emily, no answer. I didn't bother leaving a message. I could sense Eric didn't want to talk. I saw Leslie standing in the parking lot looking hopelessly lost. I went down there and turned up the heat on her, grabbed the gun out of the Jeep and brought it up. I had had enough. I called Eagle when I got back upstairs. Her number was disconnected. I went numb. I was ready to die.

I found some pills and chewed them. I wasn't sure which ones they were. I felt nothing. I started talking to the cat. I played with him some more until he was worn out and curled up for a nap. I started searching the apartment for another bottle hid someplace. I spilled something I couldn't drink on me and stripped out of my clothes. I stumbled around the apartment in my boxers looking for booze. I found a bottle of wine. I couldn't find a corkscrew so I tried a big knife that I did find. I cut myself pretty bad and bled a good bit. I found a screwdriver and got the cork pressed down inside but I spilled much of the wine. I tried to clean that up and slipped in it, smacked my head good, almost knocking myself out.

I sucked what I could out of that bottle then found half a fifth Rachael had left with me a while ago. I drank that and remembered the gun. I said goodbye to my sleeping kitten and apologized for the mess I was going to make. I looked to see if he had enough food to last until someone came to rescue him. I asked the dark to help me. I asked The Other to talk to me. There was nothing. I put the gun in my mouth and pulled the trigger.

The gun didn't fire. I pulled it from my mouth and wept, sprawled against the kitchen cupboard there on the floor. I smacked it against my head and prayed to the dark to take me. Years in the army let my hands take the gun apart. Through the teary haze I could see what was wrong. Its guts were fused. This gun would never fire again. The Other had ruined it when we killed the cop. I threw the thing across the room and cried some more. I pulled myself up and slipped, banging my head off the fridge. I shook and begged to die.

I looked across the floor. A magnet was broken and next to it the paper Emily had given me, the A.A. schedule from the first meeting months ago. I put it there on the fridge and ignored it. It let her think I might use it one day. Now it was the only thing in the world before me, I couldn't even kill myself. I picked it up and found the Nokia in easy reach. I tried to read the numbers. My mind couldn't understand the schedule I didn't know what day it was. My hand trembled. It took a while but I strung together a jumble of numbers and pressed the green button. On the other end someone answered. "Hello?"

I hesitated afraid a moment, I hated these people. I feared them. I hid behind a terse question. "What day is it?"

I think the man on the other side understood something was wrong somehow, he wasn't mad at me. "It's Wednesday, buddy, who is this?" I heard happiness. I kept crying, through my blubbering I heard myself ask, "What time is it?" He couldn't have understood me.

"Where are you, friend?"

"The floor." My words couldn't have been English at this point but I think he understood me somehow. He said there was a meeting in an hour and asked if I needed a ride. I slurred out something I didn't even understand and hung up. I dropped the phone and looked at myself, trembling in my boxers, bleeding from the cuts I had made. I needed cleaned up. I found some pants, chewed some of my pills and went out to find the Lutheran church basement.

I still felt tremors but the fog was lifting fast. I was able to stand up straight and look human. I heard laughter for the first time, after months of visits to this room. It was always there. I hated it before. I had thought it laughter at my failures. Now it was life. I slipped in and counted six. These people were ugly and frightening monsters before but somehow now their smiles were love and open arms welcoming me with joy. They gave me light like Brittney's smile. They looked like friends to me. I only knew a few of their names. I tried to smile, I know it didn't work but they didn't care, they didn't judge. I heard them greet me but my ears were ringing in alarm. I tried again to smile and found my hand waving. Someone took it and gave it a friendly shake.

"Hey, it's me, Bob, how are you, man?" The fog, the drugs, the drink may have clouded my vision but I could see his kind face towering above me. Bob was a tall and gentle fellow, like the father I would have wished for. He was one of the first guys to greet me all those months ago, though I feared him then, like the foster fathers I had for too many years.

"I called you."

"I know." He grinned and chuckled. He got me a seat and some coffee. "I'm glad you made it, we can talk after, okay?" I nodded. Bob smiled and returned to the conversation he was having with another fellow I didn't know. I recognized only two of the others. I looked for Eagle but she wasn't there. I knew then I'd never see her again.

Aaron was there, he was silently practice reading the preamble, nervously awaiting his turn to read it for the room. He reminded me of a hundred guys I knew in the army–lean, strong and kind somewhere hidden inside. He was as afraid of this place and people as I was, but he had long ago gotten over his fear somehow and I wanted the courage he had. It wasn't envy. I felt inspired and hopeful he would share it even as I imagined he fought himself to find it.

I turned to see Sarah who had been milling about lost, walking towards me. I was the only one she talked to for some reason. She sat next to me and smiled as she usually did. She was always so sad, why did she smile? Why did she tremble so? I decided our conversations had been one way for too long.

"Hi, Sarah."

"Hey, you can talk."

"I don't like to. Everyone here terrifies me."

"Right? I'm just starting to get comfortable." She got comfortable in her chair.

"You've been coming since before me, though." I began to understand everything in its own time. Someone here had said that before at another meeting.

"Yeah, but I haven't started any of the steps or anything." She leaned in and took a closer look at me. "Are you okay?"

I didn't have the energy to lie or pretend. "Not really. I tried to die today but couldn't even manage that."

"That's terrible, I'm sorry. I don't wanna add to your woes but I just figured out that I died."

"I wondered. You didn't talk to anyone else."

"I talked to Lisa, she's like you–she can see me."

"Rachael said Lisa wants to kill me."

"That's...nice. Maybe avoid her." She smiled nervously.

"Why are you here if you're dead?"

Sarah wept now and I offered her a tissue. "Thanks, I got one." She wiped at her eyes. "I don't know where else to go. Everyone here is nice."

"Nice? Even you get this better than I do. I am just seeing these people for the first time it seems."

"Thanks but I didn't do it right either at first. I tried a few times before I started to get it. Now it's too late and I come out of habit." It dawned on me I was in a church. I tried to summon Eric but he could not come. Sarah noticed this. "You're calling your friend that paces outside, the burning man."

"You know about Eric?"

"He can't come in can he?"

"No, do you know why?"

"No, most of the dead can't, I don't know how or why. All I know is that I can."

"Can I ask you how you died, Sarah?"

"You can ask." She smiled, trembled and laughed nervously, fresh tears welling up in her eyes. She turned away for a moment.

The room began to fill. I relaxed talking to her though we were continually interrupted by people happy to see me, people I was finally happy to see. For the first time I was somewhat relaxed here. I wiped away tears and tried not to cry and the meeting got underway. I listened to the stories and adventures and hope in the readings. I joined the prayer but subversively skipped the "Amen." The friend leading the meeting asked me if I would like to speak. I declined. I wasn't ready yet. Sarah elbowed me, "You should, I can't, I lost that chance."

"Next time."

She accepted that and we listened to Bob tell a story about the wild friends he knew years ago. He talked of wrecking cars—turning them on their sides and ringing the owner's doorbells. He regaled us with tales of doing donuts on the lawns of people they didn't know or did but didn't like. He wasn't full of anger or resentment or regret about those mistakes. He drew strength from them. He told us about his struggles driving to the rehab parking lot with a few beers and how he sat there drinking and thinking about how he needed to stop.

All I could think of were the people inside the rehab looking out drooling and praying he would bring the beers in for them. Then I realized that I needed that rehab, too, I was outside in the parking lot. I wouldn't want him to bring me the booze if I was lucky enough to be inside. I wanted to throw up. I was so ashamed but Bob went on to tell how he had felt so low, too, and found redemption here, a better way of life. I hung on his every word.

Someone spoke of God and I had a real problem with it. It was the last barrier, the second step. I had already learned The Other in me was from God. It was a creature of his, a cosmic balancer, a dirtbag angel, brutal judgment and authority, blind retribution and rage. What kind of god was it out there? How could this thing help me? It had ruined Rachael when it needed not do so. It had torn her to pieces and painted the field with her insides so horribly. I wept again and the friends whose names I could not recall tried to comfort me. I talked with Aaron and Bob afterward, we had coffee and I committed to return for another meeting soon. Bob gave me a big blue book again and this time I accepted it. I wanted this.

When I got home I played with Pickles a while then decided to go for a walk. I found Sarah out near the creek. "You asked how I died today."

"I did."

"Did you still want to hear?"

"Yes, if you don't mind sharing." We walked together down in the creek bed close to the water.

"I have to tell someone, because everyone has it wrong." I sat down beside the creek watching the first firefly of the evening come to life. It brought me joy and a tear.

"Okay, I'm ready. Should I write this down?"

"No, I trust you'll remember." She sat down and caught one of the bugs and let it crawl around on her hand. "I never noticed these things when I was alive. Sad, I love them now. It wasn't long ago I had grown up not far from here and had been staying with friends. We partied a lot. My roommate at the time had a kid, a boy. He was eight or nine and had special needs." She paused to watch the bug take flight and sparkle in the dying light.

"My friend was supporting me trying to recover. She was clean but didn't judge me when I had a slip. And I had a lot of them. I managed to string a few days together, then a week. One day, her boyfriend had an emergency and she had to go to the ER to see him. She didn't have anyone who could watch her boy and she thought she would only need me to watch him for like an hour or so. She called her mom who was going to come and take over. She asked me to watch him and I agreed, she didn't notice I was drunk. I had lost my job that day and was drinking over it. I really wanted to teach my boss a lesson." She was choking up a bit and beginning to tremble. I saw tears coming.

"I completely get it." I didn't lie this time.

"Right?" Her voice quailed and I thought to tell her to stop but she continued. "So I went to the kitchen after she ran out, I was looking for a bottle I had hid. Not long after my friend left, her son was having trouble in the bathroom. The sink was clogged or something and it was sending him into a tizzy, he couldn't wash his hands according to his routine or something. I found half a bottle of drain-o and tried to read instructions but I couldn't make it out."

We were surrounded now by little glimmers, fireflies in their hopeful summer dance. Their light sparkled across the glassy water of the slow creek and filled the field across the way near the train station. We both gazed wistfully at a black oil car, it was God's chalkboard tonight and there even I found hope. In Sarah's story death loomed large. I saw only hope.

"So I went to my bedroom to find my glasses. Of course they were dirty when I found them. I started cleaning the smudges off and grabbed my drink. I chugged that and left the empty glass there and forgot what I was supposed to be doing. I wanted to get more. Then I heard it."

She looked at me and I saw in her eyes the memory play out through her tears. She had no words for what was happening in her heart. I could hear there was a loud thrashing and she ran to find the boy convulsing, viscous fluid pouring from his mouth, and an empty bottle of drain-o on the floor. I watched her try to find a phone and make a call and dial 911 but she had failed. She tried to think what to do. In a panic, she picked up the boy and ran outside. She went out the backdoor thinking to find a neighbor there. She stumbled and fell, sliding into the creek. The house was there across the street just a stone's throw away from where we talked.

"So you drowned?"

"I did. I must have hit my head when I fell and the boy fell on top of me. Pressing me under the water, not even a foot deep, it was enough to kill me in a few minutes. If I remember anything at all I remember it being peaceful, even euphoric. I killed that little boy. He died in agony and horror and didn't deserve it. I deserved to die, but not peacefully."

"I'm sorry." I tried to sound empathetic but it was beyond me.

"Don't be." She quipped, blowing a strand of hair off her face. "I killed that whole family. I waited with the dead boy until he was found. I followed him to the morgue where his mother came to claim him. I followed her home and everywhere. A few days later she was told her son could have survived the poisoning. My friend went to her dad's house and shot herself. I followed her pleading for her not to do it but she couldn't hear me. Her boyfriend had died that night in the emergency room when she went to see him. It was all too much for her."

"That wasn't your fault."

"No, it was."

"How?"

"He knew I had some strong pain meds. He had asked me for some. I shared. He was basically paying to put a roof over my head. I wanted to help. I had let him have some of my pills that morning before I went to work and got fired. Turns out, they were too strong for him or he was allergic. He fell asleep driving a forklift and mostly decapitated himself."

"How do you…"

"…live with myself?"

"No. How do you still find hope?"

"I don't know. I do know you can release me and send me to the other side. But I'm afraid of what awaits me. I want to find God in those rooms with the friends first. I don't want the God I knew, that let me kill all those people, be the one who judges me." I understood this. The God I was seeing was something nightmarish. I would find another before I try to die again.

"Will I see you tomorrow?"

"I don't know, Lisa is usually at Thursday, I would avoid it if she wants to kill you. But there is a meeting in Fairfield you could go to." She told me how to get to the Thursday meeting there and told me names of people she liked. She had spent her strength, sharing with me her secrets and laid down to rest beside the calm water. I lit a camel and wandered past the bar this time.

I got home and slept like the dead. After a shower in the morning I got the journal out and thought about writing in it. I put down Sarah's story, she wanted someone to know. She said everyone had the story wrong.

I decided I wanted to see her again. I wanted to talk to her, Lisa didn't scare me. I had the Witch Hammer, she couldn't hurt me. This was my town and I didn't much care for the drive to Fairfield. It was just boring. There wasn't much there, the town had a baseball field and a mom-and-pop grocery store. No Starbucks and no restaurants to speak of, at least not that I had saw on my two trips through it. You could miss it if you blinked, unless you drove the speed limit, then you'd have to blink twice.

I found Sarah there milling about nervously trying to be sure to find an empty seat. I tried to get her attention but she was distracted. I grabbed a cup of coffee and greeted Bob and Aaron who were both there. Aaron was new, Bob was not. The two were partnered up I learned- Bob sponsoring Aaron in a symbiotic relationship to stay alive. Bob said to me, "You really shouldn't wait too long to get a sponsor yourself, even just a temporary one." I nodded, but who could do the job and at the same time not be someone I was afraid to accidentally murder? I couldn't ask Bob, the thought of losing him to my angry angel was too much to bear.

"What about Sarah?"

Bob turned white. He looked at Aaron who just shrugged. Bob looked around. "I don't know a Sarah, and it's best to keep men with men with this kind of thing, women with women." He winked at me.

"Okay."

Aaron guessed, "Is Sarah that one lady that did all that time in Baltimore?"

"Oh, yeah, but she's not been around of late."

Another friend heard us puzzling about her. I realized she might be forgotten for a reason. Her death was so unbelievably tragic. I might stir up something and make myself unwelcome. I thought to change the discussion to asking for one of the readings to do. Aaron smiled approvingly. I got the 'How it Works' card. It had two sides to it and I thought this seemed like punishment. I didn't like my speaking voice and my brain was so screwed up still with drugs and all that I didn't think I could complete a sentence. Sarah found me and brought me courage with a giggle.

"Boo! I'm a ghost, get it?" I smiled. She must have been a delight alive.

"Hey you, I was gonna say hi earlier but you seemed to have a lot on your mind."

"It gets kinda full on Thursday. I just hope nobody takes the seat I like. I don't like to sit in a different spot. I have my spot, you know?" I remember someone told me ghosts are creatures of habit.

"You slept last time we talked, how is that?"

"What do you mean?"

"My friend Eric says he can't sleep."

"Oh that's awful. I bet he's crabby."

"Yes, the last few weeks he's been getting worse. He doesn't want to be around me anymore. I worry that he's going to let me die so he can rest. He knows that's one way he can."

"Wow, some friend."

"It gets worse. Rachael, a ghost of a crazy girl I was seeing, she wants me to kill myself and be a haunt like her."

"Like me." She smiled and lifted off her heels for a second.

"Yes, I suppose."

She relaxed. "I didn't mean to be so excited, I don't want you to join the club like that—that's really terrible. I'm sorry about your friends. It is painfully lonely but there are things we can do for fun."

"Should I ask?"

"Well, I see all the movies as soon as they come out, for free. I can't eat popcorn or get a slushy but I keep trying. Maybe one day I will figure it out. I get to hear all kinds of secrets but also have to see people do things they do when no one is around. Gross stuff mostly. You get used to that. I get to rummage through all kinds of locked up places. I ride the carnival rides free and don't get sore walking as far as the shore where I like to sit and watch the water. I've met one or two other ghosts who are around and not dangerous. They're gloomy but not dangerous."

"Are there dangerous ghosts?" I became aware that I was being watched— to everyone but Lisa, who hadn't arrived, I would appear to be talking to myself.

"Yes, there are demons too. They can kill me so I have to watch for them. I spend a lot of time here safe from them. And they don't like the creek bed, they stay away from that. There are from time to time, angels who are almost as bad as the demons. They might send me to the dark, where demons live. I don't know. I see them doing all kinds of busy things."

"Have you been able to affect the living world?"

She put her head down and sobbed. "No. I try, all the other ghosts and demons and angels can."

"I'm sorry." I sat down and she sat beside me. I knew her regular spot and I figured if I sat next to her seat people would give me room, I'm the crazy "talking to himself" guy. Her seat would be safe. "Sarah, can I tell you something?"

She wiped at her tears with that tissue she always had. "What is it?"

"You're my favorite, if I had only one person to talk to forever."

"Really?" She looked up and brightened. "Why?"

"Well for starters, I talk to a lot of people, and ghosts. Every one of them wants something from me. Some of them want too much, some take even though they know it is harmful to me. Others keep their secrets that threaten me. But you, you don't even know me except as one person who can see you and sits here and is obviously disturbed. Yet you share with me, talk to me, are patient with me and have never asked me for anything."

"Aw. That's awful. People take from you knowing it hurts you? Sounds like pretty much everyone these days, though, it's sad. I really screwed up. I was like that sometimes, especially with my boyfriend. I took so much from him. He didn't deserve the hassles I made. I heaped secret scorn and resented him but he was pretty good to me, I don't know if I deserved him. I didn't mean to put him through so much. You know my story?"

"Yes I wrote it down, wondering who you needed me to correct about it."

"Well not now, later. But the reason I was with my friends and their little boy. I got mad at him and told him I needed a break from us for a while. I was throwing a tantrum over something trivial like a pillow or crown molding or wallpaper. I was such a tornado some days."

"You seem nice enough to me."

"You don't have to live with me," she smiled timidly, "and I been coming here, what, two years now, or however long it's been since I died. It's hard to tell sometimes. Like when I sleep, once I slept three weeks. In the winter it's hard. The cold seems to sap strength very fast and I sleep a lot. The demons are all over then, too, so it's dangerous. But I'm pretty good at not getting eaten."

Someone knocked on the table and the meeting started. When it got to be to my turn, I read how it works and no one complained or shot me so I must have done alright. Lisa arrived late. Sarah alerted me. "I hope she doesn't kill you."

"Thanks pal, I'd really hate to die." Lisa ignored me, but her demeanor wasn't haughty- it was afraid. She didn't flirt with her eyes like she usually did. She was trying to put me at ease so she could kill me before. Something was wrong. Rachael!

The thought of her drew her to me. She danced in, naked as a jay bird, except for her clunky shit kickers. Sarah blushed and Rachael sat beside me, opposite Sarah. I whispered hello to Rachael. Lisa saw Rachael next to me. She flipped Lisa the bird and threated to cut her if she did anything. Sarah tittered and Lisa left after just a few minutes. Sarah offered to go and find out what Lisa was about and I cautioned her to ignore her, Lisa might be unpredictable right now.

"Why? What's going on?"

Rachael interrupted, "Baby, who is this bitch?"

"Whoa, Rache, it's okay, Sarah is a friend."

"I thought I recognized her, she's that baby killer who shot her friend Emma or something after poisoning her boyfriend. I heard it was some kinda creepy three-way gone wrong. Her boyfriend helped her rob the house, too, I heard."

"What?" Sarah jumped up, jaw agape in disbelief. She looked as ready for a fight as her slight figure could. "None of that's true!" She protested honestly.

I shook my head at Rachael. "No, it's not like that."

"What the fuck, baby?" Rachael stood up and I tried to use The Other, he stirred but did nothing more.

Rachael fixed me with a freezing glance then hissed, "What did you just do?"

"I am trying to reach you to calm you down." Sarah was composed, looking contrite for her momentary and reasonable loss of composure in light of Rachael's all-out assault on her. "I thought of you hoping to remember to ask you a question, I didn't expect you to appear."

"I'm on a hair trigger, baby, in case there's danger. But this bitch is weak, what's going on, what did you want to ask me?"

Sarah excused herself, I tried to halt her but she took two steps and evaporated. "Damn it. Lisa's behavior changed, why?"

"I told those bitches at their little witch gathering last night that you're a judge. The Judge, I figured out that it would solve our problem. They'd be so frightened they'd never mess with you. Two of the four left have already fled town."

"Why did you do that? I needed surprise to succeed against their numbers if it came to a fight."

"Ssh." someone shushed me. I left and Rachael followed me. I was beyond enraged with her now and wanted to destroy her, I should have kept her bound where she might not risk angering me.

"There are only two left, Lisa and Mara. You saw one run away!"

"What if I have to hunt them other two down?"

"I'll help you!"

I walked away in disgust. I put in a call to Brittney and asked her for some time on her voicemail.

"You want her, baby? I can live in her, I know you like how I do you." Rachael's voice faded away as I marched off to find a place to hide. I thought about a bottle then decided against it. I had numbers in my phone. I knew half of those people I would talk to were busy, in the meeting I had just left.

The rest, I didn't want to talk to, I hadn't warmed up to them yet. So I went to the creek to find Sarah. She was gone. I didn't know enough about her to know where else to search. I gave up and went home thinking of how Rachael had hurt the best friend I had left in the world right now. I thought how pathetic it is that poor Sarah can't really even be a part of it. I was disgusted with Rachael, I wanted to destroy her and worried she was too much for me. She is the first of the witches I've faced that knew more about me than I did.

CHAPTER 21

RECALL

A few weeks later, early one morning there was a knock on the door. It was an army captain. I called Eric and he appeared. "Want me to kill him?"

"What's he want?"

"Fuck if I know. I was watching the skanks from the titty bar, turns out the one who saw me was just having a bad trip. But now I can go back there when I want to...so what did I miss? I really don't want to be a part of any more killing."

"Did you know that Sarah from the meetings is a ghost?"

"I didn't know there was a Sarah, are you banging her too?"

"She's a ghost, how would that work?"

"I'm sure you'd find a way, fucko."

The knocking continued. "So can you help here?"

"Doubt it. I think you can do this."

I opened the door and the captain introduced himself as Sillwell. I thought that was the dumbest name I had ever heard.

"What do you want, sir?"

"I'd like to come in and have a word with you, Sergeant."

"I'd rather not sir, I've got company. It's a very bad time."

"I'm sorry but I must insist."

"I'm sorry but you can't come in, asshole, unless you got a fucking warrant."

"That can be arranged, Sergeant." I slammed the door in his face.

I turned on the TV. I caught a news story about remains recovered from the fire on the mountain—the fire Eric started, those remains would be Rachael's I was sure. The news continued and sure enough she had been positively identified. They didn't say anything about investigating it as a homicide but I was sure that was coming. "Put the game on, we already know Eagle told them about the dead girl, didn't we?"

"Yeah. I think so. I didn't put it in the journal but I should have. I recall you telling me on the mountain."

The phone rang. It was Emily, I answered it. "Hello?"

"Are you okay?"

"Yes, I'm okay now. Thank you. How about you? I been calling."

"I'm sorry, I know I don't have good service here."

"I was going to mail you a letter, like an old-fashioned letter but the international studies people didn't have an address for you."

"I'm at home now. I need to see you, can I come over?"

"Yes, please. I need to pick up a bit."

"No you don't, I just need to see you."

"Okay, I'll leave the door unlocked and get a shower, if you get here and I don't answer just come in, okay?"

"Deal. I could use a shower too." She hung up. I was still in the shower when she arrived.

Eric sensed her and told me he was going to get lost.

"No, please stay in case she wants to talk to you."

"Alright but I'm going to stay out front and watch the game."

"That's why I left it on, so why are you in here?"

"I just came to tell you, oh never mind there she is, I'm out."

I yelled from the shower, "Emily, I'm still in the shower."

She made her way back to me. "May I?"

"I can't stop you."

"Thank you. I'm sorry I worried you."

"It's okay, I'm just glad you're back. I was angry that you had lied to me but I been working on letting go of that."

"I'm sorry, I really am. I had to. I didn't know what else to do and you were…"

"Unstable, erratic?"

"Yes, basically, I worried so much about you and couldn't add to all of that. You were dealing with enough real and serious problems." I opened the curtain and she stood before me, she had gained a lot of weight, it looked good on her. I know I have no poker face and she flashed a look of anger and consternation then embarrassment, she blushed and looked down.

"You look great! I missed you. I'd almost forgotten how beautiful you are." I wasn't lying.

"I'm pregnant."

"Are you sure?"

"Look at me." She threw her hands up.

"Did you still wanna shower? We got about five more minutes of hot water."

"Do you still want me?" I leaned out and kissed her and pulled her in to her surprise. She giggled and fought me off. I let go and she stripped down and climbed in. The water got cold before we finished so we made our way to the bed. Then we laid there in silence knowing there was so much to talk about.

"So you're pregnant now?"

"Yes, please don't ask me if it's yours."

"God no. I wouldn't, I know it's mine. Do you know if it's a boy or a girl yet?"

"Do you want to know?"

"Yes!"

"We're having a boy."

I was going to have a son. The world changed in a blink. I wasn't ready for this, I had no idea what to do. Anxiety now, fear, anger.

"So why did you go away? Why the strange disappearing act and the silent treatment?"

"You're mad. Please don't be mad, the baby can feel it."

"I'm sorry."

"No, it's okay, I was kidding. You should be mad. I did lie and ignore you. I was not in control. Mother is very insistent things be done a certain way. She had me out of state to stay with friends who were to care for me. I was basically a prisoner. I meant to get an abortion. But I couldn't do it."

"An abortion? But why?" She wept and wrapped my arm around her. "I'm sorry."

"I can straighten out and be a father."

"I wouldn't ask you to do that, to end your life to be with me and the baby. Mother would make your life a living hell."

"Forget her we can go anywhere we want, we don't need her money. I have enough coming in. I can keep us alive until I can get through college and make some real money."

"Please. Let me finish."

"Okay I'm sorry, I just - I'm overwhelmed."

"Like I said I was put up with her friends. I thought I would be free to get the abortion but they wouldn't have it. Then I tried to arrange an adoption. Mother wouldn't allow that either. I was afraid she would hurt me, her friends would. So I relented, Mother wanted me to have this baby. I'm almost doing it for her. She won't let you be a part of his life. I'm not telling you this to ruin your life and make you change your plans or asking you to do anything. I just have to have the baby and..."

"You don't want me around. That's why you didn't tell me before. I'm in no shape to be a father. I know that. I don't blame you."

"No, that's not it, if you want to be–I want you to be. I want you around for the baby, I do. But I want you healthy. And you need to know what you're dealing with."

"So, the baby, is that why you did all this for me? The apartment, the doctors, the phone, I had hoped it was because you loved me." She got quiet.

I may have pushed too hard. I should have felt gratitude and love but I was scared, anxious and overwhelmed with dread. I might still face prison or execution for the murders. Now a baby's life would be ruined too. It wasn't just my life I was destroying. My skin crawled. I wanted out of this. It all felt like a lie.

"I didn't want to pressure you. My family, I have a family and plenty of resources. Relatives, and family friends, money, all of it, and you were a ward of the state, an orphan before the army. You said before you never had a proper father. I didn't think you would feel comfortable being in Mother's world. To be honest I've never been either. Eric wasn't and I think even Dad regretted joining her world of country clubs and gala balls. He hated golf and yachting."

"You're right. I wouldn't be comfortable but I'd do anything for you, I'd try. I've been trying. I'm sorry I've been failing. I don't even know who I am. Besides his own death, Eric blames me for killing others too."

"Others, in the war?"

"No, here in town."

"That's can't be true, if there were murders it would be on the news."

"Rachael."

"I thought she died in a fire?"

"Her mother."

"Her mother, Leslie? Didn't she die in an accidental slip? Broke her neck I heard."

"No. That wasn't it."

"It's not important. Maybe we should sit down with Eagle or someone and have a family session?"

"I'd like that but she won't answer my calls."

"Why is that? Did you have a bad session or something?"

"You could say that."

She sat up and looked at me. "Do I want to know?"

"It's not pretty." She got out of bed and started getting dressed.

"Please don't tell me you had sex with her."

I had to lie. "She took me to a retreat to have a sweat lodge ritual. Things got mucked up and I had the sweat with her. There she saw my ghosts. She didn't believe in them but they were now undeniably real and it was too much. One of the ghosts, Rachael, told Eagle I had murdered her and her mother and Eric. She ran out and told her uncle I was a murderer. She abandoned me at the retreat."

"You did sleep with her. She told me once how she always takes guys she wants up there for that, since her husband can't." She cried as she left half dressed.

"Where are you going?" She slammed the door. "Eric, stop her!"

"What? She's going home, I can't stop her safely. Calm down. Her story doesn't add up there is still something else we're not getting. Just let her cool off. Why didn't you just tell her 'no?' She wanted to believe you. She would have, just for the sake of staying with you, jackass."

"Should we follow her?"

"Give her room, maybe a day or two, she just got back in town, look, her car is still full of stuff she had up in Maine with her. She'll call. If she doesn't in two days, I'll talk to her on the voicemail."

"Why not now? She's driving, she probably won't answer."

"If you'll calm down, I'll do it."

A knock at the door. "Who is it, Eric?"

"Fat white guy, looks hung-over. Wearing a suit like he's trying to pretend he's on duty."

"He's not?"

"Nah, no way, not that hung-over, if he is, he's got problems." I thought everyone's got problems.

I answered the door stirring The Other and feeling it fill me, ready near the surface. I was not going to wake up in another hospital bed. Eric rolled his eyes and faded away as the door opened.

"What?"

"Hello, Sergeant…"

"…No, no, stop right there. Those days are behind me, I'm just a regular guy now. What do you want?"

"You mind if I come in, son?"

"You're that cop, Oldham, right?"

"Yes, Corporal Oldham, State Patrol. I just want to ask you a few questions."

"Yeah, I mind, you can't come in. Fuck off, I got the DA on speed dial, we're drinking buddies, so anytime you wanna get fired, come on back. He told me that case was closed and your agency is not involved." I went to close the door. He stuck a foot in it and held up a photo of Leslie's patrol car.

"I'm investigating a separate matter, on a state road. You recognize this vehicle, son?"

I have no poker face, he surely saw my reaction. I had to scramble and lie or kill this guy. "Yeah, it's a cop car, right? I seen a lot of 'em, so what?"

"Do you remember seeing this particular one?"

"Do I need a lawyer?"

"I don't know, do you? I've seen your record, how many times you been in juvie?"

"My record? You mean the fucking year in Iraq? The year in Bosnia before that? Is that the record you're talking about? The Purple Hearts, the Bronze Stars? That record?"

"The car, where it was found, there were some tire tracks, same model as on your Jeep. They were new, like your Jeep."

"It's the single most popular SUV on the market, thirty years running. Look behind you, there are twenty in the parking lot right now. It's my second one."

He knew he wasn't getting anywhere. He changed tack. "The Mexican."

"He was from Costa Rica."

"The Latino fellow, I was there when you killed him, you know that? I felt the heat coming off him when I pulled you off. They thought I killed him. I got put on leave for that. For asking about it, I got suspended."

"So fucking what? You smell like you're still suspended."

"You got me. I'm on my own time."

"Then get your foot out of my door or I'm going to consider this a home invasion and kill you."

"Excuse me?" He pulled his coat back to reveal his gun at his hip.

"I knew that was there, who do you think I am? You think that scares me after what you seen me do to a man? Don't try to intimidate me. I ain't some high school punk stole beer from the liquor store. I've killed people I like better than you, and forgot about it. You get a warrant or you charge me and you roll the dice. You got a personal problem with me, you got a death wish? That cholo had a gun too. The shape you're in, you gotta be fucking kidding me. Get your foot out of my door or tell me where to send the flowers."

He had a moment of clarity and removed his foot. Rachael appeared and pushed him over the railing. He fell and landed twitching on the pavement below.

"Rache, why?"

"It' a part of the package I bring to the party, baby. I told you, don't underestimate me. I'm murder."

I wondered if I was safe from her. The Other slid back down into the dark. It thrashed about to show its displeasure. It was annoyed. But not sensing danger, it fell back into its slumbering puddle to await the next summons.

I looked down, he was alive, barely. He twitched and I saw a neighbor calling 911 on her phone. I called Walter right away and left him a message at his office about what had happened. Oldham had dropped his file on the landing and I took it in for later study.

Eric appeared. "There are still gun parts behind the trash can."

"Not now, man, there's a dying cop on my doorstep."

"What? I was gone for two minutes. He's dead now? I want to go, you gotta release me or destroy me whatever you and homemade porn star here want to do to me. I can't take it anymore."

"What's wrong with you now?"

"I think. I think Emily might be one of them. She might be a part of this whole mess, the plot that got me killed."

I didn't know how to hear that. I had the same suspicion for a second at the retreat. Rachael's revelations made me wonder. Now Eric had found this suspicion. Her story didn't make sense to me, but she had my son now, I couldn't risk hurting her. But I needed to see her. Waiting time was over. Eric wandered looking lost back into the kitchen.

"Where's that cat? How long have these gun parts been lying around back here behind the trash can anyway?"

I needed to get rid of that. I bagged it up, scratched the cat for a moment, checked his food and spent fifteen minutes trying to find my keys. I finally got into the Jeep and tore off to Emily's house. I saw the Lutheran church and friendly cars in the parking lot. It was a meeting, I decided to step in.

Sarah was slipping in, avoiding a demon patrolling the intersection looking for an easy meal. I parked the Jeep and approached the demon. It spotted me but didn't flee. It hunkered down for a moment looking like it was trying to size me up, I knew it was weak. I drew into certain killing range and it only then realized it had to flee. For the first time without blacking out, I unleashed a dark tendril and seized the demon. It unleashed agonized howls as I drew it into myself to feed The Other there in the dark. As I made my way inside I felt a calm come over me.

I greeted the friends inside, grabbed a coffee and pulled up a seat next to Sarah who was happy to see me, though her happiness was tempered by some apprehension about Rachael and the others. I whispered, "I'm sorry about Rachael. I tried to send her away but she has sorta staked a claim. Like a crazy ex-girlfriend stalker." I looked around worried mention of her would summon her, she stayed away.

"It's okay. I didn't mean to react to her. I heard that story a thousand times. Only you know the truth. It doesn't really matter, though. Even if the truth were known, people prefer the lies it seems. It's like an urban legend now."

"A lie gets around the world while the truth is still trying to get its pants on."

"Pants?"

"It's one of Eric's favorite Churchill quotes."

"Oh, are you okay today?"

"No, this cop is harassing me and Emily, my girlfriend, she's pregnant and I don't think she wants me around."

"Why? You're a terrific guy."

"Thanks, but no, I'm a monster."

"You have a monster living in you. It's not you, though."

"You know?"

"I thought you told me about it?"

"I don't remember that."

"Well I can see it, I didn't say anything. I didn't know what exactly to make of it."

"Did you see the demon on the corner?"

"Yes, it's been trying to get me a few days. It's figured out where I live, I think, so I don't go there anymore."

"You can go home again. My monster ate it."

"Wow, can I borrow him? I know where there are a lot of others!"

"Really?"

"Yup. The worst is a serial killer, a man who became one of the demons."

"I didn't know it worked that way."

"There is a place I will take you later if you want you can clear it out, it's like a den of them."

"Deal."

Bob arrived and came over to me and shook my hand. "Good to see you, what's going on?"

"I got my girlfriend pregnant but she doesn't want me around."

"Is the pregnancy cause to celebrate?"

"I would say yes."

"Well congratulations. Were you talking to someone on a blue tooth ear piece a moment ago?"

"You wouldn't believe me if I told you."

"You're a strange man, my friend."

"You got no idea, but I'm okay, thanks, Bob. Where's Aaron?"

"I don't know I talked to him last night. He said he might not make it today with his work schedule."

Another friend grabbed Bob and he excused himself.

CHAPTER 22

BATTLE

I turned back to Sarah and she was weeping. "What's wrong?"
"You're leaving, aren't you?"
"What? No, I'm not planning on it."
"I see it, Lisa won't come back. There won't be anyone to talk to."
"I'm not leaving. Look let's skip this and go find your demon nest and make sure you're safe walking around out there, okay?"
"Okay!" We left. I ran into Aaron coming in late, he shook my hand with a smile.
"How are you, pal?"
"I gotta go, emergency. Tell everyone I'm sorry, call me later, okay, and let's get coffee again soon."
"Awesome, will do, bro."
Sarah joined me in the Jeep and she guided me to a famously-poisoned and sealed spring near the battlefield memorialized by the locals. There I saw dozens of them lurking about the tall grass, most of them seemed to be in a stupor. "They're usually like this in the daylight, they're not particularly dangerous or alert. They can get agitated though, if something bothers them or they smell food."
"What kind of food?"
"Like an unbaptized child, a weak ghost like me or a lost drifter or junkie." I climbed out of the Jeep and looked around. Sarah called out, "The spring is the den."
I nodded and made my way there slowly. The Other didn't stir, it didn't seem to care. I had to force it to respond and it wiped the field clear of the dark spirits in a swath like the reaper's scythe. It cut them down, leaving them broken and disintegrating. Those beyond the reach of my scything tendril were becoming alert. Eric appeared. "What are we doing?"
"I think we're hunting demons, the spring is their lair."
"I always thought this place was creepy as hell. You want help?"
"You can help?"

"Yeah, unless you run into a high ranking one this should be no problem."

"Were you ever going to tell me about this power of yours?"

"I keep trying but keep forgetting and we get busy. I really just want to be gone. I don't want to exist anymore."

"Help me here and I'll see what we can do, I think Rachael can help."

"I hate her."

"I heard that." She appeared. Even the slightest thought of her brought her in all her naked glory.

I looked and Sarah was hiding in the Jeep. Rachael didn't seem to notice her. "Yeah, I can help you, baby."

"Thank you, Rache."

The demons were beginning to call some sort of alarm, a howling call that was low and dull, like the echo from inside a rusty pipe dragged through sand. The sound slowly rose in volume, until it was rolling thunder. Flocks of demons appeared like bats taking flight, from the spring they rose in a cloud of wickedness and I brought more tendrils to bear, I became a black heart at the center of a writhing mass of seven muscled tendrils smashing, crushing or cleaving the weak and petty demons. Rachael and Eric combined their burning beings into a new form. They were a burning angel with wings and whipping tendrils like The Other's. They could run, fly and spring after the fleeing demons. I heard Sarah scream and turned, a few were swarming over the Jeep and she was struggling to fight so many but had felled a few without assistance.

I raged and turned all The Other's power against them, it was too much for me. The violent surge blacked me out again. Damn. I wasn't out long. Rachael was the next thing I saw. I could hear Eric continuing the slaughter around me. Rachael was her beautiful self, holding my gaze fixed on hers. "Breathe damn it, your crush is fine, look at me and breathe!" Then after a moment she rejoined Eric and I resumed a more cautious assault into the spring.

I spotted Sarah safe behind me, this time not staying outside the protective radius of my writhing deadly coils. She followed and pointed out danger and soon it was over.

"Rachael, what happens to Eric if I try to release him?"

"He is weak, but marked. He would go to Hell."

No! He didn't deserve that. "How can I fix that?"

"He has to come back into grace. I don't know that, I'm only trained in corruption."

"I need another teacher?" Rachael only shrugged.

Sarah tapped on my shoulder smiling. "Thank you for getting rid of them! They kept me from going to see my boyfriend. They always blocked this road. I want to go see him, okay?"

"Sure, of course. Thank you for this, Sarah, I needed this. This felt good to do."

Rachael sneered. "She's so weak, can't teleport."

"Why do you feel it necessary to belittle her so?"

"I'm a pissed off murdered junkie going through withdrawals. I'm jealous of how you look at her and defend her. I had the emotional maturity of an eleven year old and I'm having my period. Maybe, I don't know, fuck you, baby, why are you a pill? Your crush isn't coming back. When she finds him again she's not coming back. She told you she was in those rooms out of habit only. Now you know she didn't go home only because the demons. You cleared them out, now she's never coming back."

"You don't know that. She wanted to find God in there with the friends."

"There are other demons out there, she could run into a whole army of them and not even know it until it was too late. I don't think you'll ever see her again."

I felt a sting, a twinge, loneliness. We had something special, she was a good friend. I would miss her. Rachael was probably right, she was wise. My phone rang. It was Brittney.

"Hello?"

"Hey—it's hard to hear you. What are you doing?"

"Wondering where you've been, I haven't heard from you in a while."

"I'm sorry I've been sick, hon."

"Darn, did you miss work?"

"Yeah, if I didn't live with my mom, I'd be worried about making rent."

"That's great, then."

"No, it sucks. I'm finally feeling better but she's using that an excuse to go on some kind of bender. Wants to drink tonight which means I'm babysitting unless I can tell her I have a date!"

"You do then. I want to see you and talk to you, anyway."

"Not that dump Kildare's, though, can you come down here? Pick me up?"

"Sure, I can do that. What time?"

"What time can you get here?"

I drove south from there. I came up on Sarah dreamily meandering down the highway, and I offered her a ride. "No, thank you, I want to enjoy this walk, I haven't been able to enjoy these views for a long time and I want to soak them up."

"As you wish." Without another word, I drove off. I fought back most of the tears watching her fade into memory in the rear view.

When I got to Brittney's, she answered my call by flashing frantically a light in a room identifying her apartment and shouting out a window for me to come up. I made my way up the stairs and she embraced me at the door. "What were you doing?"

"Me and Eric were fighting demons at a spring near the battlefield."

"Oh that's that smell, come inside, you can freshen up here, I'll find some Febreze or something you smell like burnt butt."

"Sorry."

"Don't be, you're saving my life." I followed her in, she dragged me, really, and I closed the door behind me. Her mom had already started on the wine. She rose from her couch unsteadily to greet me. "See, Mom, I have a date! I can't stay home and hose you off when you get so sick you puke."

After a brief slurred introduction, she made a pass at me and Brittney pretended to be astonished. "You know what, you smell like that, I don't need to get fancy, let's just go."

"Dirty Brittney it is!"

"The one you know and wuv!"

Her mom called after us, "Don't forget the condoms."

We climbed into the Jeep. "Wow, your mom is interesting."

"No, that's the booze. She's got no personality except Zinfandel."

"Damn. Ouch. Where to?"

"Your place, I brought overnight stuff." I hadn't even noticed she brought a duffel I was so distracted by trying to escape her mother. "So it's been a while, what's been going on?"

"You remember Emily, right?"

"Yes, you guys go to Vegas and elope? Bringing me home to sacrifice to the demon living in your basement?"

"No, but she's pregnant."

"A lot pregnant?"

"Nah, just kinda pregnant."

"Oh, well, so…"

"She doesn't really seem to want me involved. I don't know. I need to talk to her about it."

"You aren't taking me to that dance, are you?"

"Ha! No I'm taking you for dinner, drinks?"

"Are you two keeping the baby?"

"I think so, she went away, remember she had disappeared? She went off to have an abortion but changed her mind. She didn't tell me. She tried to arrange an adoption, gave up on that so she's keeping the baby and I…"

"You want to be with her, you want to be a dad, don't you?"

"Yeah."

"So you aren't going to marry her, are you?"

"Her mom would kill me before she let that happen."

"So we don't need to rush a bachelor party, then?"

"No."

"Is she going to murder me if she finds me at your place?"

"She's not coming back. The last time we talked she left angry at me for having cheated on her."

"I thought she said you could be with me, you showed me the letter."

"It was someone else." That hit her like a sledgehammer. She shook her head and fought it but the tears came in a river. She put her head in her lap and cried.

"Can you just drop me anywhere and never call me again?"

"Brittey, please."

"No, I really… I don't want to be in your collection. How many girls have do you have right now? I remember Rachael, Candice, Emily and now there is another? I didn't mind having to deal with some competition, but if I'm with you, I'm not sharing. I can't do that. I'm sorry—there, that gas station there will do."

I pulled into the gas station and she nearly fell on her face scrambling to escape. She tore her duffel out of the back and ran inside without a backward glance. "Why did I tell her that?"

"You're so stupidly sweet, you chased her off so I wouldn't possess her didn't you?"

Afraid to anger her I lied. "No, I didn't, at least not consciously."

"You're a terrible liar."

"You can read my thoughts too?"

"Don't have to, no poker face."

"I can still take her."

"Don't, I could never enjoy doing that to her."

She looked at me strangely like she could scarcely believe that was true. "You really wouldn't, would you? Is it me, you really hate me so much?"

"No, I just really care a great deal for her. What should I do next, Rache?"

"What do you mean?"

"My next move. Mara was trying to kill me, Emily might."

"I told them about you, they're afraid, why don't you believe me?"

"What if Mara provoked The Other? What would that mean for us? If I kill Mara, her demon would take Emily, then the baby."

"Yup, so?"

I wished I could figure out her move, what she was planning to get what she wanted. I worried I couldn't stop her anyway. I wondered if I should try. It was dizzying and overwhelming.

"Can you help me at all?"

"Baby, I told you, you're safe, I don't know what you're worried about."

"I'm worried about the baby, and Emily, she deserves a normal life. You said there was a way to fight just the demon, tell me how to do that!"

"No. You're being a total shit right now. I should just crash us and keep you to myself." I found myself near the Salem Estate. When we arrived the gate was closed but Rachael said, "I can fix that in one second." She vanished

145

and appeared on the other side of the gate and somehow triggered the sensor opening it. She just stared angrily at me as I went past her to the circular driveway in front of the house.

CHAPTER 23

RAID

Eric was standing out front. "Please don't hurt my sister. Please, let's all talk, okay?" I remembered he can read my thoughts I made sure he knew I wasn't planning to hurt anyone. It was clear he didn't trust me. He hovered.

Emily answered the door, happily surprised to see me. "I was just thinking about calling you, babe! The main house lost power and I lit a fire." She wrapped her arms around me unaware of the storm churning inside me or Eric behind me begging me not to kill her. Her belly was large and hard against me, I embraced her and tears slipped free of my restraint. She felt one of them fall on her ear.

"Babe, did we ever decide on a name?"

She hesitated for a moment, pulled herself away and looked at me with terrible worry. "What's the matter?" and Eric closed the door behind me as I stepped inside to stay close to her, still loosely holding her.

"I love you." My confession seemed to puzzle her.

"Why are you telling me this now? You've never before, I...what's wrong?"

"Do you love me?"

"You know I do." She clutched her hand to her chest, now there was a twinge of fear in her. My head turned downward and I touched her belly.

"I love both of you."

"Babe, what's wrong? Why are you crying?" Her eyes watered.

"Nothing, I was just thinking. Can you make some tea?"

She sniffled and brushed her hair back. "Yes, the wood stove is working, yes. Are you sure you're alright?"

"Yes. I know you worry, it's just day-mares again." She nodded and excused herself. She knows it's been hard on me, getting attuned to emotions after being medicated so heavily for so long. I took Eagle's advice and convinced the VA doctors to wean me off the hard stuff and without booze and pills I had been a bit erratic, emotionally. She kept talking from the other room, her voice shaking a bit, I had clearly distressed her. Lightning flashed across the sky and I saw through the glass doors at the back of the house, there in the garden a surprise. A thousand ghosts languishing and moping about.

I went through the doors and out to see them. Eric followed to illuminate their faces in the dark. They were ghosts from across time, like at the clearing where I killed Rachael. Some were hundreds of years old judging by their dress and hairstyles. They were all begging for release and called me by name. I wept and touched one on the forehead, she vanished. There was a tearful elation from the rest.

I walked around, hands outstretched, touching them two at a time. Some took a few moments of concentration to send them to the light. That's what I felt I was doing, releasing them into oblivion, peace. It must have looked strange and alarmed Emily. She came into the garden with an umbrella shouting something like, "Come back in!" I ignored her, intent on finishing this mission.

Rachael appeared, "Baby, this is dangerous. These are Mara's, there is no telling how she'll retaliate, don't do this."

I came to a large weathered stone and I was filled with rage as I read barely visible glyphs that had once, long ago, been carved more clearly upon this rock. I felt a living hand on my shoulder, Emily. Then lightning struck the stone and knocked us both to the ground. I blacked out a moment, I was hurt, badly. I didn't know quite how. The rock had been split. The ghosts were still surrounding me, now trying to help me to my feet.

I rolled over and started to raise myself up. I saw Emily beside me, unconscious. I pulled her to me, she wasn't breathing! Her heart had stopped. I was frantic and afraid The Judge would come, but he didn't. I reached into my pocket to find my phone was melted, fused to the pocket fabric. I screamed for Eric and fell to her side. "How could you do this!?"

"What? No I didn't! CPR, start now!" He gawked at me, "Damn it, Sergeant Salem, there is no one else! Do it!"

The ghosts hauled me up. I found my footing and lurched into a dead sprint. The house phone in the kitchen still worked, the voice on the other side knew the Salem estate and swore an ambulance would be there in moments. I rushed back to Emily. Eric said we had to get her onto the kitchen table, it wasn't safe out here, and CPR would be easier there. I was unable to lift my Emily. My left arm was almost useless. I think it was broken from the lightning. Eric and Rachael helped me carry her inside and put her on the kitchen table. I took a try to perform CPR, Eric had no more strength. I asked Rachael to help. She just looked at me and said, "You sure you want her to live?"

"Please, Rache!"

"If they die, we take Mara, you're safe forever. You have a normal life."

Eric looked at me and then at Rachael with hatred burning in his eyes. I didn't wait. I told her to help, my arm was broken. I tried with one arm. But I was hurting her. She was steaming. Eric had burnt her, maybe the lightning, maybe me. Rachael said, "I don't have the strength left to do that after the demon fight."

"You have to try."

"Invite me in. I can give you back your arm at least. Inside I can do that much, then you can do it." It happened in a heartbeat, Rachael was in me and braced my arm. It hurt and more than once the pain brought me to the brink of passing out. I held on for dear life, for her life, for the baby. I think I broke one of her ribs. The paramedics finally arrived. I fell off of Emily, off the table and Rachael fell beside me.

I asked Rache, recovering on the floor panting, "Where is Mara?"

"I don't know."

There were six responders, four firemen and two paramedics. The EMTs said they could find a pulse and she started to breathe again but she didn't wake up. They couldn't keep her breathing on her own. The firemen shut the back door and the EMTs peppered me with questions I could barely hear over Eric trying to answer them and the ghosts coming into the house from the garden begging for my help. The medics assured me she would be okay but that they had to transport her right away. It wasn't like in the movies where you give someone CPR and they pop back up and help you fight the bad guys and win at the last minute. It wasn't going to work like that. She would face a lengthy recovery.

"The baby!" Eric screamed, "What about the baby?"

I think one of the paramedics heard him, a redhead, she looked in his direction and said, "They'll be okay." I rode with Emily, the firemen said they'd see to the fire in the hearth for me. I released as many of the ghosts as I could on the way out. Then in the ambulance I asked the redheaded medic if she knew the family. She studied me. "Yes, our families are friends. Don't worry, I'm not one of them."

"Rachael says you are."

"She's not as smart as she thinks."

"So, what's your story?"

Eric appeared. "I'll be careful and not set anything on fire, I promise." She looked at him. He looked at her. She smiled.

"You do see him!"

She talked like she was directing battle. Between reading information off to the driver or the hospital over her radio, she told us what she could. "Yes, I'm gifted like my mother. But I'm not chosen to be her inheritor. I have early stages of MS. I won't last very long. I don't know how much longer I can work, so I'm not desirable. My younger sister has been selected instead. She's only six but she's already being groomed. She's defect free." She looked sad,

"So my disease has doomed us both. I do understand, though, that you are fighting them. If I can help, I will, for my sister."

We arrived at the hospital. They took her back and I was left in a waiting area assured I'd be allowed to join her in recovery when she was stabilized. A doctor came to ask me if I was with Ms. Salem, if I was the baby's father. He didn't seem particularly concerned. He said that Emily was going to be in for a few days and the baby was okay. I was allowed to visit with her. From beyond the curtain, I overheard the nurses talking with a doctor. They were discussing Emily's cancer and whether or not they should perform a C-section now. One of them said that admin said that since she was unwed the father didn't get a say, it was the doctor's call. I wasn't invited to participate in this discussion.

Eric popped in to tell me Mara was on her way but I didn't let that affect me. I stayed by Emily until the doctors told me I had to leave. Mara was arguing with the nurses at their station down the hall and when she saw me she raged and charged. "This is it," I thought, "I'm going to kill 400 people burning down this hospital in a deranged fit of self-defense."

Eric intervened, pushing me through a set of doors and kicking his mother square in the gut. I skidded across the floor, rolled to my feet and fled to the lobby of the emergency room. I could hear the old hag terrorizing the doctors. I heard a code announced over the PA system and two policemen went running past me. Soon, Mara was being led out in cuffs.

She was bloody and bruised, she had bit one of the officers and she stared daggers at me as she was dragged out into the night. I watched a trio of nurses patch the officer up as I gave a statement about what had happened with the old woman. The nurses agreed I hadn't done anything to her, the old woman's injuries must have occurred elsewhere. Eric had kicked her hard enough to severely bruise her but no one saw anything but me tumbling through a door and the old woman fall down and then attack a nurse who tried to help her up. Nervous small talk with one of the officers revealed that trooper Oldham was there and survived his fall.

I asked Eric if he knew something about Emily and cancer and he shook his head again, "No." He knew what to do, he went to check her chart and listen more closely to the doctors talking.

I found Rachael at the vending machines. She was sweating. "Withdrawals, I'm still having them…" It had been weeks. How awful, I thought to myself, offering her one of the peanut butter cups I had purchased. "I don't think I could hold it down." I bought a coffee and noticed my cup said I had a full house. I didn't feel like a winner. That felt like the last bit of good luck I would have for the rest of my life. Rachael added then, "The paramedic, the redhead that talked to Eric, her mother is one of us, I've seen them both at Mara's "book club." She's Lisa's daughter. I think I warned you about her before."

"Melissa, was that her name?"

"I don't remember. I'm in a lot of pain right now again. Fuck, I'm cold. You might have to kill her anyway, eventually."

"No, she said her sister would inherit the demon. She offered to help."

Melissa came back to find me. "My shift is over, I'm heading home but I'll call you as soon as I'm rested or if I hear anything that can help you." She gave me her number on the back of the card for the doctor supervising Emily's treatment. I wrote my number down for her on another card and I headed home.

On the drive, I picked up a fellow at a stop light. He just hopped in. "Excuse me, who the fuck are you?"

The Other surged, danger. "I'm a penitent soul. I was Abner in my life. Abner Burnside. I killed something on the order of a hundred people when I got home from Vietnam. I don't know why. I was a good man when I went. But something infected me there. It came back with me and I fed it booze and drugs. And you killed the horde of demons that grew from that, that kept me prisoner. You freed me. I want to thank you and ask you to complete your task. I need your help, Sergeant."

"I'm kind of busy not giving a fuck right now."

CHAPTER 24

TROLL

"Don't feel obliged, young man, I know you got your own worries but I spoke to an angel after you left the spring. She found me and told me I could still be redeemed. But I need you or another like you." I gave him Melissa's card and he dropped it in the cup holder. "Do I look like I have a phone?"

I pulled up to the house and got out. "Don't follow me. I got problems of my own right now. If you come inside I'll cross you over into Hell, unredeemed."

Eric was there with Leslie and Rachael and the cholo and dozens of others from Mara's garden. I released all of them and watched the cholo and Leslie be sucked into a horrible dark nightmare, the same place I dreamed of where I had to kill Emily over and over again. I couldn't get rid of Rachael so I came finally to Eric. "Alright, you earned this. Are you ready?"

"No. It was selfish of me to ask you to do that for me. Emily and you still need me. And I'm not convinced we can trust blondie here or that you can handle her on her own."

"No jokes?"

"I'm exhausted and I thought I'd leave them to Brittney."

"She's gone, I lost her."

"How?"

Rachael chimed in. "It was to protect her, he's a big softie."

Eric looked beyond exhausted and irritated. "Just keep her away from me, I'm not learning anything exciting yet, I'm going back to Emily and I'll alert you if anything happens."

"Thanks, bro."

"Get some sleep, Sergeant." I found myself alone with Rachael. I sank to the floor. I was sprawled against the cupboards again where I tried suicide. It was late. Pickles came to see what I was doing and curled up on my lap. Rachael pet the sleeping kitten and he didn't seem to mind.

"He runs from Eric. How did you do that?"

"I don't know."

"Did he tell you how bad Emily was hurt?"

"No. I didn't hear."

"How are you feeling? You were having some issues earlier?"

"Yeah, I was. I heard the doctors talking about her imaging and lab results. Eric, in his panic soft-boiled half her lung capacity away. You, we, broke a rib. She is a mess, baby. She won't recover quickly if at all."

"What do you mean?"

"The doctors were not talking about a C-section so they could help Emily recover, that was to save the baby. She might not make it, baby. Between the advancing cancer and the damage the lighting and we did."

"Wait, was the lighting god, nature, an angel, me?"

"You don't want me to tell you, do you?"

I sunk still lower. I needed a drink. My mind screamed for it. It subsided as I pet Pickles. "If it was me, wasn't it The Other, anyway?"

"Baby, the line between you two is blurring, it may one day disappear totally."

"I thought I was getting control of it? I had unleashed him at killing power and not blacked out twice, at lesser power several times without blacking out."

"Yes, but that was owing to you fusing with him. You're becoming him and he you. Every time you call on him, you become more tightly entwined. You always called on him without control before, but at the spring you were like a ninja or a surgeon. So deadly and accurate, even when you lost control, you killed around your crush and didn't harm a single hair."

"The lighting wasn't so well controlled."

"I didn't know you could do that! That's a new one by me. I thought it was sexy as hell."

"It almost killed Emily and the baby, it could have killed me."

"I love you alive or dead, baby."

"Did you ever care or were you always just sent to watch and then kill me?"

"Not funny. Not nice. I was going to use what's left of my strength to blow you tonight so you could sleep, but you know what? Fuck you. I'm going to go before I kill little Pickles, asshole."

I fell asleep on the floor. In the morning, Abner was still outside. I could see across the field and saw Sarah back at the creek. I was happy to see her, but it was selfish. She shouldn't have been back. She should be with her boyfriend. I went down to see her without a thought of hygiene or a change of clothes. I went barefoot and smelly.

"Sarah, what are you doing here?" I stumbled into the creek with a splash.

"Hey, are you okay?" She looked like she had been crying again. She tried to steady me as I climbed back out of the creek but she had not the strength for such a feat.

"What happened? Did you get home okay? Or do you need more help?"

"Oh no, I did make it home. It's not for me anymore. I'm replaced." She shed a few tears and shook it off. "It's what's right, it's my punishment. He couldn't see me, he couldn't hear me. He thought he could smell my perfume a moment, he mentioned it to his new wife. She recognized it and said she had found it in the closet and had tried it on that morning. Not thinking, he wasn't even upset by it. He just didn't care. I spent all the strength I had saved up, everything from a whole year to bring that scent to him. I probably wouldn't have tried if I knew she was there. I didn't notice her stuff everywhere or her car outside or all the other signs of another woman. I ignored it until she was there explaining it to him."

"I'm sorry, Sarah."

She smiled again. "No, it's really okay, he's happy that's what I wanted for him."

"Are you okay?"

"No, I'm terrible. And now I'm going to ruin us."

"What, how?"

"You said you liked me because I never asked you for anything."

"Yeah, for starters. You have other qualities."

"I want to go. I want to be over now. I can't take this life. Let God punish me, I need to accept it."

"I saw a man yesterday, a man like you who said there was an angel that come through, told him he could repent with the help of someone like me, have a chance at redemption."

"I don't want it. I talked to angels. There isn't redemption for me, for what I did."

I dropped my head. I sat down and I cried. "So we have to say goodbye now?"

"Please, I don't want to ask you. It's my last redeeming quality that I never asked you, that I was such a good friend."

"You didn't ask. I know it's what you want and it's the least I can do. If I was starving and you had a sandwich, you'd give me half."

She sat beside me again one last time, she wrapped an arm around me in half a hug. Her endearing voice quailed as it did so often before, "Okay I'm ready." She closed her eyes and I put two fingers on her forehead. "I'm sorry, Sarah." She was gone. There was no light, no darkness. I don't know where she went. Whatever god claimed her didn't leave me any hint. That was hope enough it was someplace better than where I was.

The hobo ghost Abner was still sitting in my Jeep. "We'll start tonight. Don't tell any of your friends, and don't fuck with me or I'll feed you to The Other, understood?"

"Aye."

"You were navy?"

"Aye, I was a boatswain's mate, special boat units."

I went upstairs and summoned Eric. He appeared and I told him what I had gotten from Rachael and what happened with Sarah and about the hobo killer. I asked him to stay and watch his sister, I'd call him later. He just nodded. I was losing him. He was drifting into madness now. That his sister might have been involved in killing him, that he might have to help me kill her, his mother, and who knows who else was really all too much for him. He had asked weeks ago for a break, a vacation from me. I didn't give it to him.

So I was going out on the road with the hobo and I was going alone. Eric tried to dissuade me once, only once. "You probably should stay in case Emily lives, if she wakes up and you're not there. Or if she dies and someone has to take care of the baby."

"Mara would fight me. Should I talk to her?"

"Put in a call, make one. Please try once."

"I need a new phone, again. Those things aren't very tough."

Rachael appeared. "Mara has sent a killer demon after you. She summoned it alone, so it's weak, it can kill you but it can't go far and it will only live while the kid she sacrificed is still...fresh."

Eric and I both recoiled from that revelation. He looked at me with a sad resignation that suggested he would be happy to help me kill his mother now. Rachael went on, "I'll try to ambush it for you. Get your cat and some clothes and get out of here a while. Cross a big river if you can. I'd say fifty miles should do."

I sent a check for two months of rent to the property management office. I loaded up some clothes and my cat and put the doors and top back on the Jeep. I went to the hospital to see Emily, probably for the last time. I guessed this hobo was going to kill me, he said he was a serial killer. Eric went in searching and found that Mara was not there so I went in. I left him to watch for her at the main entrance. I found Emily with the help of a volunteer in a bright yellow vest. I thought of Brittney and I wanted to kill myself for all the hurt I had caused just to her. I wondered if Sarah regretted her choice and if I would remember her in a week.

Emily was on life support in a medically-induced coma so she could heal the doctors explained. They were hopeful she would live long enough to deliver the baby. I asked why she wasn't given the C-section and they said that Mara had convinced her companions at the hospital not to risk harm to the baby unless absolutely necessary. I had forgotten she was once a surgeon here. I said a quiet goodbye to her. I held her hand and talked to her for an hour. I remembered Pickles in my pocket. He was getting too big for that but he still liked to travel this way. I put him on the bed at her side so he could say goodbye too. He gave her a lick and I put him back in the pocket. I kissed Emily's forehead and left my family there to die.

I asked Eric at the entrance not to tell anyone where I was going. He replied that that would be easy he didn't know where I was going.

"I don't know yet either. I haven't gotten any directions from Abner yet."

"Good luck, brother. I hope you don't need me. I'll be here."

I climbed in the Jeep and turned Pickles loose in his kennel in the back seat under my duffel.

"Which way?"

"We have to go west. Head to Pittsburg, then we'll go all the way west. Down through California, Mexico, Texas, Alabama, Tennessee and back to West Virginia to my family church where I will find the angel and finish my penance under his direction."

"What is this about?"

"We have to recover remains, bring them to the law and give the families closure."

"Won't that just make me look like a serial killer?"

"No, you might become a famous crime solving psychic or you can tell the world you're haunted by a serial killer and see which they believe."

"In my experience they'll believe the craziest thing."

"The truth it is, my boy."

"So you're a serial killer, but you can do penance?"

"I guess. I suppose the angel could be lying, I wouldn't put it past 'em."

"How many did you kill?"

"Hundreds. Most were found, at least partial remains. Usually, I'd read about them in a paper sometime later. I'd dump the bodies where animals would make it look like nature had done it, or at least so no one could obviously pin it on me. I wasn't looking to be famous."

"I thought you guys all wanted to be notorious, known for your crimes, played games with the cops so you could get caught and bask in a moment of glory."

"Nah, that's the TV, movies. It ain't like that. Every year in this country something like five to six thousand murder someone and get away with it. You'd be surprised how many murders go unsolved. A good chunk of those killers have done it more than once."

"Those are like gang shootings and stuff, though, mostly, right?"

"Nope."

"It's a long ride to Pittsburgh, go ahead and educate me while I try to figure out how we're going to do this and not get me arrested. I've gotta tell you, I've killed a few people and worried it's going to come back to me, I'm not a serial killer—in that I never intended to kill—but I could use pointers on not getting caught and hung for it."

"Alright, so, there are different types. There are about two thousand of us out there at any given time. That's a lot to keep track of so they get grouped into types. The way the FBI looks at it, there are missionaries, black widows, bluebeards, angels of death, trappers and the trollers. I'm a troller. There might be one more in there but those are the main ones."

I lit a cigarette and got a ticket for the turnpike heading west. There was a demon gnawing on the addict in the booth who looked like she was going to suicide after her shift. I wanted to reach out to help but there was nothing I could do. She wouldn't even make eye contact.

"A missionary kills those he judges to be undesirable, usually one specific type he don't like—say whores or addicts, and he usually sticks to that type of victim. The black widows kill men, usually for money, insurance that kind of thing. Bluebeards kill women for money or to feel powerful. Angels of death are nurses that kill patients, pretty common and easy to do without getting caught. Trappers are the ones you see with elaborate schemes to trap someone they stalk, sometimes for weeks and let their victims come to them. They have the torture basements and the panel vans. A troller like me is a gambler, thrill seeker. He doesn't worry if his victim is important, just that they're vulnerable at the moment their paths cross and he feels like killin'."

"You say it's easy to not get caught?"

"Well yeah, the TV makes us all out to be geniuses, but it ain't true either. Most of us are average or less intelligent. I heard agents, profilers trying to find me talking. Said our average I.Q. is like 90. That's not that impressive I don't believe. I'm pretty sure I'm not even that smart."

"So why the Hollywood lies on this, just marketing?"

"I don't know, best guess is someone decided it was more interesting to have an intelligent character on screen or to portray for the actor and to make it look harder for the cops, even though it's impossibly hard even with dumb serial killers. Most are never caught or detected. Lots of killers do a spate of murders get their fill, get bored or find satisfaction and move on then with more or less normal lives."

"That's truly disturbing on so many levels." I thought about shredding this ghost now.

"Well, that weren't me, I weren't never normal. I was like you."

My heart skipped a beat. "First, fuck you, man, and second what do you mean?"

"I was an orphan. I went in the navy, I was a volunteer not a draftee, most of the guys what died over there were volunteers, not draftees. Another Hollywood lie. The PTSD, they didn't know it then, but that got me and the demons filled me to spread the pain. Just like you."

"Were you haunted like me?"

"Not quite, you got that good one, the one the other angels even fear to disturb. Why do you think you ain't met one yet? They're scared of ya."

"That sucks."

"Angels ain't no fun anyway, trust me, you better off drowning in demons."

"Well so why are we going to Pittsburgh?"

"Well I threw a lot of bodies in the three rivers there. Most would be found floating down river somewhere. They'd get spread out over some good distances. Wash into different jurisdictions and nobody would connect the dots. God didn't care. Most of them I killed were damned, irredeemable or stripped of their souls in life and it didn't matter. But I made one mistake.

I was sleeping off a drunk in a houseboat. A big ole Gibson thirty plus footer, she had all the bells and whistles. The owner kept it just to show off at football games, he'd take it out and BBQ and tailgate by the stadium to shoot off fireworks. Well I thought it was safe since that week the Stillers were on a bye."

"I can't watch them play."

"I don't like football but that town is crazy about them Stillers. Well, the owner thought he'd bring his little one out for some fishin.' They surprised me and I don't know what I thought, they were robbers or junkies come to trash the place, I stabbed him dead. Put a knife right in his throat and watched him kick and dance the death rattle on the floor there in front of his little girl. She just stood there and cried holding her fishing pole."

I started to cry, I didn't know why but then I thought of my parent who had to die to give me my judge in the desert so I could live.

"Well I reckon I didn't want no witnesses, and I thunk it better she not grow up an orphan with no daddy like me so I put my hand over her mouth and nose and held on tight as she shook and skittered trying to get away. I shushed her and whispered it was going to be alright over and over until she died there watching her daddy go still too."

I had to stop and pull over. I stumbled into the turnpike traffic lane and threw up. I stumbled into the center Jersey barrier and summoned The Other. This time it was different. I burst into flame and the tendril writhed about me on guard for an attack. "Stay the fuck away from me, man, this was a bad fucking idea, just forget it get the fuck away from me."

"You asked me, boy, you ain't got another way out of this. I can help you, remember? You ever wanna get back to that filly of yours, that baby as a free man, not see them from death row in an orange jumpsuit, you'll do what we gotta do!"

I knew with one thought I could send him into oblivion. A truck drove past honking at me. I was in the left lane now advancing on him, ready to strike.

"Boy, I won't tell you no more, just show you where, alright?"

The Other lifted me out of the way of a car not paying attention and put me back into the Jeep. It returned to its slumber and I was aware of how close I was to being killed. I took a deep breath and counted to ten.

"Finish the damn story and tell me what I have to do already." I put the Jeep in gear and we resumed the trip west.

"I didn't know you could fly."

"I can't, didn't you see The Other?"

"I know he's there but like the witches, I'm full of evil and broke the laws, I can't see him."

"He lifted me, I can't fly."

"Looked pretty fucking cool to me."

"Finish the damn story."

"Oh, right well I realized what I had done. I took the man's keys and drove that boat out. I tied 'em to an anchor. I dropped 'em into the river and sailed the boat as far south as I could go. I crashed it in a drunk later and escaped as I always did."

I thought God loves tragedy, he let that little girl be murdered and this ass accidentally survived, drunk, a crash and boat sinking, so he can continue his murder spree. Fuck God.

"Well it turns out that little girl was something God cared about. He set a hound on me. My demons murdered it and the next one too. Then they sent a bigger one later. I been on the run since, that big one–like you I can't win that fight. Anyway, the cops, they found the dad but not her. Her mother was driven mad searching for her. It's been a dozen years but she's still alive and we'll bring her peace. I know where the body is and you can talk to the little girl's ghost for her. It won't put right what I did but it'll stop that hurt from growing in the world. And let that little girl rest and be with her daddy."

That seemed worthy, putting a daddy and his daughter back together. I was all in now. I didn't see how it would help me but I didn't care. It was something to do and it was better than watching Emily die in that hospital bed.

When we got to Pittsburgh we had to turn south, I didn't get to actually spend a lot of time there. Pittsburg. It wasn't as ugly as I had expected it to be with a name like that. I thought it would be fun to explore it but that would have to wait. South it was to a town upstream where he crashed the houseboat.

"So wait, the Mon flows north, how did the body get lost south?"

"I sailed the boat that way I dumped the bodies there. The dad, he washed or floated north, it's how they found him. And because the river flows north, they didn't think to look too far south. I crashed north of the stop. It was just terrible luck for that little girl, she stayed right where I dropped her."

"I was hoping to get some French fries on something unexpected here."

"You been here before?"

"No, I had a friend in the army that went to college out here. He used to put fries on everything in the chow hall."

"I haven't had a damn fry in, well I can't, so."

The roads didn't always let us get close to the river where my ghost companion could get his bearings. We backtracked a lot thinking we passed the spot. We rode about for two days like that. He would look around and I'd take Pickles for a walk on a harness he didn't mind wearing. I enjoyed having him with me. He was the only good thing on this trip. I bought a new phone at a strip mall and put in a call to Walter. I needed to know what would become of the mess with Oldham.

"Hello?"

"Hey Mr. Ewing, guess who?"

"Thanks for calling me back, I been trying to reach you—was trooper Oldham at your house when he fell?"

"Yes, he was threatening me and obviously hung-over if not drunk."

"He had been warned. Your neighbor said he tripped and fell but the PSP wanted me to get a statement from you denying that you pushed him."

"I didn't."

"Where are you, can you come in?"

"No, I'm out near Pittsburg I'm on a road trip. I don't know when I'm getting back."

"Let me get a recorder we can do this over the phone." In a few minutes we did a recorded statement over the telephone and I was able to honestly say I didn't push the pig over that railing. I know Rachael did it, a neighbor gave me cover, too, so I didn't need to be afraid. After the brief interview I asked Walter if Oldham was okay. "No, he killed himself after he was released from the hospital and his employment was terminated."

"They fired him?"

"Yeah, he was drunk and carrying his service revolver and badge off duty. I guess it was too much for him. He had a lot of problems. He was probably never going to walk again so he shot himself with an unregistered weapon stolen from the evidence locker several years ago."

"Dirty cops."

"I told you they all are."

My ghost companion finally found the spot. The little girl was still standing there not knowing where to go or what to do. It had been many years and somehow with demons, witches, everything out there that made being dead so dangerous, she was safe if frightened and terribly alone. She saw me see her and she ran to me arms wide to grab me, I knelt to catch her and hug her back.

"You can see me!" She cried a lifetime of tears.

"Yes, I can see you, sweetie. We're going to take you home, okay?"

"I miss my mommy!" She cried and wouldn't let go. Then he appeared and she shrieked and tried to disappear like Sarah did when Rachael threatened her. But I held her and motioned for Abner to back up. He did.

"The body, it's just here. Can you swim?"

"No, but I don't have to." I called The Other and an ebony tendril whipped the water away as it spiraled down into the muddy Monongahela.

With the greatest care it pulled what was left of her, still wrapped in a rough sailcloth sack with an anchor inside and it laid her before me. I called 911 and waited.

Every flashing light, emergency vehicle and news van for a hundred miles showed up. I was allowed by the news people to stay anonymous and the police were happy to enforce that–I was interviewed like a suspect until they realized I would have been nine or ten when the murders happened. The little girl never let go of me not until her mommy arrived. She was escorted by a host of family members. She was only about forty according to the police and reporters but she looked much older.

She had been crying but was withered and dried out now. Her daughter ran to her and hugged her crying and blubbering. "Mommy I missed you, Mommy I love you!" I began to tear up. The shattered woman embraced me and thanked me. I told her there was no need. I asked her if she had a message for her daughter and she stared at me blankly. I asked the little girl if she had something she wanted to tell her mommy and she said only that she missed her she was lost and didn't know how to get home.

"Is she here?"

"She's always been here."

"Who are you?"

"I'm just a guy who talked to a ghost that told me she was here waiting for you."

"Can you tell me what happened to her?"

"I wouldn't dare. No. I know she's happy to see you."

"She can see me?"

"Yes, and she's overjoyed."

"Can she hear me?"

"Yes."

I pulled one of those recorders from my hoodie, one that Emily had given me. I turned it on and asked the little girl to talk to it, tell it what she wanted her mommy to know. When the little girl was done I played it back for her mother. We cried together and someone brought us coffee. We used the device until it ran out of batteries. The ghost was losing her power too. The family insisted on taking her home and they wouldn't let me go on my way. I stayed with them for several days until the little girl was laid to rest with her daddy in a family plot overlooking the river where he was found. The priest released the little girl and I went west again. The priest! I needed to get one to help Eric find grace.

We drove for days. We found other ghosts, and along the way they made up the bulk of our acquaintances and companions. We avoided the living and their questions. I made time to let Pickles play and let him roam off harness on a number of stops, keeping an eye out for hawks and other raptors. One tried once, a turkey vulture, I think. It was the size of a Winnebago–it dove at him and I snapped its neck with a flick of The Other's tendril. The bird crashed into the ground, its head bounced hard enough to separate it from its body. Pickles was alarmed and ran into my coat pocket, painfully climbing my leg. I decided to trim his claws and wondered where Abner was taking me next.

Finally in South Dakota, which seemed almost completely empty and abandoned, he spoke of our next task. We bought food at a truck stop gas station casino where I could get a shower and a blow job from a lot lizard. I got the shower but skipped the almost certain venereal disease or robbery that would come with the meth head blow job. I did hear some truckers comparing notes about the quality of their respective lizards in the showers.

Abner said, "Near Sturgis, I killed one of them lot lizards because I wanted to. The sex wasn't enough. I was still in denial that I liked the killing. It was sloppy. I threw her in a canyon where there were critters aplenty to clean her up. You'll need to make a hike into it. You're going to need some equipment I'd reckon."

"I have him, I don't need anything else."

"The cat?"

"No the other cosmic balancing witch hunting demon eating burning death machine that lives inside me."

"Right, I knew you meant that."

"What the hell was the cat going to do?"

"You think that little varmint's gonna survive this little quest of ours?"

"Don't say that."

"What?"

"Quest, makes me think of *Monty Python and the Holy Grail* or some stupid Nintendo game."

"What the hell's that?"

"Don't worry about it. Show me the canyon."

We drove out into the middle of nowhere on some side roads and parked next to a fence. There were cattle here, content to ignore us. It was incredibly windy. Abner pointed to where the dead girl could be found. I thought to ask him how he made sure this murder looked like animals had done it, how he knew they'd devour her but decided I was better not to know. I followed him on the ranch and began to worry. "What if the owner decides he doesn't like us on his property?"

He looked around, "There ain't nobody for thirty miles in any direction. The guy who owns this place lives in Montana. He only gets out here but once a week."

I had no way to know for sure.

Then I spotted her. She was radiant. Her long flaxen hair glowed in the sun. She was wearing bell bottoms and a tiny bikini top, bronzed skin shining with life but she was not happy to see us. She howled in rage at Abner and I just stood back as they fought. He struggled to explain to her why we had come, what he wanted with her. He had remembered her killing wrong.

She was a hitcher not a lot lizard. He thought she was but she screamed her story at him, setting the record straight. She was just another runaway who had had enough of the free love, sex, drugs and rock and roll lie. She was returning home. She was only a few short miles away when she ran into him and he offered her a ride the rest of the way for a little loving. She changed her mind as they were beginning but he wouldn't stop. He raped her then murdered her. I don't know how I was going to make this trip with this guy without ending him right now.

I had one question. "Is there anyone still waiting for you or looking for you?"

"I doubt it. They had given up on me when I left, I'm pretty sure after more than twenty years they've completely forgotten, if they're even still alive."

"Then I can release you."

"Please, can you?"

"Are you at peace with your maker? You may not like the other side."

"I don't care."

I touched her forehead and thought of love and light and she was gone in a glimmer. She would be free. As for her remains, I noted the location, found the address for the ranch on a mailbox not far down the road. A piece of mail inside showed the owners name and I made a note of that as well. I called the police from the next truck stop casino and turned my attention to Abner.

"So, why were these killings so far apart? This woman you kill some forty years ago, at least 30 judging by her dress. The little girl though, that wasn't all that long ago ten, twelve years. What the little girl the last one?"

"Yes, she was the most recent that matters."

"Any more waiting to be reunited with the living or is this just to help you?"

"This is to help us, friend."

I destroyed Abner without a second thought. This work was for him. I didn't need to cultivate good karma. I should have done it when I found out what he did to that little girl. I don't know how I didn't, or how long I could have stayed in his company without becoming more like him. I guessed I could find the other ghosts without him. I could release them and there were others like me out there doing the same work. I wish I could find another. I could do so much with the help of another.

CHAPTER 25

RESPITE

I wasn't ready to head home, though. I was going to keep going. I was going to find a place I wanted to see. I called Emily every day to leave a message so if she woke, she'd have some way of knowing I thought of her. I drove to Mt. Rushmore and tried to pronounce the sculptor's name. I wished it was easier to say, you couldn't work his name into a conversation to impress someone with your trivia skills and not sound drunk. Borglum, yeah, I will always sound drunk saying it. I remember having to pay to get to the parking lot then being underwhelmed in the extreme. It always looked towering and enormous in movies. But in real life it was much smaller than imagined. I thought, "Meh, that's it, huh?"

I thought it would be more impressive if it was easier to find. It was an impossibly long drive from the nearest town, there was a little village (Keystone) near the base of the mountain but it was of little interest to me. Why didn't this ass sculpt it closer to a highway? Was he worried it would look bad and he didn't want his critics to see it? Disappointed in one of our great national treasures, I meandered off towards the Devils Tower but sensing trouble as I drew near, I went instead towards Yellowstone.

There was a fire when I got there. I was relieved it wasn't my fault and that there was no way I would be blamed for this. I stayed in the village known as Gardiner at the north base of the mountain for four days watching news of the fire, watching crews go up to fight and come down for beers. I found an A.A. meeting. I went fishing with another A.A. guy named Bob, who while friendly was not half as cool as my own Bob back home.

I went fishing and didn't drink. I had a giant $14 elk burger. I painted a landscape at an artsy coffee shop with a lesbian whose face was mostly made in a metal shop. I couldn't count all the jewelry in her face. She wasn't a bad-looking girl, I had to wonder why she did all that to herself and I wondered how heavy it was, how much it cost. No matter, she was a great artist and fun to talk to. She had some great stories and helped with my piece.

I donated my painting to the coffee shop and the weather took a miserable turn. The fires would be put out by the storms coming but I decided to head out and try this park another time. Maybe bring Emily and the baby, I thought. Can babies eat elk? I was thinking crazy thoughts on the road. I was alone again, except for Pickles and I didn't know what to do with my mind. It seemed you could drive for eight hours and never have to see anyone if you didn't want to. There were ghosts and demons about but they were few and far between. I managed to get lost in some rock canyons and bought a spare gas can to mount on the Jeep bumper after a close call lost in a reservation. I saw a real sweat lodge being repaired on that adventure and just kept going. These were the guys that killed the Custer fellow.

I found myself in southern Montana. I pulled off to get gas in a place called Garryowen. It's a town, with a population of two. There was a Conoco gas station, a Subway and a tiny memorial to the end of 'Lakota–Cheyenne and USA violence'. The monument made claim to be the resting place of an Unknown Soldier. Being less convenient than the one in Washington D.C. it wasn't guarded around the clock but nonetheless, here was another soldier nobody cared about. He even had a monument but I'd never heard of it. I doubt anyone I knew had either. I bought some tchotchkes and a buffalo hide for Pickles to snooze on. I let him try it at the next rest stop after he got tired of chasing bugs. He really liked it. I had succeeded in bringing some happiness into the world and felt a little better about myself.

Was she still alive? Her phone hadn't been disconnected so there was a good chance she was still alive. Eric hadn't appeared with news, which must be a good sign, unless a demon ate him. I looked around for one. There were almost no spirits around. I was careful *not* to wonder what she was up to, so as to avoid summoning her. What was Sarah doing? I needed to talk to someone. I found a ghost in the hotel parking lot. It wasn't friendly, though, so I sent it over, into darkness it went. I went into the bar. There were cheerful and happy people there. I had to take care of my kitty and drive in the morning. Before I sat down I decided to get to my room and get some sleep.

Next thing I knew I was in Washington, on the shore I had hopped on a ferry to explore the Olympic peninsula. I hiked to the hot springs that are full of gross things you don't want to get into for a soak. It's full of toxic shit, at least according to the rangers and signs. I went on a boat cruise of the harbor looking for whales or something. It wasn't peak season or whatever so it was cheap and there wasn't much to see but there were no ghosts either.

I hiked trails all over Mount Rainier and little Pickles was my constant companion. He was a great ice breaker. I was enjoying the gentle easy company of strangers in safe, digestible bits. No one frightened me, no one took from me and no one cared about my name. They always wanted to know the kitten's name but I didn't matter and that worked for me. I spent a day in the ass end of the wrong exit during a detour around a freeway fatality clean up.

There was a town there about halfway through the detour called Osbourne, near the army base and Yelm. There was a saloon, like a wild-west saloon with a wooden sidewalk and those miniature doors and everything. It was like a movie prop. It was steak night and the parking lot across the street, beside a railroad crossing, was jammed. I expected everyone to be in cowboy boots and long dusters with oversized hats but it was regular people. All in sneakers, sweats, hoodies and baseball caps with football teams on them. It had an electric bull and a pin ball machine. I got a lousy steak and a warm soda. Eventually people could be heard excitedly leaving because the highway was reopened. Everyone resumed their trips home but I went home with a bartender.

I spent two weeks with her. She was older, had the kids and a family and all that but her marriage was on the rocks, he was in jail. It was probably a typical story around here judging from the billboards advertising for DUI attorneys, divorce lawyers, casinos, rehabs and psychics. I got bored and tired of her drunken escapades, loud friends and left town. It was for the best not to remember her at all. Every other night in the bar with her someone would try to pick a fight and I was glad I didn't drink or I'd have to explain another death. The one time I had to fight I was able to do it without The Other. A civilian with a knife and a snoot full wasn't going to require the kind of soul-rending overkill that The Other could bring.

I drove down the coast past Portland which was keeping it weird. The city was swarming with ghosts and demons and I didn't even stop for gas there.

In California, which should be three states, I got pulled over twice and hassled. One of the cops was a host to a demon. I thought for half a second to ask Rachael again how to kill the demon but not the person. She didn't come and I was grateful. The demon didn't bother with me and I decided to leave it be. I already had my own coven to destroy. I didn't need a new world of problems that a group from such a densely-populated area as Los Angeles might bring. I shivered at the thought of it.

I didn't stop overnight or for longer than a few minutes at a donut shop. I cleaned the litter box and let Pickles play then went to Tijuana for some mole and marveled at how easy it was to get into Mexico and how it was inversely difficult to get out of that shit hole. I decided not to go there ever again. My mole was delicious, though.

I drove into Texas and dodged a tornado in a hotel bomb shelter. They didn't charge me for a room to hide there. I decided to go ahead and get a room anyway, it was a long day and I wanted to give Pickles a chance to run around and play. Then I saw something I hadn't thought of. In the hotel, on local television news, a story about a collection of occult works protested at the San Antonio library. Why didn't I read something? I bet some books exist about what's going on with me! Next morning I used the hotel business center to find the nearest library.

It seemed it would be San Antonio so I headed that way. I stopped at a gas station BBQ joint called Rudy's north of town near a Sea World and had the best two pounds of brisket, sausage and ribs I've ever had. I thought about living here permanently. I ordered another two pounds to go and grazed on that in the car for the rest of the day. I got lost in town, ate some more and noticed the Alamo was near where I was stopped trying to read this damn map.

I decided it would be something cool to see so I threw more change in the meter and put the kitty in my pocket. There were no ghosts, but there were demons lurking about in the shade. I set The Other after them. I learned for the first time to do that. I let him go, off leash. He didn't go far but he made my work easy, devouring the entities with ferocity. I hadn't been able to witness such power when letting him fight in defense of myself. I was not strained or stressed but only slightly distracted by the divided focus on where I was walking and what I was doing and what he was doing and seeing. It was like playing a split screen video game of *Mario Kart* with a friend. I was keenly aware that I was vulnerable in this state. I could not magically defend myself separated from my judge. I didn't want this curse, but I'd be damned if I let him stray. I brought him back quickly and felt him lumber back into the pit for sleep.

I followed a group of marked inheritors, young girls being prepped by their mothers. I was curious if they might lead me to a den. They led me to the Riverwalk and I lost them there, until I found a little store along the walk called the Crystal Wand. I went inside and overheard a conversation between two older witches about preparing their wands with their sexual juices and I pretended not to hear any of it. I looked around and saw a little red book with a title suggesting it was for good witches. I flipped through it and went to the counter to pay for it.

The witch behind the counter asked me, "Is this a gift, sir?"

I grinned, remembering that Rachael could feel The Other stirring in me when we were close, I roused him. The witch shuddered and I said, "Guilty." Pickles stuck his nose out of my pocket, probably annoyed by the heat, and he meowed at her.

"It's free, then." She stammered and I nodded, took the book and walked slowly back to the Jeep to feed my little companion.

I wasn't followed but I did catch one of the witches I saw in the store snapping a picture of me when I turned to look back. I don't know why I was looking for trouble. I must have been bored or The Judge was affecting me. I was feeling good, strong.

I enjoyed watching the kitten eat. He wasn't getting bigger but I couldn't call him a kitten much longer.

I flipped the book open to the section on the expulsion of demons. It was some Old Testament shit but there was an English translation of the one chant that seemed like a good start.

"Come out, daimon, since I bind you with unbreakable adamantine fetters, and I deliver you into the black chaos in perdition."

The text described a bunch of writing and symbols to use in preparing tools, and outfit and the like but another which identified the "magician" who is invested with the same powers as the god. I wondered if I qualified as a magician of this type. I had a power, "King of Judges" Rachael called it, living in me. Was that sufficient to use the first person expulsion enchantment contained in the text?

'I conjure you, daimon, whoever you are, by this God,
SABARBARBATHIOTH SABARBARBATHIOUTH
SABARBARBATHIONETH SABARBARBAPHAI."

These seemed like they would be too easy. I read on and found a ritual that took some two days to do at a safe place made ready for the ritual and the chant to bring something like my judge into the magician. It was thought to be a path to gain exorcist-like powers. It was incomplete in the book referred to as theoretical. There was enough information that I thought I might be able to summon my judge, remain conscious, perhaps send him off leash to fight then use these powers to bind, expel or trap the demons. To pull them out away from Mara or Emily if need be.

With Eric and Rachael we could win perhaps and save my family. I began devoting the chants and Psalms in the text to memory, the ones that were said to be offensive for attacking the demons. I learned those, trusting to my judge for defense and hoping this was not a mistake. I found the library and the protested occult section, now under guard. I was allowed to read one work at a time under supervision. I found what I hoped would fill in the blanks and asked the librarian to make some copies for me. I paid for the copies and hit the road for home.

I crossed into Alabama before stopping for the night. I met a sweet blonde in the hotel bar. She didn't beat around the bush, she wanted me to pay her for a night. I proposed I give her half the money she asked for if she would kill half the time with me talking so I wouldn't drink. It was weird. Her demeanor changed and she refused the money but asked me if I was one of those A.A. people.

"I'm trying to be."

"Do you have a chip on you?"

"I have a one month chip. I think I can get a three month but I haven't been in a meeting for a while, been on this road trip." I pulled the chip out of my pocket.

She smiled. "My real name is Freya. My family is from Spokane, it's not an unusual name there. My dad was an A.A. guy. A lot of my friends are in there. I should be but I haven't been able to make it work. Tell you what, I'll be your friend, keep you company. I have a meeting schedule in my room. I'll go get it, okay?"

"Okay." I thought I probably shouldn't be sitting in a bar. But look how even that is somehow turning out well for me. She wasn't gone long.

She smiled and said, "There is one in fifteen minutes not far from here" She grabbed me up and took me to the parking lot. She pointed to her car, a blue Hyundai Tiburon coupe. "Follow me, okay?"

I asked The Other if there was danger. No stirring, no ringing in my ears. I nodded and followed her to a church in a sketchy part of town. There were the typical smokers gathered outside and the collection of shady characters that always looked harmless up close. She waved from her car and pointed to the entrance. I nodded and she drove off into the night.

I enjoyed the meeting, ran into another Bob and enjoyed some homemade donuts but otherwise it was the same as any other meeting in any other town. It was a large group of wonderful, kind, gentle people with hearts open, arms outstretched, ready smiles, handshakes and patience to listen to me whine. I helped clean up afterward and got some restaurant pointers. I learned Freya's dad was in the meeting and that his daughter died last week of a heroin overdose. Someone in the after meeting had a newspaper with the obituary handy and showed me Freya's picture. How did I miss that?

I went back to the hotel to find Freya but she was nowhere to be found. Her car wasn't there either. I didn't know what to do. I could release her as a favor but would she even want that? I had to see her. I hoped she was okay and that I could find her in the morning. I fell asleep with the spell book on my stomach. I had dreams of death and war, blood rituals, rape and murder. I saw Hell and the crash. I woke up under an upturned couch. It was the worst night I could remember in a long time. I found some pills kept for these kinds of emergencies. I wasn't relying on them as heavily as I had been but I needed them from time to time and had a small daily maintenance dose.

In the morning I couldn't find Freya but I swore I'd return to find her as soon as I could. I got a hotel waffle and loaded Pickles into the Jeep. He didn't seem his usual happy self and I worried, that's part of my condition. I told myself not to listen to my fears.

I pulled into one of those restaurants recommended at the A.A. meeting and got a delicious meal. Pickles looked terribly ill after lunch so I asked for directions to a vet in the area and detoured thirty minutes to reach one. There the vet informed me he had leukemia. I didn't even know cats could get that.

He was apparently lucky to have lived this long. He was so advanced he might not make it another week. I cried with him. I asked the vet what could be done to make him comfortable. He shrugged, "Cuddles."

I held him in a hotel room then, making sure he had what he needed but he stopped eating and drinking. I used an eye dropper to get water into him but he just lay there waiting for the end. I cried like a baby. I was about to be completely alone again and I wasn't ready for that. I called Eric.

He appeared but just stared at the ground. "I don't need anything. Just stay here with me."

"Gay."

"Pickles is about to go."

"So is Emily. You need to get back home as soon as you can. I still want you to end me. Let me go to my judgment. I can't do this, I can't kill my mother and my sister and I can't let them kill you."

"Catch 22 man."

"Catch 22?"

"There might be another way."

"I'm all ears."

I showed him the spell-book, my notes, the copies from the library collection, the Psalms and the symbols. "See?"

"This looks like something from that *Beautiful Mind* flick, bro, you know that, right? Next thing you know you're going to have all this on a wall and string everywhere."

"This might work! There is a chance. Even if the odds are against it, we have to try, don't you think?"

"I agree. It's worth a try. But I have to wonder why the haunted would have a book to help you defeat them in their store?"

"Good question...there is something else."

"What?"

"What *you know who* told me once. That you were in grace most of your life, you can still get to Heaven instead of Hell when I do release you. We just have to get you back into grace somehow."

"Blow up doll told you that?"

"Sorta, she said you were a virgin when you died. Is that true?"

"Yes."

"Wow, man, I'm sorry."

"If you pass a catholic church on the way home, stop and we'll talk to the priest. For now, start getting home." For the first time since before he died, I heard hope ringing in his voice.

I wondered how to make Pickles' passing painless but before I could pose the question to Eric or call Rachael who I'm sure would know, he was gone. I cried some more and took him back to the vet to get him cremated. I gave the guy cash and told him the address to ship his remains to in Pennsylvania.

I drove through Pensacola to see the beach for a quick distraction. I liked the ocean. I didn't see any ghosts out there. It felt like life, home somehow. I fell asleep on the beach and woke up being hassled by the cops. Not real cops but the kind in shorts they put on bicycles. I gave them my ID and they said I had a federal warrant and arrested me. They were lucky I was sober or there'd be two dead assholes burning in a trashcan at the beach on the news.

The cops didn't make a mistake. The army had put out a warrant for me, I didn't believe their threat in the letter or from Captain Sillwell or whatever his name was, but it was real. I spent a few days in an army lock up, got a free haircut and a new uniform set. I thought about burning the place down just over the lousy food. I went through the fastest court martial in history. I was acquitted providing I complied with the requirements for re-entry into service. I agreed. I was almost eager to try out my new superpowers and get some payback in Iraq. I lost friends there and well, fuck those guys. I wondered if I could burn them from here the way the witches tried to burn me from around the world. But I also knew I would never pass the physical or psych exams.

I failed the army psychiatric exam for re-entry and as I had blacked out during a blood draw and choked one of the medics. I got to keep the haircut and the new uniform anyway. I was given a medical discharge and was told to file a claim with the VA. I was already getting disability from them so I just went on my way.

Eric was going back and forth from me to home. He had news for me when I hit Tennessee.

"I know why Mother is so mad. Emily's cancer can't be cured, not now. She refused treatment when there was time. She was depressed and so Mom thought she would outlive her daughter and have to pass the demon on to me, a stronger host. With my death her demon would lose its place in this world, all its work would be undone and the judges, the god she hates will have won."

"Why did Emily refuse treatment?"

"First, she wanted to try holistic approaches, she had seen a friend's mother go through fruitless cancer treatments. She knew her chances were slim, pancreatic cancer, so she thought about just enjoying her life, what was left. She wanted to finish college just in case she did live. Mother thought to incentivize her to get treatment, she told her what awaited her, tried to seduce her with the power—come to the dark side, all of that rubbish. Emily became suicidal over the prospect of being possessed. She went through a whole grieving and acceptance struggle with it. It's probably why she never thought you were imagining me. Mother had taught her some about the magical world. It's probably why she wanted to help you. There wasn't anything left for her in this life."

It was why she gave herself to me, why not? She was going to die anyway, so much for love. "Why do you think she let herself get pregnant? Why did she keep the baby? Can we save her?" I was now ready to strike a bargain with God. I was grieving, I was running and she was going to die. I was missing our last days together. Eric only shook his head

"Her journals said she just wanted to feel alive, knowing she was dying didn't think about birth control. Then she wanted to give you the baby. She was going to ask you to name him for her father. Maybe it's a power we don't know we have yet—the power to heal? Maybe we can."

"Start trying to figure it out. Rachael might know—find her, ask her. I want to save my son." Speaking of her didn't bring her. She was resting, or throwing a tantrum. I had managed to irritate or enrage another woman without knowing why. None of my relationships made sense, least of all the one with myself.

I sped home calling Emily at every stop, leaving messages for her that she didn't return. I hoped it was only because she didn't want to. God let her just be angry and alive to hate me.

CHAPTER 26

GRACE

We found a Catholic Church in Birmingham. There were several and we chose one randomly, following a sign on the highway. The historic marker indicated the church had been here since 1871. It was odd to see a church as a tourist attraction.

"Only in the south," Eric was smiling, as best a burning cinder of a man could. I think it amused him.

"Why can't you be normal?"

"What, like you? You look like a can of smashed assholes. I'd rather be burnt jerky thank you."

"Seriously, Rache comes in stripper and BBQ flavors, why are you only available in crispy and extra crispy?"

He thought about that a moment and of course, Rachael appeared.

"This is hard coming after you when you're off your meds, baby, can you please have a Xanax?"

"Fresh out."

"Yeah, and your roots are showing."

Rachael checked her hair in the Jeep mirror out of habit and Eric laughed himself into a snort.

I was amazed. "Ghosts can snort laugh?"

Rachael glared at him a moment then faded away to preserve her strength without a word. It was unusual for either of us to get the better of her so we silently savored the moment with a grin and a fist bump.

We made for the church, it was crawling with tourists and most of them were clean, in grace. Practically everyone who came out of the church was in a state of grace, protected from the demons and evoking a sense of amity from The Judge inside me. There was a notable exception. A priest was being walked by two others away from the building to a waiting car. He hosted a demon and one of the priests escorting him was hollow, ready for one to move in, though the third priest was in grace as was the waiting car's driver.

"Child predator," Eric explained. "He was on the news the other day and I'm surprised there isn't an army of press hounds around looking for an interview."

"What is he doing free?"

"The church handles most of those cases internally. The legal system rarely hears about it and usually can't do anything about it."

"I can."

"Yes, but then you'd be one of troller Abner's 'missionaries.' Do you want to be that guy?"

"My monster is called a judge, maybe I do. Maybe I'm supposed to."

"I don't think helping you kill a priest who may be rehabilitated yet, is a path back to grace for me."

I asked The Judge deep inside. He was resting and ignored me.

Eric read a sign to himself and turned to tell me, "We'll need to come back tomorrow, we missed the confession times."

"What?"

"Look at the schedule."

Confession Schedule
Saturday: 3:00-4:00pm
Monday-Friday: 11:30am-12:00pm

"I don't know what that means."

"That's when confession is available."

"So wait, how does this work? I still want to know why a child predator gets a pass!"

"Strike a nerve? The church is full of them. They're kind of an open secret. It's almost a rite of passage."

"Did it happen to you?"

"No. But I feel like I'm one of the lucky ones. My family had money and power and nobody would mess with us."

"I don't get it. Your witch monster mom marries a devout catholic—she lets him raise you like one. How does that work?"

"She was probably planning to sacrifice me or use me as a henchman or try and put a demon in me. Best I can guess from stuff Rachael says."

"You guys on speaking terms now?"

"Yeah, we're cool right now."

"That thing where you guys formed up in the big weird transformer thing, that was intense."

"It scared the shit out of me. Rachael wore me like a suit of armor, she just jumped in and took control."

"She drove the whole thing?"

"Yep, she's very powerful. She just grabbed me and took me. I couldn't do a damn thing about it. If I really angered her, she could snuff me out but together we were ferocious. While I need to keep on keeping on to help you and sis, I'll keep doing what I can to get along with her crazy ass."

"I hate to admit I love that ass."

"Wrong brain."

"Not sorry, Boss. So we have to come back tomorrow?"

"Yup. Might as well get your bone bag a place to sleep I'll hang out here, see what I can learn."

"You got to explain to me how this works. The whole confession and how it will restore you to a state of grace or whatever thing. I don't understand."

"Let's get a place for you to stay first."

"You know Sarah slept?"

"Rachael can too."

"You really got the shit end of the stick then, didn't you?"

Eric shrugged in response and followed with, "At least I didn't have to have sex with you."

The church was in the heart of downtown so I decided to get something to eat before I got a hotel. We explored town after finding a vacancy at a place near the cathedral. We found a lot of demons and I let The Judge roam a bit feeding on demons wherever he could find them. Cities are wonderful breeding grounds for evil.

Eric tried to explain this to me. He said it stemmed from the age of conflict of farmers vs. shepherds. It went all the way back to Cain and Abel and I knew nothing about that. Something about how farmers made laws and rules to oppress each other where Shepherds had a different approach to managing the self and the sheep sacrifices that God preferred. All I got from his rambling Sunday school lesson was that God would laugh at vegetarians.

I finally had to ask him to explain the confession, how to get a priest to give him absolution while he remained non-corporeal.

"Non what?"

"Dungeons and dragons word, I read shit."

"You can say that again. Shit."

"So why don't I find a priest who can see you? I bet there is one or two."

"You're right. I would expect the church to be a place the gifted might be drawn to, for a profession."

"Yeah, some churches are safe, and ghosts that can enter might stay there, or look there for help."

"Makes sense, but if we can't find a gifted then we should just go to the confessional. I'll walk you through it and he'll prescribe penance. I'll do it and hopefully that works."

"But you can't get into the churches."

177

"This one I can."

"How do you know?"

"Remember that pedophile? His demon didn't have to wait outside. I'm guessing I can get in too."

"I still think you should let me kill that priest."

"When you get rid of me after this is over, you still want to be a serial killer, be my guest."

"I like vigilante superhero, I'm not a serial killer."

"Spoken like a missionary."

"I should never have told you about that adventure with Abner."

"Well you did, dumbass. It sucks to be alive, doesn't it?"

"It does suck, it really does suck!" My sarcastic taunt didn't please him so he punched me in the arm leaving a stinging blister and evaporated. I got some sleep and thought about the task ahead of us tomorrow. I worried it was too simple, that surely this god who seemed to love tragedy wouldn't allow such a simple fix to such an enormous problem for us.

Sure enough the next morning we did run into a media circus outside the church. One of the alleged victims had killed himself after he felt justice was denied and the internet trolls leaked his identity. There were a bunch of tortured, partially consumed souls and hollow shells out front crying for blood. There were some souls in grace with them. I wonder if the priests—the predators, were taking souls and leaving their victims like that, hollow and broken or if the rape left them vulnerable to hollowing out. There was a lot to learn about how all this worked.

There were ghosts too. Ghosts of other suicides who had not been damned right away but held on and I found one who was not in a murderous rage. I asked Eric to talk with him about the situation here. Sure enough one of the priests here was a gifted mortal who we could reasonably expect to help us.

We had only a small window for confession. With a sense of purpose I wove through the mob of protestors, penetrating the wall of sorrow and indignation by way of a somber section of sedentary or fatigued participants. It was easy enough to get through them without disturbing The Other or having to be pepper sprayed by the police.

I explained to one of the officers at a control point that I was here for services. I must have seemed harmless enough. The badge, a metro cop, checked me with one of those handheld metal detectors and waved me in. Inside the perimeter there were more cops and parishioners talking and making their way to and from the cathedral. I stopped and looked at Eric a moment, he looked at me.

"You know what? You're right. I don't need you to come. I'll be able to find this gifted mortal and you and The Judge might only muck things up with your black out fuckery."

He was reading my surface thoughts so naturally now he didn't think to give me the courtesy of talking and thinking I was a separate entity. It annoyed me and without me saying anything he apologized, promising not to do that again. He complained that my thoughts had the same sound as my voice so it might happen by accident in the future. I thought that that would be fine and the quicker communication could come in handy in a tactical situation.

I went in and sat in a pew while Eric went searching for the gifted human priest. There I picked up a book I guess was a hymnal or a missal. I pretended to read it. A square of paper fell out. It was a folded piece of composition book paper. It had yellowed some, suggesting it was old and the book hadn't been used in a while. I unfolded the paper and noticed some symbols in what looked like a coded message. Something kids might pass to fight boredom.

The Judge didn't stir. I looked around me to see if there was anything I needed to worry about. There was nothing. I was becoming restless and watched people line up to do their confessions. I wandered a bit then sat back down. I didn't do waiting very well these days. I went outside for a camel and saw the alleged predator priest and different priestly escorts coming through a police barricade to a side entrance.

The church wasn't safe, demons could enter here. I had to be more vigilant! I raised an alarm inside and The Judge stirred to life. I felt his wrath welling up inside. I don't know why but I found myself walking towards the demonic clergyman and he seemed to sense me coming for him. I called the tendril up to strike but though I felt The Judge lash out, the fire and the crushing black whips didn't appear. The priest turned to face me. I felt a burning and I nearly blacked out from the surge of power. A pillar of lightning crashed into his party. Sadly the escorts were killed too. I was knocked from my feet landing on my ass and palms.

The lighting came from above. It was a sunny day, without a cloud in the sky. This happened in front of at least a hundred witnesses and dozens of news cameras. I picked myself up and wiped the grit from my palms. I went into the church as a crowd pressed in around the dead men outside. Some were praising a miracle, a sign of God's love and divine justice. I laughed as I entered the cathedral. It wasn't God, just an angry near-indestructible orphan with a chip on his shoulder and an aeons-old cosmic demon killing monstrosity at his disposal. If that wasn't the makings of a superhero I couldn't think what would be.

It was chaos as ambulances, police, firemen and mortals scrambled. The demons and other evils fled, knowing the source of the lightning. The Judge was roused and looking for more. Knowing everything had left the immediate scene and for the sake of the people in the area I turned The Other loose and I let him range far and wide.

Eric found me as I stood before the altar area–my eyes transfixed on The Judge's view of events not the world before my body. He found a witches' den with souls needing me. The Judge couldn't release them without me. I learned something new, barely aware Eric was standing there. The Other was going to start murdering haunted women, the witches, I couldn't let that happen, could I? I wasn't at the scene. There was nothing to tie me to it. I could let him rampage and later after the crime scene was clear, enter and release the ghosts. Time didn't matter to them, certainly not a day or two.

"You have to call him off!"

Eric heard my thoughts. I was beginning to smile and Eric must have sensed malevolence in me. He struck me with his own ghost fire and there in the church before the people already startled by the death of three ranking members of their diocese, I began to burn. My clothes did anyway. Then there was rage–I saw Eric and I saw The Other rushing home to defend me. Eric was doomed, but I was in real danger too. Eric could hurt me even with The Other tethered to me. Without him, I was feeling his full wrath and if he had a little more strength and the will, he might have been able to maim or even kill me.

I ran to the water on that pedestal near the other entry and extinguished the flame as frightened civilians fled in terror. The Other came tearing in at full tilt and anchored to me, whipping spectral flame about in defense. Eric didn't back down but advanced aware of his power now and the reaction of The Judge he might have mistook for fear. It went back down- I pushed it back down and fled from the church.

Eric followed. When he came out I could see his mark was gone. He was restored to grace. He shouted an apology as I backed away from the church in disbelief of his attack. I was still burning somehow, the wounds stung. Some of the humans around could see The Other and they fled in a panic or collapsed in a faint. He was whipping the walls of the chapel around the entrance Eric was standing in but it couldn't strike him there. It wanted to. I wanted to.

The Other made a line in the pavement before me, whipping a black burning gouge. Someone had to diffuse this now! It was going to get ugly. We weren't the kind of friends who could fight and hug it out afterward. Our "fists" were lethal. One punch could end either of us. I had the advantage but Rachael may have taught him...paranoia. That was my paranoia talking. She came and stood between us crying with outstretched arms for calm. She tried to take Eric like she did before, join with him but in his grace she couldn't touch him. He was mighty and she was the weakling.

She came to me, grabbed my face as The Other was surging. It didn't fear her, it let her in close she got in my face and spoke softly to me, talking me down. She kissed me and I pushed harder so The Judge would retreat.

Satisfied I was in control, it slumbered again but it was a fitful slumber waiting for Eric to drop his guard.

I couldn't hear their conversation as she went to him but she calmed him. They had a language all their own it seemed. They could think at each other. Eric came out and just asked me if I was finished trying to be a hero.

"Are we done here? There is a den we need to cleanse. Then we can finish the trip home."

"I don't want to kill anymore," Eric said. Rachael hung her head in exasperation.

"Everything kills, it's just what we do. If you stop whining I'll teach you to sleep and eat again."

Eric's demeanor completely shifted at the prospect of a meal.

"Will I taste it?"

"If you calm the fuck down, I can teach you to, yes. It's expensive and painful, can't do it often…but I can show you."

"Okay." He turned to me. "What do we do, Boss?"

"I'm not insensitive to your aversion to killing. I don't want to draw more witch attention so, I'm sorry I was giving in to anger, revenge, hate. I was letting something take me. The Other's appetite maybe, I needed stopped. So thank you both. I want to keep you in grace, Eric."

I turned to my trash fire, "If he kills, will he be corrupted?"

"Absolutely, if he lets you kill, same thing. Self-defense exemption or defense of the innocent but the kill has to be absolutely necessary, if it seems excessive it is and it will break you."

"Okay, we don't do it. Next trip, but I need you guys to help me watch the den. We're going to surveil it and learn their identities and their routines then raid the den and liberate the souls. We can stage a distraction in case we need one, got it?"

Both ghosts nodded.

In three days we learned this den was led by a single demon, one of modest rank and power. The others were all initiated and ready to inherit and were cousins and other relations. Rachael wondered why they hadn't all found their own demon, what kind of weird "perverted" ritual set or rules they were following.

"Kill them because they're 'wannabes' and more dangerous in some ways than the real thing," Rachael advised.

Eric seconded the warning citing the danger of a novice with drive, or the power of stupid people in groups. He didn't want to kill anyone, though, and again made his opposition to that clear.

Rachael apologized and we started to work up a plan as we continued watching them. We followed them and learned they worked in hospitals and nursing homes. They took sick babies, coma ward patients and other "easy pickings" as Rachael called them and kept them in their den. They would feed the demon one from time to time and keep the rest to grow their group's power.

During this time Rachael taught Eric to sleep and eat. He enjoyed a bucket of fried chicken and mashed potatoes and gravy, biscuits, potato wedges and a bottle of champagne and said he felt a bit queasy. Rachael said it was his imagination.

"You had withdrawals, too, though, isn't that imagination?"

"It was. I have a powerful intellect and imagination to match."

"Touché."

Eric dozed and slept the sleep only the dead can know. I took the opportunity to spend some time with Rachael alone. "Can he hear us talk when he sleeps, read my thoughts?"

"No. He is dead when he's sleeping." She came closer and was intrigued, "What did you have in mind, baby?"

"Can we kill the demon, while he is 'dead' asleep, without harming him?"

She nodded. "I thought you might want something else. I can love you, baby."

"Would you still have energy enough to kill the head demon?"

"No. But we wouldn't want Eric to know we broke our agreement would we?"

She was right, that might be too much and end our partnership. "I can't lose this friend."

"Then let's play, baby. You need it, it's been a long time."

"Can you?" She pressed her fingers to my lips and took control.

We roused Eric after enjoying each other and a long nap. Then it hit me.

"Rache, the chants and stuff I was trying to learn. Can we use those on this weaker demon? Break it loose in practice and kill it and not her host?"

She gave it a long think. "Yes."

I reviewed the Psalms and chants I had introduced Eric to earlier on this road trip. Rachael had heard some of them and watched us practice. She offered tearful congratulations. She helped with the proper way to say the words and the chants rhythms. She helped prepare a garment with the symbols that would strengthen the attacks and commands. The symbols would be placed under my street clothes. So concealed their power, she assured me would both be effective and surprise the foe.

We learned they were having a mass on this very evening so I ate a good meal and we prepared. We brought restraints we bought at the Walmart and went into the den we had spent several days watching. It was a home, an old three-story mansion on the northwest corner of a major intersection. It was a historic building and made of locally-quarried stone. There was a servant entrance, still being used and a gate surrounding the entire property that occupied half the city block. The rest of the block was divided into smaller homes, probably once servants' quarters.

They were eight small bungalows with their own generous gardens. The house was lit brightly. Servants were preparing meals for the witches meeting in the basement and beds for them after their black conjuring.

Rachael went in first to take a look. She was evil and would not attract their attention or invite an attack as Eric would. She returned from her reconnaissance to inform us that they had all assembled now and that though there was little reason for it, this evening they were initiating a new member. Rachael believed it was because this new one was rich and it was almost being done as a lark.

I asked Eric what lark meant and they laughed. After explaining that, we decided it would teach this one a lesson seeing what we were going to do.

"Will the servants be a problem?" Eric wondered out loud.

"Nah," Rachael declared, "the basement is sealed and soundproof. They murder children in there so we just lock the door and do our thing. No one will know. We didn't see any kind of alarm or panic system so we can get in and sing our little Psalms, chant our little chants…"

Eric interrupted, "…Get down tonight!" He started dancing. It was terrific to see him like his old self. I forgot he was dead except for the skin on fire and melting all over the furniture.

"Rache, is there a way you can teach Eric to not look like a dumpster fire?"

She looked confusedly at each of us in turn, then again. "Yeah, but why, if someone we don't want to see him sees him, they react to it–I mean he's fucking terrifying and our automatic detect-a-witch alarm. And no one else can, so who gives a shit?"

"It's disturbing to me to see, I think it's freaking me out. Like when he was dancing. He threw his hip to one side and a chuck sloughed off and fell on the floor with a plop and a hiss. It was horrible, I almost threw up."

"You're such a softie, baby, I'm sorry I forget that all the time." And she kissed me three times. I thought of Brittney and her kiss hello, stay with me, goodbye. That routine of hers, she was good for me and to me and honest.

"Baby, you're drifting…I can still go take her, be her…"

"Don't you tease, I love you dead anyway, that meat bag will get old."

"There's the spirit, oh let me kill you already?"

"You can't, remember, The Judge?"

"Well let me show you how and pretend I did it."

"You two wanna do this today?"

We focused and made our assault. We looked like just one guy in a hoodie. Rachael teleported in and opened the door. Eric distracted the kitchen staff with a small pan flare up and I went into the basement. Rachael opened that door for me and we descended. Eric casting a light only I and the demon would perceive. Rachael hearing this thought whispered into his ear. He turned into the man I had known before the crash. But his light was gone. I could only see him by the faint reflected glow of candles coming from somewhere down below.

"Why do these cults always light everything with candles?"

I thought of the guest house and Emily that first night. Rachael looked back at me from her position on point and Eric smacked my head from behind me. Both said, "Focus." Together, we were becoming a team. We would need to be when we faced Mara.

Down below the ceremony was near its climax. The sacrifice, in this instance just a goat, was in the center of the Hollywood spectacle of a salty pentagram on the floor, black candles, symbols painted with supermarket butcher shop blood on the walls and very perfectly cut robes with vented flanks and silver piping and runes. I could hear Rachael rolling her eyes. She entered first and doused their light sources with her dark will.

They were unable to react then to me entering and binding the nearest robed fool. I started the chant and Eric brought the candles to roaring life, all but one of the figures fell to the floor trembling. Eric was strong enough right now and furious enough to be seen by the living. He was beautiful, not the ugly hateful hellfire of the first days but a burning fire of life and cleansing with bright sparkling embers like fireworks. He chanted and commanded the demon release its host.

Rachael beat one of the witches who tried to attack me as I bound yet another. She spent a lot of her strength to do it but she assured me she had plenty to spare. Eric paralyzed the demon but I had to hurry to join him. It would gain strength while ours would only ebb as the battle went on. An initiate on the floor, armed with a dagger tried to stab me but The Other struck her dead on the spot before I could react. I looked to Eric, he was unaffected. He remained in his God's good graces.

I understood Eric had his own god, a major power no doubt, but The Judge answered to another greater still, something as yet unfathomable. Rachael beat another cultist. I rose to chant with Eric and saw progress. Rachael kicked one of the witches and told her to look at the frauds she was giving her soul to and to watch the gods save her and punish the wicked. She rejoined our chanting and we pulled the demon free in less than fifteen minutes of this willful struggle.

As soon as the human was separated, before she even fell to the ground from where she was floating, two tendrils seized the demon. It was quickly broken, killed and The Other devoured it. We cheered. It was over. Eric lit the room with his spirit as the candles had disintegrated during the raid. The bound witches were sat up against a wall that they might see and hear Eric speak. He was visible still, his power had grown magnitudes beyond anything what he had before and he was not tiring it seemed.

"By Jesus you have been saved. These two were here to murder you in judgment for your crimes but through me, his humble servant, Jesus did speak, "Mercy be upon them who are led astray by the dark pretenders". So I convinced them to spare you. Will you turn your hearts back to the son, to the Lord and receive His mercy, His teachings and renounce this infernal craft and demonic powers forever?"

All were in agreement, the head witch herself an unwilling inheritor pleaded with her followers to turn to the light and do as Eric was telling them. "But how?" One asked him.

Rachael looked at me and said, "Some of these souls may yet be revived. Release them quickly before the hospital harvests their organs."

I began my work and as I touched the living souls, they became visible too, their living strength so great that they showed themselves to their tormentors to scar their memory and shame them. Eric started into some sermon and Rachael said, "We won, we have done a great thing and saved so many souls, even I must admit it feels good. I'm touched by your choice to do this, baby. I'm sorry I wanted to kill you so I could have you all to myself." She cried and carefully stepped close to me and rested against me. "Hold me." I did.

Eric remained behind in Birmingham while I travelled north. Rachael and I saw on the news that night at our hotel stop that a dozen vegetative patients awoke from their slumbers simultaneously that evening and were being hailed as some kind of new group of apostles. Each claiming to have been visited by a friend of Jesus, one of his prophets not yet known, his name was Eric. There was pandemonium in the national media as several other coma patients, other ill or paralyzed people got their souls back and revived singing the same story. They were visited in some awful dark place by the prophet Eric and two angels that traveled beside him. One, a sword he called Rachael, the other, his shield.

I had become a sidekick. I was amazed at how something like this could take off in the media and take on a life of its own. Then the crazies took it to a whole new level. Other people saw Eric rescue their cats from trees, or named their children born that day after him, Eric or Erika. We followed his exploits, real and what we guessed were imagined, all the way home to McKnightstown where I summoned him to my side. He knew about the adventures, the hoaxes and all the craziness. He said only he wished he hadn't let it get so out of hand but was glad for the good that was done and the focus on Jesus's word that he had shared. He said he didn't want to talk about it and I said it was fine with me so long as he was ready for this next mission. He nodded. We spotted our highway exit and began the final leg of our journey.

CHAPTER 27

CHOICES

I rolled back into town passing the estate. Eric said that Emily was inside with some nurses, a doctor, a whole team of medical types. Lisa was there but Mara was not found. Despite our Alabama adventure, I found myself unsure about Rachael and her loyalty and Eric's as well. I needed to prepare. I went to the apartment and sat. I had a good long chat with the team.

"What odds do you give us, Rache?"

"You can win if there is any luck in the universe, we will win."

"I feel like we might be missing something."

Eric chimed in, "Good, you're thinking right, Sergeant. You're ready, looking for that one more thing you can do."

"Alright, that seems legit." Then it dawned on me, "You should lead the op, you're senior."

"You've been promoted to magician, and 'King of the Judges,' so I'm out. Plus I'm dead, they might be able to beat me easier than you."

"We need guns, bro."

"Why do we need guns?"

"I'm new to the whole magician thing. I'm not confident I can do everything with these powers. Play to your strengths, right? I'd rather have 'em and not need 'em."

"Okay, well, sounds like paperwork we can't afford now."

"I'm not doing paperwork. It'll be night soon. Rache, you're good with precision movements, what you did to my eye, the battle with the demons, fighting me."

"Yes, I'm way more precise than either of you lunks."

"Did she say lunks?"

"Can you open locks?"

She nodded mischievously.

I prepared what seemed like a last meal. We went and got lobsters and steaks and a bottle of sparkling cider. We cooked together and ate together. We laughed about what we had been through and things we forgot to do in life, falling in love, having kids, making love outside. Things we would miss the most, ice cream, blow jobs. Things we are glad we didn't have to do, that first colonoscopy, taxes, awkward first dates or head colds that lingered.

We parked down the road from the hardware store. McKnightstown was the kind of place where the "hardware store" sold guns. Rachael went in, Eric followed. "I wanna see this, I need to learn if I'm gonna be like this a while."

She whistled from the back door after a few minutes. I met her and Eric there. "The alarm system is just for show, it's never actually worked. Come on in and take your time." I got a tactical vest and a Kimber custom 1911 in .45. It had a match grade barrel and all the bells and whistles I would not need or appreciate. I found a holster and attached it to the vest. The Kimber didn't fit so I dumped it for a stock 1911 in a matte finish.

I loaded four magazines, eliciting a puzzled response from Eric. "Four. Four mags, that's for my one sister, couple of nurses and my mom?"

I shrugged, "Never know, remember that time we ran out? The whole squad ran out?"

"That was a shit show."

"Yeah, we were throwing rocks and helmets."

"Okay, 'nuff said. Better grab a long gun in case you have to reach out and touch someone. And an extra box of ACP"

"Snipers?"

"It's a big estate."

We got some flashlights and I selected a simple lever action Marlin scout in .45-70 government. There was only one box of ammo for that, it was dusty. I loaded the gun and Rachael handed me an attractive sling which held a dozen rounds giving me enough stopping power to drop a herd of elk. Rachael continued searching, "Do you think they have grenades?"

Eric and I chuckled. "Doubt it."

"I always wanted to throw one."

I thought about the back room or basement safe. Rachael went to search and found it, opened it and discovered grenades. They were flashbangs but those seemed like they would be fun for her, I took two and promised her I'd let her throw one, either in the fight or to celebrate afterward. She liked that idea and we loaded ourselves back into the Jeep.

We drove to the estate. On the way Rachael said she was having so much fun she felt like she was in the army with us. She lamented not joining and said if she had to do it over again, she would. Eric said, "Yeah, it was great for my career and future." We all laughed.

When we got there Rachael opened the gate. We parked at the edge of the gravel circular driveway. We surveyed the place. My ghosts vanished, fanning out in a spectral search of the property. Finding no threats they returned to assure me it was safe.

"I never thanked you for teaching me how to eat as a ghost, Rachael. I take back all the shit I talked about you."

Rachael was taken aback by this. "Oh, well, you're welcome."

"Focus, guys." I slung my rifle and made both guns ready to fire.

I entered the house. Three nurses were having a meal downstairs. I pointed the .45 at them. "No one has to die. You stay put do what you're doing. I'm just here to talk, understand?" They nodded. "Are any of you armed?"

"We're nurses, we're just here to make Ms. Salem comfortable."

"Good, one of you come with me, I want a volunteer or I might get shootey." They looked at each other and they decided the on-call should go. She stood up and said she'd come with me. "What's your name?"

"Sarah."

"That's a nice name, Sarah. I had a friend named Sarah, that's what we're gonna be right now, friends. Let's go and see Emily, okay? You go first." I followed Sarah upstairs to Emily's room.

Mara was there with a pair of lab coats attending to Emily. A tear fought its way free at the sight of her. I had missed her and only now did I know how much. I wanted to kiss her. I touched her hand. She was cold, her skin dry. Her beauty was fading but she was still that woman whose gentleness and beauty threatened to crack me. Today she was dying. She was still and unconscious. I cleared my throat and thought about shooting everyone. The Other stirred and my ears rang. No one attacked me, Mara was calm. Eric and Rachael were behind me. Mara looked at them saving her most vicious gaze for Rachael. Mara then turned again and spoke to Eric.

"Eric, my boy, my dear, sweet boy, Momma's sorry. I was only trying to protect you."

"So you could feed me to your demon."

"It's not like that, son, you'd have been a god."

"I'm the man with the gun, maybe you should save your breath for me, old woman."

She scowled at me. "No manners, what a pity. You think that gun frightens me any more than it might you, boy?"

I relaxed my stance keeping the gun ready but showing her I was ready to talk. I looked at a chair and Rachael brought it to me, I sat. "Okay, I just came to talk."

"You want a truce?"

"No, demon, I want you away from my family."

Mara stopped pretending to be human. Her eyes turned over white and her voice was that of some otherworldly nightmare, not the frail old woman before us. Even Rachael cringed. "You think because you weakened me by stealing my cattle that I can be drawn out of the blood that is mine by right?"

I chambered a round, "I didn't come here for a confrontation, I can just start shooting and see what happens if you want to go there."

The demon relaxed and was Mara again, at least in appearance and voice. The lab coats there were terror-stricken and unable to move. I turned my attention to them. "What's Emily's status?"

The older fellow in white spoke. "She's no longer in a medically-induced coma, but only sleeping peacefully. Her baby is fine, though Emily has maybe a month at the outside. She is having some extreme difficulties owing to her sustained injuries, the lightning strike, as much as the cancer. So she is on bedrest. If you need to speak to her, we can wake her."

"Not yet." I was hoping to be able to wrap this whole thing up and tell her afterward that all would be well. No need for her to be awake and see me kill her mother. I wanted to get Mara in another room to talk. I didn't want to chance injuring Emily. "Mara, can we talk in another room, leave the doctors to their work?"

She thought a moment then decided it would be wise, for neither of us wanted harm to come to the baby. Mara, sensing her time was up perhaps, began to offer a bargain. "I can make you wealthy, boy, give you all the earthly pleasures if you leave this place and never return. Take your monster to hunt and feed elsewhere. There are many easier meals in California."

"You're mad. I want my son. I can't leave him with you."

"You are young, you can have more children. Many more. Much time, you have a full life ahead of you, a life you can start now."

We went downstairs where the other nurses were no longer to be found.

She was right and I hated her for it. She was desperate. I had time, she did not. The baby, my son was her last chance for renewal. Had she planned for this? I worried about why she was so calm, had I walked into a carefully-laid trap? I decided I would buy time for Rachael to do her work. Rachael had remained behind, upstairs with a supply of my blood. Her tasks was a special part of our mission, one that neither Eric nor I could perform. I trusted her to paint Emily with the powerful writing and symbols that would stop Mara's demon from finding refuge within her.

"What are you offering?"

"Anything your heart desires. You know you can have the women you desire. I command many, I can gift you the most beautiful companion for you."

"And she would kill me in my sleep."

"The Judge will protect you, no doubt."

"You'd know where I was, you'd need to know. You'd never let me be. My family would always be under your threat, control."

"I can protect you, them, even from you and your monster."

That should be enough time. Rachael should be done. I began a series of chants and Psalms to paralyze the demon. Mara contorted into her true form.

She was a hideous caricature of a living thing, nothing like the old woman. Her head was beaklike with rows of misshapen teeth jutting from it. Her eyes were bulbous and milky white, sitting atop her head–she could probably see all around her. Her limbs cracked and snapped, having many segments like a spider. Her arms and legs split into eight of these legs. Her body floated near the ceiling, her tongue was like a bullwhip, it lashed at me but the runes hidden in my clothes deflected her attacks.

The demon seemed to suffer great discomfort from my chanting. She was not separated from Mara however, nor was she unable to fight. She raged and hissed and threatened us. She hurled furniture and anything not tied down at us. Eric pleaded with his mother to help him in his battle with the monster. I could sense the spirit of a young girl inside the demon. Mara was taken as a young girl. I felt bad for her. Was she a victim too?

Eric burned protective writing around me in the floor and joined me in singing, though he couldn't make his voice heard by the living now. He hadn't the strength restored yet. His week of playing Jesus had sapped him. We hoped against hope his effort would lend some strength to our magic. Mara didn't seem particularly alarmed, more surprised at our inventiveness than anything.

We managed to achieve a stalemate until Rachael rejoined us. "Done!" She joined the chanting to separate Mara and her demon. Mara was becoming angry and lashed out, it was working! Now she lashed me with fire trying to burn my garments and their protective runes away. The Other was trying to respond, to counterattack. It was unthinking and only wanted to kill the demon but it might kill everyone. I couldn't have that. I struggled to keep it in check until the moment was right. I had been wounded. If I was knocked out or killed it was all over. The demon was getting to me. I had to let The Other out like at the spring. I fell into the center of its writhing coils with its powerful tendrils shielding me.

Mara summoned a horde of powerful warrior demons. They came in a horrible and perverse assortment of shapes and sizes. They all appeared an impossible combination of parts of other creatures, things themselves that should not have been. Seeing them I remembered fear, thought long forgotten now behind The Other's protection. The demon's army came up through the floor, the walls, the windows or lumbering in through the doors to the backyard. They howled, hissed and spat hatred, fire and venom at us. The Other loosed all of its limbs and with effort I was able to guide most of his strikes and continue the chanting to free Mara from the demon that possessed her. But it was getting stronger and we were getting tired.

Rachael fought with the grace and precision of a ballerina on fire. She could only kill one at a time but she could keep others off her as she murdered the monsters methodically. I had trouble keeping my eyes off my beautiful trash fire. Eric could not be touched by the demons and he chanted on, though his strength waned.

I and The Other cut down demons, handfuls at a time, but we were damaging the home. We splintered walls and furniture, atomized the stair rails, shattered chandeliers and left exposed wires sparking, torn from the walls. Mara kept calling them from the beyond. I could see that while the foe was gaining strength, its host body was unconscious, it was exhausted and dying. Then the demons captains arrived to see what was depleting their army. Upon spotting me the demon lords joined in our attack on Mara, hoping to dislodge her from her body and end this costly battle.

The demon lords were fearful of their losses at my hand and avoided attacking me. Mara fought them off, hurling them away and The Other would catch them, unwilling to let them live once it had sensed them. It seized and crushed them in tendrils but it was costly in time and energy to do it. Each wave of demons was stronger, took more to kill. For a time each tendril was occupied with a demon wrapped up in a crushing grip. The Other was clubbing foes with the dying ones that it was constricting as quickly as it could.

Eric kept chanting but he was fading fast. Rachael hid within my shield of writhing coils. She said she was catching her breath but I knew she was depleted. Her spirit was dying and Mara was only getting stronger. The Other strained against me, trying to kill the demon. It had sought this quarry for a hundred years or more and was going berserk trying to get at her. He was hurting me and draining my strength. Demons swarmed over us now, it was hard to breathe. Only Eric was untouched by the foul beasts. He stopped chanting and was back to exhorting his mother to fight the demon and help him.

Mara's body was now limply capering about like a puppet on a string, still possessed by the demon. She looked human again. She was helpless now, awaiting final destruction. Though the demon could still whip me with fire, rake me with sharp metal whips and bring demons to help her attack Rachael and I. Emily appeared at the stair but she was enraged at the sight of her mother's frail form flopping about in midair. She looked at me with the same blame and hate-filled eyes Eric did in the early days all those months ago. "Why have you done this?"

"Emily, I'm trying to take the demon out so I can destroy it!"

"But how?" Emily seemed genuinely surprised, "Can you do this?"

"I think so!"

The demon then shook its head joyously snickering with a hateful intent. "It's too late. I'll take her now!"

I was realizing what I needed to do but resisted it, trying to find another smarter way. Mara was lost, perhaps, and would never survive this battle, but she was a victim too. She was not my enemy. Generations upon generations had been victims of a bargain of blood and souls for infernal powers. I had to destroy this thing but I was alone now. My allies had faded away. Even Rachael with all her boasting had seen her strength fail her against the full fury of the demon's wrath. I could crush Mara but would need The Other's full power, something I could not yet control and still feared.

"Emily, get out, run quickly before it's too late!" But it already was.

Rachael found some last measure of strength and stood beside me whispering into my ear, "Baby, it's too late, we failed. There is only one way. Do you understand?" I did. Rachael was fighting back tears, "I'm sorry, only now because I love you, have I realized why you must do this, why it's the only way for you. I hate the world and the gods for this!" She held my face in her hands keeping my eyes locked with hers a moment.

Knowing the way out, the only way to win made The Other thrash about ferociously. He knew what I was planning. The demon struck Emily, cutting her legs out from under her, spilling her on the ground. "No!" I screamed nearly losing my grip on The Judge. The demon looked at me.

"I can kill her, boy. And take the child. The doctors will ensure it lives. So I will enjoy renewal. If you release the Hexxenhammer, it will kill us all, you will fail. If you keep the enraged beast so close to his quarry, you will smother him and he will kill you with his last gasp trying to escape your control and you will lose."

Emily struggled to her feet, accidentally wiping the runes painted in my blood away from her skin, making herself vulnerable to the demon. The monster abandoned Mara and took Emily. Emily was stronger, healthier if only by a small measure, giving the demon new power and further enraging my judge.

Eric cried out with what little strength he had left, "Revive my mother if you can, she can help!"

I moved to the old woman just in time to deflect a whipping attack that was meant to finish the old woman. "Rache, can you help her?"

"Yes, baby!" Rachael tried to revive the old woman and I tried not to murder my family while defending them all. Rachael turned her gaze to Emily, "I hate you, I wish I had killed you when I had the strength."

Emily laughed maniacally and shrieked at me, whipping me with renewed fury. I was bleeding and burnt terribly. I felt reality cracking, my mind was fracturing. I couldn't think what to do. I felt trapped. I didn't know if I could contain The Judge much longer. Three of his tendrils were broken, severed and nearly useless. It was mad with rage and hunger.

Mara came to and looked around. Rachael helped her to her feet and the two chanted at the demon in Emily, Eric resumed his prayers and chanting for his sister, this time appealing to Jesus directly. The demon seemed to realize it made a mistake letting the supremely knowledgeable Mara go before she was completely incapacitated or dead. She tried desperately to kill the old woman. She pulled a section of the floor above down, spilling a bedroom suite onto the old woman, or rather me and my writhing barriers. The pain was becoming intense, not just from the bruising attacks but from The Other trying to fight its way out. It was cooking me like it had the cholo, rage burning inside my blood.

The struggle proved to be too much for Mara, she collapsed again. The heat and choking dust, the smoke and the wild magical energies took her out of the fight. I looked to Emily, "I love you Emily, please, baby, fight this thing!"

It laughed at me with her face and voice.

I turned to Rachael, "Have we lost?"

She nodded and a tear rolled down her cheek.

"Rache, is The Judge immune to the cancer?"

"He can cure it as he heals you."

"Will the baby be as I am?"

"Yes."

"And Emily?"

"So long as she and baby are together."

I raised the gun to my head. "I love you."

The demon howled, "No!"

I pulled the trigger. I never heard the only shot that rang out that night.

EPILOGUE

I watched my brother limply fall, his head splattered into a million bony shards and droplets of gore. I wept, too weak to take any other action. Rachael fell beside him crying and shaking, pounding the floor with a balled fist. I watched The Judge emerge from him and dive into my sister's belly. My sister shuddered as the demon was forced out. It crawled back to the refuge of my unconscious and dying mother. Emily was filled with strength and life. She was healing and drawing strength from the monster now in her womb. The demon tried to kill Emily before The Judge could protect her in a mad spasm of vengeance, but it was too late. The demon's razor whips and flames were repulsed.

The Judge had possessed the baby and he had no ability to suppress it or fight it as his father may have done. With the power of a new life full of promise and his mother's love, The Judge was finally able to let its full power loose. In one terrible swift stroke it ended the demon and Mara. It destroyed most of this ancient home and the surrounding buildings were also left in ruin. Every living thing on the property was extinguished, every blade of grass, insect, everything. Emily emerged from the rubble, shielded by a writhing mass of deadly consequence.

That's how I saw that thing. It wasn't of my God, it was something else.

She could see me now. "Brother, I'm sorry."

"Did you help Mom?"

She nodded. "Some, I should be sorry."

"I loved him, you know, as much as I loved you."

"I'm sorry I didn't. I could have."

"I know. It was a shame what you did, what happened to him."

"What will you call his son?"

"I wanted to name him after Dad."

"William? Dreadful."

"Did you have a better name in mind?"

"Yes."

There was light in the rubble, Rachael lifted my brother from the heap of broken timbers and plaster. He looked to us with a tear in his eye then faded into nothingness. Rachael unfurled her new wings and followed him into eternity.

He had heard what Emily said and went away hoping for happiness in the beyond for there was none in this world for him no matter his best efforts.

"Will you stay with us, Eric?"

"Yes, I owe it to him. I had thought it was I that was suffering all this time. I was selfish and self-centered. He was a leaf in the stream, helpless. I blamed him for it and it wasn't fair. You could have ended his suffering, you knew the spells, didn't you?"

Emily didn't respond to that. The sound of the house being crushed had attracted attention from neighbors a mile away, sirens and lights. Emily was taken to the hospital. The Judge had cured her cancer, the doctors hailed it as a miracle. The baby was delivered the next day. I knew it was his gift. He gave her his life so she could raise the boy. That child would see me and I would tell him of his father over his mother's objections. I would protect him, so he wouldn't be the last Salem's son. I followed the pair ever after.

Over the years, Emily would discard our family's legacy of magical meddling with the world and the lives of others. She never admitted to planning to take The Judge in this way but I had my suspicions. I never spoke to her again. She knew I was there, sometimes she counted on it. She would leave the baby unattended and I would, having grown stronger than Rachael ever was, save the baby from some danger, a fall into a pool, an aggressive neighbor's dog and the army recruiters.

I have never encountered another haunt or judge since. From time to time I work a miracle here or there, though, and let the beneficiary praise their god, chance, luck or fate for it. While I never found another witch or judge I did meet a harvester, an angel of death who called herself Debt. She had murdered whole worlds and would be my first love.

AFTERWORD

The book you hold in your hand has taken shape but slowly. I had originally thought to write about my annoyance with government, hence the references to *Catch-22*. I was in the air force in 2004 when this idea first was discussed at a bar with a woman who might have done for the inspiration behind the hero's love interest. I had decided when I started writing that I would never include a superfluous love interest in any of my works. So why so many love interests in this work?

It was a rather accidental thing.

Originally the witches were to be just ghosts. But ghosts were too amorphous a nemesis. There was no tension with them in danger, there was no danger. So the hero could destroy them and no one cared. So I decided to put living beings behind them.

Why not other men, you may ask. Well, that turned the story into an action movie screenplay and diluted the focus of masculine energy shared by our nameless hero and his incendiary companion Eric.

More masculine adversaries meant the hero didn't stand out. Trooper Oldham was originally to be a woman. With Leslie behind a badge, the two sparely revealed characters ran together so Oldham became a rare male opponent (overcome by Rachael). Who better then to cast as the relatable human powers behind the ghost foe? Witches. Yes society has been scapegoating them for centuries. Witches are women.

Women are not simple creatures and defy description by this writer's humble skill, so I had to write many. A single witch is no threat, but a coven—that's a problem. With many female personas to craft (if poorly), I could exaggerate each to some degree to differentiate them and not have to worry if I didn't get the ONE perfect. That was a major obstacle in the beginning.

Originally, Emily (at one point Sarah) was to be the heroine opposite the hero but she was too stabilizing an influence and I would have to craft her perfectly with all the pages she would occupy. She then became an obstacle and—you might decide for yourself now if she is love interest, enemy or friend. She's a little bit of all of it, because she is a woman and I can't explain her. She took on a life of her own and I will never claim to understand or own or control her, she wrote her own bits.

The hero was supposed to struggle with PTSD, something I was at the time only beginning to understand myself and was not yet willing to accept I suffered from. Nor was A.A. to be a part of the story as I was writing this in a bar (as I wrote the hardest bits of Sigrunn's Saga). Facing my own addiction issues allowed me to explore this and as I learned in treatment these two problems often dovetail, I decided they would be further challenges for the hero to overcome. I needed a feminine nurturing influence in there to lift him in the parts that would see him recovering so he could fail again and suffer still greater anguish.

Some might wonder why I destroyed the traditional hero arc, the departure, death/rebirth and return three basic act arc. I didn't. We just begin the story *in media res*, with act two opening the story. We learn about act one in the rest of the tale because it's just boring war stuff: burning shit, digging holes, dodging bullets, fixing tank treads, replacing radio batteries, yelling about stupid shit, trying to find a place to sleep, shit and eat and the perpetual waiting. I didn't set out to write a war book.

Others may wonder why (and how!) I kept the hero nameless. Short answer–Dashell Hammett's model for Sam Spade was nameless, he could do it why not me? The hero originally did have a name, it wasn't finalized and I never liked it for him. Fumbling with a name was an annoyance.

Long answer–the hero represents so many anonymous forgotten Soldiers I didn't want to stick a moniker on there that failed to live up to the many great names that deserved to be honored or memorialized. I had one ship to name and too many heroes that deserved that honor. If I had fallen short in portraying him, and the name was done as a tribute to a friend's son who died in Baquaba in 2008 (CPL Luke Runyan 2nd Infantry Division), would that be ill received or cause slight or insult? I didn't want that kind of controversy to detract from the story. So keeping him nameless, while difficult or clumsy at times (as when Brittney points to his surname on his coat) was to me worth the effort, an enjoyable challenge and not a marketing gimmick. If the story was good, his name didn't matter.

Any offense to those anonymous and forgotten folks the book is dedicated to is purely accidental, with the exception of the government types. To the rest, I apologize for any insult. It wasn't intentional but rather accidental owing to my lack of talent.

A note about witches and alternate faith paths, I borrow liberally and make up a lot of stuff. None again meant to offend, appropriate or insult anyone. I take from the Old Testament, the Lakota, even making a subtle nod to the controversy surrounding the misappropriation of the sweat lodge, with our hero siding with the Lakota here (despite similar traditions in Nordic and other peoples' traditions). I mention traditional faiths that I have an even poorer understanding of but cast them mostly as bystanders in the cosmic war of good and evil that is the backdrop for our hero's journey of self-discovery, healing and ultimately failure.

Or success. I believe in a life beyond, I believe I've glimpsed it. It's not pretty but it is there. In my mind the hero doesn't fail in the end. In the Stoic, traditional masculine sense, he wins. It takes tremendous courage to do what he does in the end. He had gotten past being suicidal earlier in the book and was now not only devoted to living but hoping to save his family. That family was at the finale, about to be destroyed by 1) cancer and 2) an ancient supernatural being. Discovering he had one path to defeat these foes, and knowing the cost he didn't hesitate. That's what is "best in men" the example set for him by Eric's selfless act. Our hero himself observes Eric's example of self-sacrifice as being the fatherly apex of masculinity in the first part of the story.

He also knows his own parent, his mother (or father), did the same for him.

So is it about masculinity? To some degree, yes, but only as a dramatic tool and motivation for the masculine energy beset by the (twisted and evil) feminine energies of the witch. This isn't done as a commentary about society's current imbroglio over "toxic masculinity" and "third wave feminism" that it might perfectly analogize. It's just classic dramatic structure (yin-yang). I have no intention of wading into current societal conflicts. I'm a Stoic and Cynic, I don't care—these things are like the weather to me. I might have decided to pursue such an angle for marketing but I don't want to alienate any audiences. I cast male and female characters in good and bad lights.

Oldham is an evil bastard. Rachael is at once good and bad. Brittney and Sarah are only light. Our hero and Eric both switch back and forth. Abner is pure evil. So clearly the book is not trying to assign virtue to a gender and wade into such nonsense. The cholo is a very bad dude too. Yes he is a commentary on illegal immigration, in so far as it highlights government incompetence.

I make a couple of references to homosexuals, it might seem superfluous but in once instance, it's just the hero's observation. How does he know she's a lesbian? She probably told him to ward off his flirting way. Her tattoos and jewelry made it obvious, I don't care and it doesn't matter.

In other places, "gay" is used as a pejorative. I make no apologies for that, people still do that, no one is perfect and, well, in 2004 in the army it was still normal to do. Most characters don't and Brittney is accustomed to warriors' humor and just making a harmless joke, trying to fit in. She may actually be gay or bi. We'll find out in the sequel. So don't write me about being not friendly to gays. I hate all stupid people, gay, straight or alien.

So how does the magic work in this story? Why are some ghosts weak? Why are the witches so weak? Why don't the demons make more trouble?

I won't answer all of these but hint at the mechanics for those inclined to fixate on those details. Remember, not all the ghosts, gifted, haunts or demons can see one another. That includes the hero, though his judge can perceive all, he is lazy and that's explained twice. He is often beset by demons he can't perceive and aided by angels who don't want to be.

The "weak ghosts" are only weak compared to those trained to participate in the cosmic war of good vs. evil. They are unfortunates who through tragedy are strong enough to retain coherent form and not dissipate into the cosmos as static electricity. They remain a mind and spirit and can exercise their will, the key evident of a soul. They are remarkably strong and in time with training can become warrior spirits the way Eric was learning and our hero learned. Rachael was trained for many years and was strong only because she was ready to be dead, and live in the magical world she was adapted to even before out story opens.

The witches are terrible trouble for the living. The judges are custom built to destroy them, punish them, for their transgressions. They are the terminators, optimized for the job and can kill them by the bushel with few exceptions. They're otherwise useless. Where the judges kill, the witch can learn the future, summon demons, steal your soul and torment you to take your secrets, and a myriad of other things. To mortals and lesser spirits, a fully trained witch allied with even a modest demon familiar (or vice versa) is a powerhouse.

Mara is a tougher demon, one of the toughest. The Judge is kept in check by her and is so held because its symbiotic bond with the hero has improved by the end. It is aware and sympathetic to the hero's limitations and by virtue of its own experience knows better than to risk serious injury or destruction at the hands of such a powerful demon. There was reference to a demon that could kill our hero as well. While he avoids it, with help, there are still more nasty things out there not yet revealed.

Things like the Shoggoth for example. Yes, the reference is a salute to the master H.P. Lovecraft. Eagle's uncle teaches at M.U., that is Miskatonic University. That wasn't obvious enough but I sprinkle that chapter with Kthulu mythos references because I can't help myself. Eagle's Subaru drives into the mountains of madness, those things can do that.

One more thing about the witch tradition as hinted at in this story. I made them up but they are modeled after certain extinct traditions from central Europe and would claim to trace their lineage even further back.

What about Pickles, why didn't he have a soul, why did the animals sometimes react and sometimes didn't? How did the kitten perceive and avoid Eric and ignore Rachael? What gives?

For you animal lovers, the animals have souls. When they depart, though, they generally are not hung up. Being natural beings without our level of complexity they pass on according to nature's laws, usually. Ghosts are an aberration. The animals ability to sense the ghosts ebbs and flows with the ghosts manifest power at the time, determined by a number of factors including distance from their grave, host and the spiritual condition of their host (if they have one). In the case of ghosts without a host, their own power follows the moon's waxing and waning and changes with the seasons. Pickles may be haunting the hero or Eric if there is a sequel.

How can a judge's host suicide if this is a sin and The Judge is there to fight sin or law breaking? Self-sacrifice and suicide doesn't violate a cosmic law revealed by the gods in this version of our world. The host of a judge, a judge can judge all and judge when its own shell should be discarded in favor of a new one. Think of it as a crab molting, shedding one set of armor for another.

Why are all the women throwing themselves at our hero when he's so clearly a disaster? The Judge is an insanely powerful masculine energy. They're attracted to that. They don't see it so they don't understand it's not the hero. They're victims really of its powerful draw. The witches (Emily and Rachael) and spiritually-open Eagle are particularly vulnerable. The sexually dead Mara is only enraged by his energy. Her hatred is increased by his draw.

Further, Emily is drunk and making bad decisions. When she's pregnant she hatches a plan and keeps it on the backburner. She manipulated her way into a pretty good spot without having to be possessed. She's opportunistic. Rachael is a junkie. When she's in the washroom she's dosing. She's a bad decision maker. She also hates Emily and most every other person in the book during most interactions. She is going to have what Emily had if it's at all possible, in the end she realizes she loves our hero but it's too late for their relationship to grow then.

Eagle is a predator with a specific taste, the hero gets lucky and thinks he's God's gift to women but he isn't. Brittney? She's not trying to steal him from Emily but she's not going to shrink from competition. She's making herself available and making a solid effort to win. She's unlucky in love and regrets it. Not being one of the particularly vulnerable magical types, she breaks free like any normal person might. This hits him pretty hard.

Now for the elephant in the room, post-traumatic stress and hallucinations; no, the whole book is not a hallucination or a dream. Writing for PTS or any disease is god-awful stuff. I thought it would be cathartic but it was agony. I spent three chapters in his head with a cigarette and a spider web and some other garbage. I didn't want this to be a 400 page story about what one guy was feeling. I need to show the impact of the sufferer's actions and how it affects his life. PTS isn't a simple problem to describe, it comes in degrees and with various add-ons creating a cluster of issues for writing so I opted to keep it simple as possible instead of describing a snicker doodle, I give you a dog, fill in your blanks. I tell you it has a tail and feet and barks, done. I didn't set out to minimize the difficulty those of us with the diagnosis suffer with only to make it fit into the adventure. Our hero suffers insomnia (at one point he can't remember when he last saw daylight), impulsivity (road trip with Abner) and depression (his suicide attempt). He does suffer from hallucinations but all the characters are real, most of the time. The demon in the theatre wasn't there. The medications made his symptoms worse disrupting his sleep cycle, hurting his connection with Eric which was probably the healthiest relationship he had (gay I know). He had difficulty with relationships and never held a job. He abused alcohol and experimented with other pharmaceuticals with Rachael in a black out. He lost his memory, he was hypervigilant and he sought danger. He experienced rage, picking fights (with Eric even) and threatening to murder a cop. It's his rage that often fuels The Judge or stirs it to do its job (lazy slumbering cosmic horrors). He experienced numbness and was technically homeless for a bit of the story. He had other issues as well but they are as fun to read about as they are to suffer so I kept it as spare as possible. Again, if there is insult or injury to the sufferers of this—it's only a result of my lack of talent, perspective and never done to further increase society's negative perception of those who suffer.

Post-traumatic stress is NORMAL. Acute PTS is not a disorder but the norm. Compounding trauma while still coping makes it worse but the "D" disorder can occur even with one event. Estimates vary but 11-22% of our Soldiers suffer from the prolonged variety of PTS (I hate the stigmatizing "D" and don't use it whenever possible to ignore it). Having spent 22 years in uniform I would say the numbers are higher. Many of us suffer in silence for years hiding our symptoms in a bottle or under pills or behind a mask of rage, bulging muscles and isolation. Some of us think it's just our personality we're quirky, dark, sullen, brooding—so what? Fuck off. But even the worst PTS can clear up or be managed and free the sufferer to function. Sufferers of sexual trauma prove this in our community every day anonymously.

Sexual trauma is sadly rampant in our (and probably every) society. I take an angry swipe at institutionalized, weaponized child rape and let God (capital G) write himself a cameo. In no other place does God make a personal appearance expect when he snuffs the priest out (well he was in the church basement with Bob and Aaron and Sarah). Nothing is more insidious than this atrocity and epidemic of child rape, institutional sex trafficking and the church cover ups which *requires* the complicity of lay members. I think the recent revelations about church rape in Pennsylvania would give H.P. Lovecraft a nightmare. The priest was evil before the demon infested him, don't blame the demon. God gets involved when The Judge does his job. He's not just after witches, he can judge the whole naughty list of demonic infested sinners (and innocent bystanders, God does this, too, ask Sodom and Gomorrah).

But back to Post-traumatic stress, there is help. The VA while much maligned (often rightly so) has made terrific strides serving *this* generation of veterans. I was skeptical and went into their system expecting to have the wrong leg amputated during my psychiatric exam. They get a bad rap and it's not entirely undeserved. That said in my experience, the health care half of the VA is amazing. Those people need more of anything they say they do to do their job. And they deserve better attention that I give them in this tale. I portray them mostly in a positive light but barely at all. They provide the drugs, they make treatments available, provide a place to escape his demons (nothing bothers him at the VA, this is metaphorical) and he meets Brittney there. She more than anything represents the welcoming loving care and support provided. Yes, that develops into something more but don't be gross.

If you know a Veteran suffering or who might be, if you need any help, the VA has a dizzying array of resources and partner agencies that can help the sufferer and caregivers. Here are just a few I want to highlight next.

SALEM'S SON

RESOURCES

https://www.ptsd.va.gov/ this is the home page for the National Center for PTSD at the VA. It is a central source for information for sufferers, providers, friends and family. They recently added a mobile app page I recommend; there are some great tools there.

If your Veteran is in crisis there is a link on the site, accessible from a mobile phone that lets you call or even text chat with a caring provider immediately. Or call the Veterans Crisis Line at 1-800-273-8255 and press 1 at the first menu prompt.

For trouble with alcohol, Alcoholics Anonymous is a good (but not the only) place to investigate. This year they celebrate some 85 years of success in outreach and sobriety. Congratulations to them. https://www.aa.org/

If you or someone you care for has issues with substance abuse or emotional (mental) health challenges and you don't know where to start, try here- https://www.samhsa.gov/find-help/national-helpline or 1-800-662-HELP (4357). SAMSA's help line is a confidential, free, 24-hour-a-day, 365-day-a-year, information service, in English and Spanish, for individuals and family members facing mental and/or substance use disorders. This service provides referrals to local treatment facilities, support groups and community-based organizations. Callers can also order free publications and other information.

You can always write the author for questions about his ghosts using the email provided at amazon.com/author/mchandler.

BONUS FEATURE
SALEM'S SON, BOOK TWO
"HARVESTER OF TOMORROW"

CHAPTER 1

Psalm 89:48 "There is no man who lives and, seeing the angel of death, can deliver his soul from his hand."

I read that passage once and it has always stuck with me. It was in the frozen grip of a dying man who would not look. I took him anyway. Though there has always been death, since the first creature sprung to life, when men came to give things names, death received many. Thanatos, Marzan, Ankou, Mictecacihuatl but *Śmierć* was the one that seemed to fit best. Like her, I wear white.

Men are a puzzle. They spread across the world in an instant. They left almost no space free from their yoke. In an instant they turned their boundless energies to murder. Death could not keep up as they lay waste to one another and the world around them. So it gathered the harvesters, we angels of death from a thousand murdered worlds where we slumbered.

It was the birth of something called industrialized warfare. The harvesters call it the *"Mech,"* the age of mechanized or machine killing and it hasn't ended. It was what ended most worlds, though some were accidents or punishment handed down by the gods. Living beings that man or other sentient beings create. I arrived during what was called the Great War. War is a pretty and small word, like a jewel or perfect shell on a beach. It does not mean the things that I have seen.

As a harvester what I have seen doesn't matter. Death has always been, since the first living things. We had no soul or will or ghosts of our own. The sky gods, the all fathers, the other deities have made their own angels, including harvesters with their own rules and ways. There were once harvesters who only took the bravest given the name Valkyrie, there are only a few of them left now. There is one angel who kills only kings.

The gods, they feast on a mixture of blood, misery and sorrow. Some called it ambrosia but there are other names for it. I call it tomorrow. I harvest tomorrows for the gods. I serve one of elder gods who slumbers eternal awaiting some forgotten reason to rise. One of the young gods here made harvesters of the living. They were born with a soul, had names and a will. They brought the first questions about my own being. When they were created I found could experience dreams, so I sometimes slumbered with my lord.

My dreams were of the many deaths of this world. I saw my own work, riding a bullet into your brain. I remember stretching myself across a valley to drown a hundred thousand souls in a moment. I was a stone that fell from the cosmos to break a continent. I crept along on a blanket into the plains with the fleas and flu to kill slowly by a hidden hand. I was for a while the tool of a vengeful murderer who wrote, "revenge is an art form, its medium is misery, blood and sorrow." I took him when he failed to see his quarry had heard another axiom about revenge and digging two graves.

I and my sisters lay some millions to rest in the Tai Ping Rebellion, the Black Plague and The Great Leap Forward. We follow seasonal floods, droughts and famines. But I dreamt most of my own work here beginning with the *Mech*, the first Great War. I was poison in water supplies, disease and exploding murder that cut men down by the dozens. I took thousands a day and there have been few rests for me since. I remember one strange day when I was given a short rest.

It was near a ruined village called "Festubert." A truce honoring one of the gods was declared and war bid me take no one within reach of my shadow. I watched as men conspired against their god and I took two to break the truce. I ended that day covered in blood. It seems stupid to honor the gods with murder and then to try and stop it for anything like a full day when murder is why you pray.

Men don't see their faiths as cults of death but they are. Death is greater than the young gods and faiths. These fledgling gods fear death and rely on us to inspire the necessary fear for control, obedience. Those eschewing violence are no exception. The monastic Buddhists harbor murder in their hearts as all men, all races do. In the hearts of men there is something else, too, something that stuck with me and changed my own path.

The *Mech* left bits of souls clinging to me and I began to *feel* like they did. I began to feel fear first. I thought it was the only emotion there was. I didn't see happiness or joy. A rare euphoric drowning from time to time perhaps or an overdose, a mad man's suicide but, fear was almost always there. The other sensations made no sense, they were just like the static of the cosmos, X-rays and sun flares. Present but meaningless emissions—sweat or skin flakes, just cast off debris.

I kept to my work never letting fear bother me until sometime later. I fell on an island. I hadn't taken so many in a day since the last world died unknown aeons ago. I wept for a child that saw me come for her. So many would never see me in that flash of light the walking dead there would call a *Pika*. When I fell from the shiny plane, I landed gently and took a wide stance above a surgical clinic. I coiled tightly and swung my scythe in a far-reaching arc. I turned and struck again with fire, then again with the magic in the atom.

Then other harvesters came from the ten thousand gods of that land. I walked amongst the doomed as the lesser harvesters arrived. A mighty sister fell on another city nearby, even as I worked. I thought that soon I could rest again and could clean my bones of the residual souls, thoughts and fears beginning to infect me. What stood out most in memory were the murders that happened after my first strikes.

There were men not satisfied with the death I brought, they needed more! Such arrogance and greed, such appetites! They set out to execute wounded prisoners and to stone their brothers to death even as they were dying by my hand. Such thirst for murder I had not witnessed on any other world. I watched the condemned men. They had no fear left in them if they ever had any. They were tired and dying and had made peace with me as I approached. I searched their faces to see what they knew. They felt something I didn't know and couldn't describe. I felt fear for them. I felt the fear that should have been in their eyes.

Then something else, I felt anger. A terrible anger, this was new. I doubled the suffering of these killers and drew time wide about them that they would suffer longer than war wished. Time doesn't like to be toyed with but he usually forgives the harvesters who do this. War was busy and I believed he would never notice. Time lives in the blood, thus only the living experience it. As one who controls the door between life and death, I can influence time.

Many years later the *Mech* had slowed, but not ended. I was asked to help *Mashhit*, who only takes children. A child was to die with her uncle, a soldier I once missed, in a simple structural failure. I stepped onto the porch and the babe glimpsed me but didn't understand or fear. The rotten wooden boards creaked under my foot. The girl stood next to the broken man, one who escaped me in Vietnam. He was comfortably reclined in a rocker that would soon be kindling.

In Vietnam he was given a reprieve by power of a prayer granted by his mother. I could see he was rotting slowly inside and was marked to die with the little one today. He was my prey. His mind was so badly shattered he couldn't perceive me. I felt pity now and marveled at the will that sustained him. He seemed to live for the child's smile. He spoke to her and she would laugh, I watched and waited, the little girl smiled at me after a time. Then his last words came to his lips and I readied my strike.

"Did I ever tell you I'm part dog now, Eppie?"

"No, pappy."

"C'meer, Eppie." He pulled his army fatigue shirt collar back revealing a six inch scar over his collar bone where I had ricocheted harmlessly away. The little girl looked with amazement upon my signature. "You see that there? That is where I got shot the first time. The bullet took that bone so they put a dog bone in there, that's all they had in Vietnam, you see?" The little girl snickered behind her hands. "You wanna touch it?" the little girl nodded. The old man leaned forward and the little girl ventured her hand towards it. The man barked at her and she jumped with exaggerated fright, giggling.

I had my scythe raised to strike but instead, I laughed with them. The porch began to crumble and I thrust my scythe into the place where the support was giving way. There was a creak and a rending noise as the porch and its roof section tore away from the house.

Eppie ran inside and the old man followed. He was as a boy again, a soldier, he moved her inside putting himself between her and I. Mashitt appeared and knocked my staff away. The porch collapsed and I called the ancient blade to my hand. It answered and I held it at ease while Mashitt gazed into me seeking explanation for my failure. I stood thoughtless, motionless and ashamed. New feelings, I had neither laughed nor felt shame before. I think I was broken by the souls' desperate pleadings clinging to me. It started with him in Vietnam, his mother's prayer, her god pushing me away. I realized that was my first failure. Mashitt slowly moved to pursue the girl. I struck him down in an instant and his god shook the sky in anger. I bent time again so the soldier called "pappy" would live, if suffer through to near the end of my story. Time and one of the sky gods were angry and so my troubles began.

SALEM'S SON

ABOUT THE AUTHOR

M. Chandler is a retired Soldier haunted by his own ghosts, not so easily destroyed be some beneficent other. In addition to writing fiction stories, he has written professionally for government for over twenty years including as a Writer-Editor at the VA National Center for PTSD. He currently lives in Gettysburg with his children and a ghost or two.

Made in the USA
Middletown, DE
07 August 2020